Indulge Me

BETH BOLDEN

Chapter One

"Did you hear who's coming in today?"

Kian Reynolds barely glanced up from the reduction he was stirring on the enormous industrial stove. He'd let his sauce scorch in the last class because he'd let himself indulge in some of the gossipy chatter, and he wasn't going to make that mistake again. He wasn't here to make friends; he was here to learn to cook.

"It's Aquino. Bastian Aquino."

Kian's gaze drifted up for a split second before he could stop himself. "It's *Chef* Aquino," he corrected. "Isn't he the head chef at Terroir?" Mark, one of the mouthier guys in Kian's class, snorted. "Isn't he? Don't you know, Reynolds?"

What Kian knew was that almost every student at their culinary academy was desperate to get the internship Chef Aquino was offering to their graduating class. As for Kian, he had already set his sights a lot higher. Napa was all well and good—Terroir, Chef Aquino's restaurant, even had a few of the coveted Michelin stars. New York City was absolutely aspirational. Chicago and San Francisco were definitely the homes of great culinary minds. But Kian knew how good he was, and he was going to accept nothing less than an apprenticeship in London or Paris.

Graduation was only a month away, and he'd sent off his applications, and now all he had left was waiting for the replies—*and,* he added, stir this reduction and try to fend off some of the nastier gossip.

Kian had figured out very early in their three years of training that not many of his fellow students liked him. His mom claimed their dislike was based entirely in jealousy, and while Kian could definitely see that point of view, it didn't make him feel any better when the snide comments and sideways glares started.

"I know who Chef Aquino is," Kian finally said, keeping his voice steady and calm. It was hard to live in Napa and avoid Bastian Aquino's existence.

"Funny, considering you're the only student in our class who didn't apply for Terroir's internship," Mark sneered.

"You're not even supposed to know that," Kian said. "Recommendation letters are private."

"Hey!" Mark held up his hands in mock surrender. "Sue me, I overheard two chefs discussing how weird it was that such an . . . *exemplary* student didn't apply."

He's just jealous, Kian told himself, but it didn't really help take the sting out of Mark's words. Maybe he *was* dumb. Maybe he shouldn't have skipped every job opportunity on this continent in a fit of artistic superiority. Except he knew he had exceptional natural skill that the instructors here had taken the opportunity to hone. Over half the teachers had personally suggested some of the restaurants he'd applied to in Europe. He stirred his reduction, eyes focused on the velvety texture, waiting until it was precisely the right consistency. Was he being obnoxiously cocky if it was true?

"Maybe you're just worried you wouldn't be able to keep your hands to yourself. He might be old, but Aquino's still pretty damn hot."

Kian knew Mark was gay, and it was no big secret how attractive he thought Chef Aquino was. He'd also made no secret out of the fact that he'd wanted Kian to suck his dick, but Kian had put a very quick end to that possibility.

He wasn't going to tell his mom that, but Kian believed that *jealousy* probably accurately characterized both problems Mark had with him.

"If you want to follow Chef Aquino around like a puppy dog, picking up his laundry and picking up the dishes he breaks every service, why should I stand in your way?"

Kian wasn't proud of losing his temper, but after three years of listening to that asswipe Mark, sometimes it was hard to reel it in. Today was apparently one of those times. Still, he'd assiduously watched his reduction the whole time, unlike the last time when he'd very vaguely scorched it during another "discussion" with Mark. Plus, Mark was *still* speechless, which Kian was definitely going to count as a win.

"I'd like to think the job is a little more than just kissing my ass," a deep voice announced, and Kian glanced up from his reduction and nearly dropped his wooden spoon right into the pot.

It was Chef Bastian Aquino in the flesh, and he was so much *more* than Kian had ever imagined.

He'd gone to a very small combination junior and senior high school in southern Oregon. His town had less than two thousand people in it. Even Napa could be small, especially when you were like Kian and kept to a strict routine of school and then the tiny studio apartment he was renting. He hardly ever did anything, ostensibly to save money for Europe, but mostly because nobody ever invited him out.

The result of all work, no play was that Kian had never met anyone who walked into a room and sucked every bit of air out of it.

Chef Aquino was magnetic, his dark eyes intense and his features generous but delicate, like they'd been sculpted by a master. He wore a simple blue blazer and an old Rolling Stones t-shirt with his jeans and made them look like high fashion. Kian could barely tear his eyes off of him, but he had to know if he was alone in wanting to drop to his knees. When he glanced around, it turned out that he definitely was not the only one. Even Marta, who made no secret about being asexual, looked fairly shell-shocked.

The man in front of him exuded mastery. You'd trust him to roast the most perfect duck breast, and you'd trust him to take you to bed and demolish you in the best way. Kian gulped air, but his lungs still felt empty. Like Bastian Aquino had command over even the elements.

He sauntered forward, casually but clearly aware that he owned the room. Kian realized as he stopped in front of him that he was completely used to owning every room—and every *kitchen*—he stepped into.

"Nothing to say to that?" he asked, raising a single dark eyebrow. He had a faintly exotic accent in the corners of his voice, and Kian ordered his knees not to automatically buckle.

Knowing the chef expected an answer and almost definitely an apology, Kian opened his mouth and shut it again. His mind was one long, circling litany of *stupid, stupid, stupid*, and he couldn't seem to break out of it, or break free of Aquino's spell.

That's what it was, right? Kian thought desperately. A spell of some kind. Aquino was a culinary magician, who cast spells on anything and *anyone* he wanted.

"I'm sure it's a . . . lot of work," Kian finally managed to force out of his uncooperative mouth.

Chef Aquino nodded once, succinctly and surely. And Kian knew that he'd work you hard and long hours, and that he would be an insanely exacting boss—and that he'd adore every impossible moment.

Suddenly, he wasn't sure he couldn't go to Europe. Could he leave Napa and get a job in London or Paris, while knowing that a man like this existed? And that he could have worked for him?

Desperation forced another sentence out. "I'm sure you're looking for the best, the most dedicated student for your internship, Chef," he added. *And that's me*, he added wordlessly. *Maybe it should be me.*

Of course he'd had no clue what Bastian Aquino was like so he'd never applied for Terroir's internship. Michelin stars in America? He could remember saying scornfully to someone that they must be easier to earn here, anyway.

In this moment, with Bastian Aquino's eyes taking him apart molecule by molecule, he wanted to drop to his knees and plead forgiveness for that rash comment. Because of course, even though they'd never met before and Aquino had no clue who he was, somehow he *must* know Kian had said it.

"I bet you know who that'd be, wouldn't you?" Aquino didn't even seem interested in hearing who Kian thought it was; he'd clearly meant it patronizingly and that might have stung, except that he reached out and tapped Kian reassuringly on the shoulder.

The contact was electric. Kian felt like he'd just been plugged into the closest outlet and then switched on high, like one of those gigantic commercial mixers that whirled away, fast as lightning, no matter how thick or goopy the dough was in their bowls.

Even Aquino seemed to react, which Kian couldn't quite believe because *of course* it was only him that had experienced the live current between them. But Chef flinched and withdrew his hand quickly, the echo of the feeling reflected in his eyes.

"It would be me, Chef," Kian said quietly.

But Aquino turned away without saying a word and left the room with Chef Charles. Kian could only think that his shot had passed as quickly as it had begun. He could go to one of the instructors and beg to apply for the Terroir internship, but after all his disdain about any job opportunities in North America, he had a feeling that was going to be pointless. But they wouldn't understand that the concept of leaving for Europe while Mark or another one of those useless idiots became Bastian Aquino's personal intern was intolerable. It shouldn't have hurt. He'd only spent five minutes staring helplessly at the man, but somehow it meant more than that and Kian was left believing that he'd always regret not trying harder.

The smell of his reduction wafted up and hit his nose just as he realized that he'd neglected stirring it for the aforementioned five minutes.

Kian picked up his spoon and gave it an experimental stir. It was definitely dark brown in spots, nearly black in fact, and the undeniable scorched smell told him the whole story. He sighed; he was going to have to start from scratch on the three-hour process.

Mark walked over and peered into Kian's pot. He sniffed, his exaggerated grimace making him look even uglier than his personality did. "Forget about it again?" he asked. "Told you Bastian was hot."

"Chef Aquino," Kian said stiffly, dumping the contents of the pot into the garbage at the end of his station. "He's not some dudebro you're casual acquaintances with. He's a . . . he's a . . . a . . ." Kian struggled to put his feelings about Chef Aquino into words—especially words that Mark couldn't exploit later.

"He's dreamy? He's hot? You want to worship the ground he walks on?"

"This isn't *Grey's Anatomy* in the kitchen," Kian retorted, trying to hide that he'd had *all* those thoughts. "He's not Chef McDreamy."

"He could be," Mark speculated as Kian walked over to the pantry and picked out more ingredients for his reduction. Mushrooms, shallots, garlic, thyme—he dumped them all in his bin. "*You* want him to be, and you didn't even want to work for him."

It was annoying his face was so goddamned transparent. Chef Aquino had probably realized it as well, but then people probably obsessed about him all the time, so it wasn't like Kian was alone in feeling that way.

"I still can't believe you were the only one in our class who didn't apply for the Terroir internship," Mark continued, even though Kian was careful to give no sign that he was even still listening. His knife flashed over the mushrooms, decimating their flesh into tiny, even pieces.

"You're an ass," Marta added in, from her own station across the kitchen. "You act like you weren't panting just the same as Kian when Aquino walked in. He's got a way about him."

The understatement of the century, Kian thought. He slid his mushrooms into the pot, drizzled in a little olive oil and started chopping his shallot into miniscule pieces.

The challenge of today's class had been to create a reduction that tasted "meaty," except without any meat used. Every ingredient had to be vegetarian.

After the shallot, Kian went back to the pantry and grabbed a few carrots. He diced those finely and added them to the pot.

His burned reduction had been good, but *expected*. And something that had always set him apart from his other classmates was his willingness to use his instincts to create something unique.

Smoked paprika was his next unusual ingredient and as he returned from the pantry, Mark's eyes were unsurprisingly on both him and the glass jar in his hand.

"You didn't use that last time," Mark said.

"Maybe I decided that my reduction wasn't very good and needed to be improved." It was usually better not to engage Mark, but he'd been shaken by Chef Aquino and needed to get his bearings back. Even though he was undeniably thinking about the reduction challenge, because he still needed a good grade in this class before graduation, half if not *more* of his brain was still contemplating the Terroir internship.

Should he convince his instructors to throw his name into the ring at this late date? *Could* he? He could ask, of course, but he had a feeling that after he'd been so adamant about going to Europe, nobody was going to understand.

What could he say? *Now that I've met Chef Aquino, I don't think I can let him get away?*

Marta walked over to Kian's station. "He was something else, wasn't he?" she asked, leaning down and resting an elbow on the stainless steel countertop.

"Mark?" Kian didn't even look up.

Marta laughed. "Silly, you know I'm talking about Aquino. You guys had a moment there. I was afraid you were going to burst into flames for a second."

It happened; you just couldn't see it.

"He's just another chef," Kian said, and Marta shot him an indignant look. *Well,* Kian thought, *if Marta's caught too, at least I'm not alone.*

"And Terroir is just another restaurant?" she asked pointedly.

But they both knew he was wrong. Bastian Aquino wasn't just another chef and Terroir definitely wasn't just another restaurant. Marta left, back to her station to watch her reduction. Kian stirred the vegetables in his pot and shook in another bit of smoked paprika. Then pepper. Then the thyme. Then, feeling like he had to be adventurous or *fail*—like Chef Aquino was somehow still watching him, testing him—Kian went back to the pantry and returned with a jar of turmeric.

Mark was watching him intently but hadn't moved to copy him yet. Which was either a very good sign or a very bad one. Kian wasn't sure yet.

He added the turmeric and continued to stir. Twenty minutes in, he added red wine, let it reduce, and then added stock, using the edge of a wooden spoon to test the flavor as it developed.

It needed something else though, a missing flavor that he couldn't quite put his finger on, something that would add depth and interest. A *zing*. After a moment of consideration, he went back to the pantry—Mark gaping at him, Marta observing him with only a little less interest—and came back with a hunk of bittersweet, dark chocolate, cumin, and Mexican oregano.

He'd realized what he was really trying to create—a reduction that was actually more like a Mexican mole. Their instructor hadn't said anything about the reduction needing to be traditionally French, and if he wanted to set himself apart, the only way he could do it was by making unexpected and unusual choices. Creating food that others didn't expect.

When Chef Charles, their instructor, came around to taste their reductions, Kian's reduction hadn't been on the stove for nearly as long as the others or even as long as his first one had, but he stopped completely short as he tasted it.

"No meat?" he asked with a raised eyebrow as his spoon descended towards Kian's pot for another taste. None of the other students in their class had warranted a second taste. Again, Kian figured, that was either a very good sign or a very bad one.

Sometimes you died on the hill of your own creation, but you never reached the top unless you took a risk to get there.

"No meat," Kian confirmed.

"It's nearly . . . a mole," Charles said with astonishment. "But it's not, is it?"

That was the fine edge; they hadn't been asked to make a mole. They'd been asked to create a reduction. If Charles decided that he hadn't fulfilled the assignment, it wouldn't matter how good it was. He'd struggled with that, in their first month of school. Just because something was delicious didn't mean it met the requirements. Creative impulses, while important, needed to be tempered by the hierarchy of the kitchen. And he, Charles had told Kian repeatedly, was going to be at the very bottom after graduation. Not exactly washing dishes, but definitely not experimenting with the kitchen's recipes, either.

"It's not a mole," Kian said decisively. Sometimes, he'd discovered, confidence could be everything. That was why it stung even more that he'd been so awestruck by Chef Aquino. Eventually he'd recovered his natural confidence, but for those first few precious moments? He'd been lost. Figuratively. Literally. In every single way that mattered.

Mark had wandered over to see why it was taking Chef Charles so long to critique Kian's reduction. "It smells like a mole," he said, with a rotten egg look on his face. Like he already knew he'd been judged and found wanting.

"This is impressive work," Chef Charles finally pronounced. "Extra points for creativity and not going in the traditional direction of your classmates. I'm impressed by your ability to impart significant flavor in such unique ways."

"Thank you, Chef," Kian said.

He'd already been wavering on his decision, but Chef Charles' comments cemented his purpose. Tomorrow morning, before class began, he was going to ask to speak to him privately—and he was going to ask about the Terroir internship. Surely, the quality of work he was currently doing warranted a late entry into the internship sweepstakes?

It was a gamble, but the chance to work for Chef Aquino was worth any risk.

***

"I asked you to recommend your top three students," Bastian Aquino said, leaning back in the chair opposite Charles' desk. "Instead of three, I'm inundated with recommendation letters. Are you telling me that everyone in this graduating class is equally untalent-ed?"

Charles shook his head, his full head of wavy, graying hair flop-ping over his eyes. Bastian had long been of the opinion that Charles was someone who fell into the category of "those who can't, *teach*." The hair was just another piece of evidence that he'd been right about him. Someone that sloppy couldn't ever belong in a truly disciplined kitchen.

"There are some very talented students," Charles said diplomat-ically. Another reason Bastian had never liked him; he wasn't really honest, he was fucking *diplomatic*. And he'd learned in a twenty-year culinary career that you couldn't ever be both.

Bastian cut right through his crap to the heart of the matter. "Who is the most talented? The one you'd most imagine fitting in at Terroir?"

Charles hesitated. Bastian, not usually the most patient person in the world, wanted to reach across the desk and squeeze his solid neck until the name fell out of his mouth. Three months ago, he'd decided he wanted an intern, so naturally had gone to the most prestigious academy of culinary arts with the intention of selecting their very best student.

It wasn't supposed to be this hard. Charles wasn't supposed to send him fifteen recommendation letters, all essentially the same. There was supposed to be someone who stood out. Someone who he instantly recognized as having the qualifications, the skill, and the talent to at least do what he told them to.

"There is one," Charles finally said. "Unfortunately, he didn't apply for your internship."

Bastian stared at him. "He what?"

Charles cleared his throat. "He didn't apply. Every single other student applied. But not this one."

Shoving his chair back, and running a quick hand through his hair, Bastian prowled back and forth in front of Charles' desk. "He *what?*"

"He didn't apply," he repeated, wincing. "He wants to go to Europe."

Just that fact alone convinced Bastian that this was the intern he needed. Someone who *knew* he was better than everyone else. That was the student Bastian wanted to hire.

"Let me talk to him," Bastian said. "I can persuade him."

"I'm really not sure you can. He's very determined. And I'm sure he'll receive job offers from the European restaurants he's applied to." Charles shrugged, like Bastian was just supposed to accept that he wasn't going to get the best student this graduating class offered. Clearly, he didn't know Bastian very well, if he believed that was going to happen.

Bastian didn't just expect the best—he demanded it. Out of the staff that surrounded him, out of the ingredients he cooked with, but most importantly, out of his own self.

He leaned forward, fists gripping the chair. "Let me talk to him."

Charles continued to hesitate. "That's not really our way here."

Holding his breath, Bastian tried to count to ten like his anger management counselor had told him to do. He made it to four.

Not success, but progress, at least.

"You want me to continue to accept graduating students from this academy at Terroir?" Bastian demanded. "If you do, you will let me speak to this student. *Now.*"

"Now?" Charles looked confused.

"I'm here to finalize this decision. I don't care where he's at. Go get him *now.*"

"He's not even here yet," Charles stammered.

Bastian stared at him in stony silence, punctuated only by a knock on the door.

Rising to his feet, Charles shuffled over and opened it, exchanging a quick word with the person on the other side. Bastian, his patience in its death thralls, rolled his eyes. Finally, Charles opened the door wider, and Bastian saw the boy whom he had seen in the kitchen classroom yesterday. The one who'd gone out of his way to insult him, and in nearly the same breath, swore that he possessed the best set of qualifications.

"Kian, this is Chef Aquino," Charles said. "He is here to select an intern for his restaurant, Terroir."

Kian was so young. Had he been this young in culinary school? Bastian couldn't remember. But Kian was definitely young, and slight, his white chef's jacket nearly dwarfing his narrow shoulders and thin arms. Only an air of fierce determination and the look in his light blue eyes grabbed Bastian's attention. This was someone who knew what he wanted, and what he wanted was Bastian.

That wasn't very unusual. What *was* unusual was that, for the first time in a very long time, Bastian wanted back.

"Kian is our best student," Charles added. "He was the one we were just discussing."

Bastian prowled a bit closer to him and tried to ignore the feeling that he was a big bad wolf, after a particularly tasty bit of prey. He glanced up at Charles. "Not available? Not even here yet?" he asked with a raised eyebrow. "He seems to be here now."

Shrugging his shoulders, Charles gestured towards Kian, like *you wanted him, there he is, my work here is done*. Maybe that was why he'd ended up here, instead of working in a restaurant or even, God forbid, some hotel somewhere: a willingness to do the bare minimum and call it good.

Bastian eyed Kian resolutely. So he wanted to work in Europe, did he? Thought, just because he was the best in this small culinary school, in this even smaller graduating class, that he deserved better?

What he deserved was someone who was prepared to remind him every second of every shift that there was a higher ideal he was aspiring to. Someone who was willing to help him unlearn every bad habit instructors like Charles had instilled in him.

"So you want to go to Europe?" Bastian asked, and took in the momentary panic in Kian's eyes. Had Charles been wrong? It probably wouldn't be the first time, if he had been.

"I do. I *did*," Kian said.

"Willing to work seventy hours a week for peanuts?" Bastian paused, gaze focused on Kian's narrow, handsome face. "Willing to scrape plates for a year, just to get into the kitchen?"

He had no poker face whatsoever. Surprise, shock, denial flashed through his eyes in rapid succession. Charles, who still thought he was needed or useful, inserted a heavy sigh into the conversation.

"You're supposed to be preparing these students for what comes next, Charles," Bastian continued, barely wasting a breath. "Instead, you're filling their heads with dreams and *ideas*. Even if they take him, they won't let him near a stove. You know that. But it seems like *he* doesn't know that."

"*He* has a name," Kian inserted testily. "And *he* wants to know the truth. If I work for you, will I get into the kitchen? And not just to scrape plates?"

Bastian knew he was a bastard. Knew that sometimes his employees even risked life and limb to call him that behind his back. Occasionally a recently *ex*-employee would even be ballsy enough to call him the Bastard to his face. But he never felt like one, not when he was demanding what he knew he deserved out of his employees—which was the very best. But he felt like one now, with Kian, all nervous naivety, not even given the basic information on what to expect from instructors who should have known better.

It felt wrong to take advantage of that lack of knowledge, but still, Bastian didn't pause. He wanted the best; he needed it. And while Charles was a fucking moron, he'd identified Kian as the best. If he had to manipulate him and his overly obvious emotions, he'd do it.

"With Charles as your instructor, I'm surprised you weren't training to be a dishwasher," Bastian said cruelly.

"I'm here to be a chef. Not a dishwasher." Kian's lips were clamped tightly together, and there was a fierce determination in his eyes. And that, more than anything else, was what convinced Bastian that he was actually the best in his class. Nobody with that look would ever settle for second best.

"Then you want to work at Terroir," Bastian said, ladling on casual contempt thick and heavy. "But it seems that you didn't think so when you sent your applications in. I don't see one here with your name on it."

Shame bloomed across Kian's fair cheekbones. "Obviously, that was an unfortunate oversight . . ."

"Obviously," Bastian interrupted.

"I would very much like to work for you," Kian finally said, cheeks still flaming, but his chin held high, meeting Bastian's cold eyes dead on.

Bastian had already made his decision, had played Kian like a fiddle to make sure he agreed with him, but it was the obvious pride that convinced him it was the right one. When Bastian inevitably yelled at him—likely in the first five minutes of his first shift, if not even earlier—Kian would take it, and with a stiff upper lip, fix whatever he'd fucked up.

He was that type and that type was the sort that Bastian liked to hire.

At least that was what he told himself as he and Kian shook hands, and he departed the academy. It had nothing to do with the fact that just touching him made his cold, dead heart race again in his chest. He'd just gotten excited about winning, something he loved almost as much as he loved his mother. That was all. In three weeks, when Kian officially started as his intern at Terroir, he would be just like any other chef under him. Under him professionally, but never personally, because Bastian didn't do that. He'd only been tempted once before, and the way it had ended convinced him it couldn't ever happen again.

CHAPTER TWO

Chef Aquino showing up at Chef Charles' office, right when Kian had been determined to talk to him about the Terroir internship, had been kismet. Even more amazingly, Chef Aquino acted determined to win him over, revealing some important facts that *did* make Kian uneasy, because clearly he didn't know that Kian had already realized how stupid he'd been.

When the internship announcement had come out, Mark had been furious, and had threatened to tell everyone that the graduating student who'd won the internship had been the only student who hadn't applied for it. It hadn't been very hard to stop him. All Kian had to say was, "Do you really want to admit to *everyone* in the whole academy that you lost out on a prestigious position to someone who didn't even apply for it?"

As it turned out, Mark didn't want to advertise that particular fact, so he kept his usually noisy trap shut, and the other students, unsurprised that the top student in the class had won the top post-graduation position, moved on.

Chef Charles had pulled him aside the day before graduation, and in his office, showed him three letters from the European restaurants he'd applied to—two in Paris and one in London.

"They're yours, if you want them," Chef had said, but the kindness in his voice didn't convince Kian at all.

"If I want them?"

Chef Charles pushed them closer to Kian. "I'm sure they're acceptances." Kian was moderately sure, too, but instead of replying, he merely grabbed the envelopes and stuffed them into his apron pocket. He had no intention of fulfilling Chef's curiosity. Or anyone else's, ever again.

Didn't Chef remember what Chef Aquino had said when he was here? Didn't Chef remember that all his encouragement to reach for the stars, and to apply at these international bastions of gastronomy, had all been based on a lie?

Maybe not a bald-faced lie, but a lie of omission, at least. Kian had no intention of slaving away in the dish room for a year at any of those restaurants. He didn't intend to scrape plates until the head chef miraculously remembered his existence. His intention was to glean as much training and information as he could, and then move on, doing the same, until he was ready for his first executive chef position. In his notebook scrawled list of goals, he'd set the age at twenty-seven, but secretly, he felt he could accomplish everything even faster.

It was very simple: Chef Aquino wanted to teach, and Kian wanted to learn.

Then there was the attraction that Kian felt. But since he was utterly convinced it had to be one-sided, there was no point in even worrying about it. It wouldn't interfere because the concept of Chef Aquino being interested in him was like the moon deciding to come down to the earth one starry night. It just wasn't going to happen, and Kian told himself that was good, because it made something that could be very complicated, not very after all.

He'd open the envelopes later, when he was alone, Kian thought absently, and then promptly forgot about them completely because when he checked his email later that night, there was an email with his contract from Chef Aquino himself.

He'd start the day after graduation, and Kian could practically hear the sweet-sour tone of his voice as he read the email. "If that's too soon, that's too bad," the email read. "And if you wanted to indulge in the sort of bacchanalian exploits that most students wish to after a graduation ceremony, that's also too bad."

Kian didn't know what *bacchanalian* meant, but he did know that he wasn't interested in it. What he was interested in was working. Specifically for Chef Aquino.

He showed up at the Terroir side door, as directed, fifteen minutes early—he'd read *Kitchen Confidential* by Anthony Bourdain, of course, and while there was a lot of crap that he couldn't imagine being applicable to a three-Michelin-starred restaurant like Terroir, he'd taken to heart the emphasis Tony placed on not just being on time, but *early*. If Anthony Bourdain, the rock star rebel of the culinary world, could do it while he was on all the drugs he could get his hands on, then Kian could do it while he was clean and sober and well-rested.

A man wearing a bandana covered in chili peppers answered his hesitant knock. His face was bitter somehow, like Kian had just caught him sucking a slice of lemon, and he didn't say anything, just stared right at Kian.

"Well?" he finally said impatiently. "Was there something you wanted? To stare?"

"I'm Kian Reynolds. I'm here to work for Chef Aquino."

Kian felt, as the chili-bedecked man in front of him examined him from head to toe, carefully, like he was a dirt-crusted organic carrot or a particularly thorny hunk of ginger. "You're the Bastard's new intern?"

It wasn't easy, but Kian kept the same pleasant expression plastered to his face. He knew everything always showed, and he'd been so determined that this wouldn't happen today that he'd spent a lot of the night before practicing neutral expressions in his bathroom mirror.

But the man in front of him must be a lot more observant than Kian was capable of fooling because he laughed, suddenly and unexpectedly. It was a good laugh, a friendly laugh, even though it was tinged at the edges with the same bitterness that existed in the corners of his expression.

"Haven't you ever heard him called the Bastard before?" he asked curiously.

"No," Kian said stiffly, "and that's really inappropriate, considering he's the executive chef and your boss."

The man leaned closer. "Let me let you in on a little secret before you walk in here. If you don't find a way to keep a sense of humor about what an absolute asshole Bastian Aquino is, then you're going to lose your soul."

This seemed unnecessarily dramatic for a man who wore chili peppers on his head.

"Can you just please take me to Chef Aquino?" Kian begged. He knew the weird man in front of him had blown through all his carefully neutral expressions already and he didn't have any extra in reserve.

He gave Kian another one of those penetrating looks, before suddenly nodding sharply. "Yeah, sure."

Opening the door wider, he let Kian walk in, and as he stepped over the threshold, he had one of those full-body realizations that nothing was ever going to be the same again. He was a *chef* now and he was working for *Bastian Aquino* at *Terroir*. This was only the beginning and it was already awesome. He could go anywhere from here; only the sky was the limit.

The door opened into an employee locker room, narrow metal lockers lining the space. "Yours is somewhere," the man offhandedly tossed out. "Your whites will be in it. What did you say your name was again?"

"Kian," he said, glancing up and down the row for his name written on the piece of blue tape haphazardly stuck to each metal door.

"Oh, you're over here," he said, pointing to one, near the end. "I'm Xander, by the way. Xander Bridges. I'm the *saucier*, and I work the line during service."

"Oh," Kian said, feeling very impressed. He'd heard great things about Terroir's sauces, in particular, and this was the man who created them. Maybe it was okay that he liked to say rude things about Chef Aquino and wear weird headwraps, if he was that talented.

"I'll take you to Aquino now," Xander said. "Come with me."

They walked through the kitchen, which was so vast, it was hard for Kian to conceptualize. The "line" itself was wide and while not exactly spacious, had clearly been designed to maximize a chef's natural movements as he prepared dishes. The range was enormous, with at least twenty burners, several which were already occupied by huge pots, bubbling away even though it was not even eight in the morning.

"I also do the soup, sometimes," Xander said, the pride in his voice betraying how prestigious being asked to make the daily soup was. "Which is why I'm here so early."

They passed though the line, which was still quiet. There were several long stainless steel prep tables, right next to a whole line of commercial-grade walk-in fridges. "Veggies," Xander said, pointing to a door. "Dairy. Meat. Seafood. There's another larger one, on the other end of the building, for wine."

Chef Aquino's office was easily identifiable. It was glass-walled, and even though there were oatmeal-colored shades, they were all drawn up, leaving Chef to survey his entire domain at any time. Kian had a feeling he rarely drew the shades. There was a single desk, metal and glass, with a keyboard and an oversize computer monitor.

Xander rapped briefly on the glass next to the open door and Chef Aquino looked up, every one of his dark hairs in place, his immaculate white chef's jacket already buttoned up to the throat. He looked pristine and perfect, and when his dark-eyed gaze hit Kian, it felt like the first time all over again. Like an electric current crossed with a wooden beam hitting him straight in the temple. But a *good* sort of pain, the kind of pain you craved all the time.

"Chef," Xander said, somehow finding his respect, which Kian had a feeling was buried fairly deep, "this is Kian. He said he's starting today."

Kian had had three weeks to contemplate them meeting again, and what his first day might be like. He'd imagined Chef Aquino shaking his hand, leading him on a thorough tour; still contained but going out of his way to show Kian the way the Terroir kitchens worked, exactly.

What Kian got was that single quick, penetrating glance and then a brusque reply, after Chef had already returned his attention to the paper he was scribbling on. "Get him changed and then take him to the dish room."

At first, Kian was sure he'd misunderstood. Xander finally had to grip his shoulder and literally pull him away from the doorway. He knew he should say something, but he didn't know what that was. Hadn't Chef Aquino convinced him to come work for him by offering to teach him? Promised him work that wasn't the dish room? Yet that was exactly where he was telling Xander to send him.

He couldn't be as callously crass as Xander when it came to their boss, but he could still, politely, make sure that Chef remembered who he was, right? But Xander didn't even let him formulate the question, he just dragged him off.

"Wait, wait," he muttered as Xander kept his grip firm around his upper arm. "I need to remind Chef Aquino that I'm not here to be a dish washer. I'm supposed to be his new intern."

Xander gave a sharp bark of laughter. "Yeah, he knows." He dropped Kian's arm, finally, when they were back in the locker room. "Get changed."

But Kian was not going to change into anything until he understood exactly what had just happened. "I don't understand."

"Of course you don't. You're like . . . a baby. Or a puppy."

Kian bristled. "I'm twenty-one. I've just graduated from culinary school. I was the top of our class. Chef Aquino *handpicked* me to be his intern."

Xander just looked bitterly amused. "Like I said. A puppy. For the record, the intern job basically means you're the Bastard's bitch, at his beck and call. And what he wants you to do today is work in the dish room. So dish room it is. Do you speak Spanish?"

Kian had grown up in southern Oregon, which meant that he did, a little. As he slowly stripped down and changed into the whites in the locker, he informed Xander of that fact.

All Xander said was, "God, where did you learn to change? Your grandmother's house? Hurry it up. You need to get to the dish room and I have to get back to the fucking soup."

Trying to hurry, Kian was surprised to discover that the whites fit perfectly. He'd never sent his sizes to Chef Aquino, but somehow he must have known. He thought about asking Xander if that was normal, but even though he seemed to be a weird guy, probably used to odd questions, his impatience was beginning to show. Kian had begun his first day by seemingly pissing off Chef Aquino just by existing; he couldn't risk pissing off the one person who'd been relatively helpful.

When he was done, Xander showed him the dish room, an already bustling space filled with steam and a single man, who seemed to be in a hundred places at once.

"This is Jorge," Xander said. "He's from Honduras, and he doesn't speak a lot of English. Good luck."

Kian looked at Jorge, who didn't smile back at him. He had a sudden feeling that this was Chef Aquino's first line of defense at weeding out the self-important and the useless that passed through his kitchen. If that was true, then Kian wasn't going to fail. Not on his first day, but more importantly, not *ever*. He straightened his shoulders and held out his hand.

"I'm Kian. I think we're going to be working together today."

Jorge looked at his outstretched hand like it was an insect. He didn't make a single move to shake it. Instead, he gestured at the front of the line, where a bunch of dirty pots sat.

Unfortunately Kian understood all too well. What Jorge wanted was for him to scrape those pots, and then the towering set of plates next to it. How was there already so much to be cleaned? The restaurant wasn't supposed to open for hours.

But it didn't really matter *why*. All that mattered was that, until told otherwise, Jorge was his boss, and he'd better do what he said, or else he wouldn't ever see Bastian Aquino again.

Jorge held out a long, rubberized apron, and a scraping tool. Kian tried not to let his frustration show in his face, but he'd blown way past any neutrality he'd ever acquired, and Jorge just laughed, and it sounded way too much like Xander's.

Maybe Kian understood after all why they called him the Bastard behind his back.

Bastian was not used to feeling guilty, but the sickly feeling at the base of his stomach followed him around during the rest of the day. Manipulating employees into becoming the best version of themselves was routine; it was okay that they hated him for it. He got their most exemplary work, and eventually they got sick of him and left. But somehow the thought of Kian hating him filled Bastian with self-loathing.

It didn't matter that Bastian knew he was doing the right thing. It didn't matter that Kian was so green, the last place he needed to be was on the line, fucking everything up during a service. He needed to learn, and he needed to prove he was strong enough to dedicate himself to this emotionally and physically grueling work.

He still saw Kian's shocked and disappointed face every time he closed his eyes, and it was *annoying*. Bastian didn't like feeling this way; didn't like feeling responsible for another person. Kian was Kian's own keeper, and it was up to him to prove himself.

It was only the force of his convictions that kept Bastian out of the dish room. He got a brief glimpse of him, face already white and exhausted, at the employee meal before dinner service began. Bastian considered sending help to the dish room, but Jorge typically managed on his own, and probably enjoyed having someone to boss around.

Bastian always kept a very close eye on how things ran during service, and tonight, like every night, clean plates and dishes and bowls and empty sauté pans didn't seem to ever be in short supply.

He almost stopped by after the dinner service ended, but that would also be unusual, and he wasn't willing to single Kian out so quickly. The rest of the staff would figure things out soon enough, if Kian was able to stick it out, and burdening him with additional shit, on top of Bastian's usual shit, seemed unfair.

He left in his Mercedes right when the service ended, depending on the other chefs to finish cleaning the kitchen to his exacting standards. The drive was only a few miles, but tonight, that didn't feel long enough, so he kept driving. It was late, but he still found himself idling in the driveway of a house about ten minutes from Terroir.

He must have been sitting there long enough, because when he glanced up, a woman bundled in a lilac fuzzy robe, graying hair curling around her shoulders, was standing on the front walk, a small smile on her face.

"It's late," was all she said to him as he got out of the car, approaching her.

"Why aren't you sleeping?" Bastian asked. He'd somewhat expected to come here and find her asleep.

Bastian leaned in, giving her a hug, and brushing a quick kiss over each cheek.

"Because you weren't sleeping," his mother replied tartly, leading him around the back of the house to the sunroom that Bastian had had built for her a few years ago. "Is everything alright?"

"No. Yes." Bastian couldn't even make up his own damn mind as he settled down in one of the wide, comfortable chairs. He propped his clog-shod feet up on the coffee table, and his mother gave him a single, castigating glance, before he moved them.

"It's very unlike you to be unsure," she said.

She was right.

"I had a new employee start today," he said.

"You are *always* having new employees start," she said, her accent still faintly musical after all the time spent in America. "Maybe because you're an asshole."

"*Maman!*" Bastian exclaimed.

She just shrugged. "I hear the stories. People love to talk. So what was so special about this new employee? Did you finally decide to hire a *sous*?"

"I have a *sous*," Bastian argued tiredly.

"And yet he doesn't do what a normal *sous* would do, because you cannot bear to let anything go. So it isn't a *sous*. Who is it?"

"His name is Kian Reynolds. He just graduated from the CIA outpost here, in Napa."

"So he is very young," Celeste Aquino observed.

"Very young," Bastian confirmed, and even though his thirty-five years wasn't old, he felt like a dirty old man, thinking about a twenty-one-year-old this way.

"And you like him," she added slyly.

He shrugged, an echo of her own from a moment ago. "I don't *dislike* him."

"Ahhhh. *Quelle surprise,*" Celeste said sagely. "You are human after all."

"You birthed me," Bastian said with annoyance. "I think you'd know whether I was human or not."

"Eh," she said. "I wonder sometimes. You are more machine than man. But this boy, this Kian, he makes you want to be more man than machine. That's not a bad thing, darling. You can't stay alone forever."

Bastian shot to his feet. It was just like his mother to assume he and Kian would fall in love and spend a happily ever after together after he'd only said that he didn't dislike him. Such an auspicious start to a romance.

"He's my employee. My new intern. And he's young." Bastian paced back and forth. "I don't know what's going to happen. *Nothing* if I'm to stay his boss, and I want to because I think he could be very good. I want to teach him, more than anything, and it's hard to be patient enough to do that."

Celeste settled back in her chair and her knowing smile drove him wild. It was like she knew he was going to fail, before he even started, and nothing ever set him on a more determined path than people assuming he couldn't achieve the goals he set for himself.

"You," he said to his mother, "are even better at manipulating people than I am."

She shrugged, but the twinkle in her dark eyes gave her away completely. "I worry for you, sometimes," was all she said.

"Maybe you should worry for him, instead," he said darkly.

"Will you be able to sleep now? Should I make you some hot milk?"

Bastian growled. *Hot milk*, his ass. But his mother was not only used to his mercurial moods, in the beginning, he'd learned them from her—and maybe a little bit from his hot-tempered Spanish father.

"No hot milk then. Take your drive home," she said, getting to her feet and swirling her fuzzy robe around her like it was a Dior or a Gucci. "I need my beauty sleep."

He brushed another kiss across her cheek. "You're beautiful, always, *maman*."

Slapping at his shoulder, she scoffed, but couldn't hide the pleased gleam in her eyes. "Goodnight, Bastian."

Despite talking to his mother, Bastian didn't feel any more settled when he finally reached his own house. Stripping down, he took a hot shower, intending for the water beating on his back to relax that tight muscle throbbing in his neck, but he still felt wound tight.

Maybe it wouldn't even be a problem. Maybe Kian, annoyed with the way Bastian had manipulated him into taking the internship, would quit after the first day. Plenty of prospective employees had. He wouldn't be the first, and Bastian was sure he wouldn't be the last. Lots of chefs, especially those who weren't fresh from school, took major offense to being asked to do dishes. But Bastian's typical trial for new chefs was rather well-known in the industry now, and most brand-new employees expected it.

But Kian clearly wasn't hearing industry gossip.

Maybe tomorrow he wouldn't show up, Bastian thought as he turned the shower controls off. If he didn't, and Bastian ever saw him again, maybe at the farmer's market or giving one of those lame culinary demonstrations at Dean & Deluca, Bastian could get him out of his system with a single night of hot, brainless fucking.

Rubbing himself down with a towel, he flopped down onto the bed and after switching off the light, attempted to switch off his brain.

It didn't work.

Instead it decided to show him, in graphic detail, what that night of hot, brainless fucking might be like, if Kian didn't show up for work the next day.

Kian would be slender but tough, all wrapped up in that milky skin, blue eyes flashing with determination. He'd want everything Bastian was willing to give him, and he'd love every second of it.

Groaning, Bastian rolled over. He couldn't jerk off to thoughts of Kian. Not if the possibility existed that he was going to have to stuff all those inconvenient and messy thoughts right back into their boxes. He knew from experience that if he slipped up, there'd be no hiding from his own desires.

You should have taken the god damned hot milk, Bastian thought, his temper spiking as he fisted his hands in the sheets. Anything not to touch himself.

What he should do was bring Kian into his office tomorrow and tell him that they'd both made a mistake, and that Terroir was the wrong place for Kian to further his ambition. It would be a lie, because Bastian already knew it was the perfect place, if Kian could be tough enough to stick it out. It wasn't like he hadn't lied to employees and suppliers and friends and ex-lovers thousands of times before; as long as he got what he wanted, it didn't matter. But something about lying to that clearly trusting face was abhorrent. Bastian didn't think he could do it.

What could he say instead? *I'm sorry, but I want you too badly for you to stay?* Yeah, that definitely wasn't going to work, because he'd seen the worship in Kian's eyes, and there was only one way that conversation could end.

There was only one option left, and that was to bury everything so deep, even he forgot he'd felt anything. He'd done it before, he could do it again. It was just a matter of determination over emotion, and despite what everyone believed, Bastian controlled every god damn emotion that escaped him. If he lost his temper, it was because he *chose* to lose his temper. There were only two emotions he'd always been helpless against: the enduring love for his mother, and its mirror, the hatred he'd always felt for his father.

Someday, he knew he was going to have to let that go; Celeste always told him that. But he *could* control what he felt for Kian.

And he believed that completely, at least until he showed up at Terroir, bone dry cappuccino in his travel mug, at the early hour of seven thirty. Nobody else would be around now, and he could get a head start on his inventory and ordering for the weekend.

Except that he wasn't alone after all. A bright cap of blond hair shone in the sun, as Kian tipped his head back, absorbing the early morning rays.

Bastian flinched, staring at the boy who hadn't yet seen him. Not only had he come back, but he'd come back *early*. As Kian's boss, this filled him with cautious optimism. As someone who was not-so-successfully trying to bury his attraction, it was the shittiest possible outcome.

"You're here early," Bastian said, making sure his voice was devoid of anything. Approval, disapproval, endless, rapacious lust. *Anything.*

Kian nearly jumped as his gaze flew to Bastian's face. "Oh, yeah. I always heard timeliness was important."

"Even in the dish room?" Bastian asked, raising an eyebrow. He typed in the code to open the back door and reminded himself to tell Xander or Wyatt to make sure Kian knew it. If he was going to show up earlier than everyone else, an insane proposition, he might as well know how to get in.

"Especially in the dish room," Kian said very seriously as they walked into the locker room. "Jorge and I have some new methods that we're looking to work into the current practices."

Bastian raised an eyebrow. Typically he didn't like anyone fucking with his restaurant, especially implementing anything new without his permission, but there was something so earnest about Kian, it was difficult to burst his bubble.

"You'll like them, I promise," Kian said, backtracking like he'd thought better of making changes without permission. "Would you like to hear about them?"

Bastian usually didn't give two shits what happened in his dish room as long as the dishes got washed. Jorge had worked for him forever and knew how to get things done. Maybe things could be improved, but having to listen to Kian's ideas was a bad idea when he'd actually slept and wasn't still fighting that pesky attraction. "Not particularly," he said casually. "Just don't fuck anything up."

"Of course not, Chef," Kian said, and goddamnit, those earnestly shining blue eyes just *killed him*.

He'd died enough last night, and right now, he couldn't take another moment, so he gave a sharp nod and departed the locker room, hoping to hole himself up in the office until he could forget everything he wasn't supposed to be remembering.

During family meal before the dinner service yesterday, one of the other chefs, a nice guy with surfer blond hair and blue eyes, had said to Kian, "Oh, so you're the new guy. Liking the dish room so far?"

Kian hadn't quite understood how he could know he'd been relegated there, but then the blond guy had laughed again. "Killed me too, for a couple of days, but what got me through it was knowing everyone's had to do it at one time or another."

As he'd cleaned up the dishes from the meal, Kian had turned this scrap of information over in his head, until he'd come to what seemed to be the right conclusion. Chef Aquino did this to *everyone* who started in the Terroir kitchens. Everyone had to put their time in, to prove they were willing to commit. Chef hadn't singled Kian out; this was the trial by soapsuds that he gave to everyone.

It sure made it a lot easier to trudge back to the dirty work he and Jorge had for the evening. It was hot, back-breaking work, but as they scraped, Kian began to think of some ways it could be less hot and maybe even less back-breaking.

At the end of the service, Xander had come in personally to check on him, which Kian felt sort of went against all that world-weary bitterness he carried with him all the time. And Kian, who didn't speak enough Spanish to communicate to Jorge what they could change to make the work easier on both of them, employed Xander as a temporary go-between slash translator.

Jorge—and Xander, as well—were skeptical of Kian's ideas. It seemed the way things had always been done at Terroir was the way things *always* had to be done at Terroir.

"My advice," Xander had said, when they were on their way out an hour later, "is if you really think this will work, just do it. Don't ask for permission. Ask for forgiveness later."

Wyatt, the blond chef, had frowned at his friend. "Aquino is going to chew him up and spit him out, once he discovers what he's done."

"Maybe," Xander said. "But maybe not."

It was a risk Kian felt he needed to take. He had to show Chef Aquino that he was different, that he was *better*. And Jorge, who had been employed at Terroir for years, seemed willing to go along with Kian's ideas, as long as they stayed Kian's ideas.

Kian had stayed up too late finalizing the plans, and then was up even earlier than the day before, determined to get a head start before the dishes began in earnest.

Of course, that was when he was dumb enough to not only run into Chef Aquino himself, squinting and vibrant in the early morning sun, smelling of freshly roasted espresso, but to accidentally confess his entire plan.

Still, Chef Aquino hadn't said *not* to do it. That was practically permission, right? Kian thought Xander might have agreed with him, if he'd been here already. But he wasn't, so he was on his own.

Sink or swim, Kian told himself, and he knew which one he needed to do. He rolled up the sleeves of his chef's jacket and got to work.

Chapter Three

Bastian had known Kian had something indefinably special from their first meeting. But he was sure of it, beyond a doubt, when early one morning—he'd had to set his alarm twenty minutes earlier to actually avoid running into him in the parking lot—he'd gone into the dish room and seen what Kian had changed.

It was a lot more efficient, so efficient, in fact, that Bastian felt a tiny pulse of shame for never trying to improve Jorge's situation. Jorge was a silent, diligent, reliable worker, and he wouldn't have ever considered changing anything because he was so grateful for the job Bastian had given him ages ago. But Kian wasn't just trying to prove his loyalty. For some reason, he was trying to prove that he deserved to be promoted from the dish room.

It wasn't like Bastian didn't have every intention of doing that. What was the point of going to all the trouble of hiring an intern if you kept him scraping plates? But he liked the hunger and the tenacity and the risk Kian had taken. It reminded him, if he was being very honest, of himself, a very long time ago.

That was both good and, frankly, sort of terrifying. Bastian knew what sort of hell he'd raised and how difficult he'd been in every kitchen he'd ever set foot in—including his own.

Definitely his own.

When Xander showed up, they consulted about the soup. He liked Xander, even though he didn't have a lot of respect for anyone else's culinary skill, including Bastian's own. There was a healthy ego brewing in that chili pepper-bedecked head of his, and someday, he wouldn't be content with making all the sauces and the soup three times a week.

Someday, Xander was going to demand more, probably *chef de cuisine* or a position as *sous* that wasn't essentially meaningless. Bastian was going to have to give it to him or lose him, and that stung. But Bastian knew it was the price of wanting to work with the best. Each of them were hungry and ambitious, and Xander was hardly an exception to this rule.

Someday, Xander would make a great head chef, but today was not that day, and to keep his ego somewhat in check, he shot down the first two of Xander's ideas for the soup, forcing him to dig deeper into his well of inspiration and find something that was really good. He looked about five seconds away from beating Bastian with the huge stainless steel soup ladle, but Bastian was fairly certain that he wouldn't resort to assault—at least not yet. At least not until Xander had gotten what he wanted out of his employment at Terroir.

"When Kian comes in later," Bastian said offhandedly, like this wasn't the reason he'd come over here in the first place, "tell him to come see me, first thing."

Bastian watched as Xander tamped down his temper, embers still flaring in his brown eyes. He knew Xander wanted to remind him that he was a chef, not a messenger boy, but Xander had a small dose of self-preservation, at least, and managed to keep his mouth shut. He gave Bastian a quick nod.

"Excellent," Bastian said. It was time to teach Kian more than just how to efficiently scrape a plate.

⁂

"Before you get started, he wants to talk to you," Xander hissed as Kian rounded the corner into the kitchen.

Xander already had a few splashes on his whites, which meant that he'd been elected to make the soup today. Usually that put Xander in a better mood, but he didn't look like he was in a particularly good one today.

"Everything okay?" Kian asked, a gut reaction. He'd rearranged the dish room, with Jorge's help, but he had yet to hear a peep from Chef Aquino about what they'd done.

He hadn't been fired either, which Kian was taking as a fairly positive sign.

"He just wants to see you," Xander said. "And watch out, he's in a mood."

"A mood?"

"A bad mood." Xander grimaced. "Though that's hardly unusual."

Since meeting him for the first time, Kian had become more than a little obsessed with his new boss. He'd read every magazine feature and restaurant review he could get his hands on. He listened to every story whispered during prep that he could hear from his own dishwashing station. He lingered over the family meal if talk turned to Bastard stories, of which there were many.

The thing was, Xander wasn't entirely wrong. Chef Aquino definitely had some bad moods. He was unbelievably sensitive to even a perceived insult, easily frustrated, quickly bored, and had a zero-tolerance policy for mistakes. But Kian wouldn't have said that he was always in a bad mood. His mood was mercurial, and he tended to react badly to stimulus—sometimes even if it was something good.

Kian had realized that what Chef needed was someone to be the first line of defense, to absorb whatever was going on before it could even reach Chef. And that, he was convinced, was the real reason Chef had hired an intern. Chef Aquino might not understand exactly why yet, but Kian believed that was why he was at Terroir.

The kitchen was comfortably staffed, and though there was always a lot of work to be done, Kian hadn't been able to identify one particular hole that needed filled—except protecting their commander-in-chief.

Chef would teach him everything he knew, and Kian would make Chef's life a little easier. He'd already decided it was a good trade-off.

He approached Bastian's office and, surprisingly, the blinds in Chef's office were lowered for the first time in the week since Kian had started at Terroir. His heart beat a little faster with the realization. Maybe he was going to be fired after all. But he'd also heard all the horror stories. Chef wouldn't care about privacy for something like a termination. He'd do it in the middle of service, right on the line. He didn't care about anyone else's pride; only his own.

Kian had been washing dishes at his house since he was seven years old and had done another healthy stint in the dish room during culinary academy. Chef wasn't trying to teach him how to wash dishes; he was trying to teach humility. Maybe his ego had been a little inflated after dominating so many of his classes. So instead of approaching the office like Xander might, like even he might have a week ago, Kian knocked hesitantly.

"Yes," Chef answered immediately, and Kian walked in. Chef gestured to the chair opposite the desk. It was made of a metal base and a hard plastic sculpted seat. It was unbelievably uncomfortable, which was the complete opposite of the modern leather office chair Chef was seated in. Kian had a feeling that particular disparity was completely on purpose. It occurred to him, not for the first time, that maybe Chef was actually a closet sadist.

"You wanted to see me?" Kian asked.

Chef was already dressed for service, but he hadn't buttoned the top few buttons of his coat, the lapels hanging open, revealing a tanned neck and even the hint of a collarbone. Kian tried to focus on the desk instead, but Chef's hands were there, clearly scarred and nicked, but strong and sure. His nails were trimmed short, and he tapped one on the glass desktop. Just the sight of those hands was enough to nearly send Kian into a fantasy spiral. But at the last moment, the point of no return, he jerked his focus back, trying to remember that Bastian Aquino wasn't just the sexiest man he'd ever seen, but also the most competent. And his boss.

Someone who, with one single word, could make sure that Kian was never hired to work in a kitchen ever again.

"I've spoken to Jorge," Chef said. "And I've looked at the changes you've made to the dish room." He tapped his fingers again, like he wasn't sure how he felt about either one.

But Kian wasn't fooled for a single moment. Chef knew exactly how he felt; he was just trying to draw out the moment so Kian would squirm, would insert something ill-advisable into the lengthening silence.

Kian might be very green, but he wasn't stupid. He stayed quiet and waited.

Chef nodded absently, but with approval. "To my utter shock, they were actually good changes." He paused again, and Kian curled his fingers around the plastic seat, fighting the urge to fidget. "Why did you make them?"

That was not a question that Kian had been expecting.

"Uh," he said, and saw the reaction instantly. Chef's dark brows slammed together, his lips curling patronizingly.

He doesn't like it when people don't know, Kian reminded himself. *He likes it when his staff is confident, but not overly confident.*

"I did it," Kian said, starting all over again, "because I saw inefficiencies, and I know how important efficiency is to you."

"And you didn't bring the suggestions to me because . . . ?"

Kian took a deep breath. He *knew* what Chef expected him to say. Knew and had to fight against his petty machinations being exposed for exactly what they were.

"I wanted to impress you," he admitted, "and I wasn't sure you'd give me the opportunity to do that if I didn't take matters into my own hands."

Chef hummed absently, fingers resuming their tapping. "*And* you wanted to get out of the dish room," he added.

"I'm here because I want to help you and because I want you to teach me. If for now that means I need to stay in the dish room and make it as good as it can be, then I'm willing to do that."

Kian was almost one hundred percent sure that this moment was the first time he'd ever surprised Chef Aquino. His eyes grew wide for an instant.

"You really mean that," he said, like he fully expected Kian to deny it. "You'd stay in the dish room if I told you to."

"If you think that what I need to learn is how to scrape plates better, it's not very flattering but you're the expert. I trust you."

Bastian leaned forward, his dark eyes mesmerizing as they searched Kian's face. "I think you really mean that."

It wasn't easy, but Kian held his ground. There was undeniably a part of him that wanted to crawl across the floor and *beg* to be let out of the wet, humid, torturous dish room and back into the kitchen, where he belonged.

That wasn't all he wanted to beg for. Before he could stop the thought in its tracks, he imagined crawling across the floor, to where Bastian sat, waiting for the head nod of permission, so he could feel those powerful thighs under his fingertips, and then raise up on his knees, mouth so close to the significant erection bulging in Bastian's white and black checked pants.

"Reynolds?" Chef questioned again, and Kian couldn't help it. He flamed bright red, making it unavoidably clear just what he'd been thinking about.

"I do mean it," he said, hating how his voice trembled a little, at the very end. And not because he'd been caught; but because the fantasy was so real, so visceral. The blinds were closed, and Chef was staring at him like he might not actually fire him if he tried it.

"Shadow Wyatt at the grill tonight," Chef ordered in clipped tones, and the heat of the earlier moment was doused by his sudden coldness.

Kian told himself that he shouldn't be disappointed, because whatever he'd just been fantasizing about was an impossibility, but it was tough not to be.

He wanted the learning and the knowledge Chef Aquino wanted to teach him, and he wanted the fantasies too. It was incredibly good for his sanity that he was going to have to settle for the former, but there was a part of him, deep inside, that yearned, anyway.

It had been a week since Bastian had pulled Kian from the dish room, but the conversation in his office haunted him still. He'd done his utmost to make sure that they were never alone after that, because the desire in those innocent blue eyes to be much less innocent was difficult to resist. And Bastian knew, as much of an asshole as he could be, there was no way he could ever fulfill any of the fantasies Kian was collecting.

Whatever passed between them was going to have to be strictly, completely, professional.

It stung, but Bastian had done much harder things, and it wasn't like a lack of sex was going to kill him. He'd already been mostly going without, because being a professional chef in charge of one of the most prestigious restaurants in the country meant excessively long hours and mind- and body-numbing exhaustion. Even one-night stands deserved better.

It was entirely Kian's fault that he'd thought about sex more in the last month than he'd thought about it in the previous six.

"What are we doing today?" Kian asked, all unvarnished eagerness.

"Do you know what the most vital part of Terroir is?" Bastian asked as they walked from his office towards the bank of large walk-in fridges.

"The line?" Kian asked, more hesitatingly than Bastian thought he normally allowed himself. He would have to be a lot stupider to not realize that Kian was trying to play the sort of chef—the sort of *person*—that Bastian normally admired. Confident but not overly cocky. Sure but always willing to be taught something new. Sometimes he wanted to tell Kian that you couldn't manipulate a manipulator. And, sometimes he wanted to shake him and demand to see the real Kian. Not the Kian that he thought Bastian wanted.

What scared him the most was that it was very possible that they were one in the same.

Bastian pushed all that away, deliberately distancing himself from those embarrassing, semi-hysterical, desperate thoughts. Just because he already knew he was screwed didn't mean he had to acknowledge it.

"Not the line," Bastian replied patiently. "The line can't prepare the fish special if the fish we receive is poor quality, or if the fish isn't available at all. The most vital part of this restaurant, and *any* restaurant, is inventory."

Kian looked a little disappointed, like he believed the most vital component of Terroir would be sexier. What Kian didn't know yet was that a properly stocked kitchen was the sexiest thing in the whole god damn universe.

"I take inventory every single morning," Bastian continued, yanking open the door to the dairy fridge. "I know you've been watching me in my office." He nearly wanted to grab those words back. They were dangerous, just as it was dangerous that Kian couldn't tear his eyes away from his boss, even when he was supposed to be doing something else. "What do you think I'm doing every morning?"

"Making phone calls?" There was an element of frustration in Kian's voice, like he didn't appreciate being asked questions that Bastian knew he didn't have the answers to.

"Calling our suppliers. Ordering. Verifying orders. Then when orders come in, I check every single one. I open every crate, every box. I examine every single piece of produce that comes into this restaurant. And if something isn't right, I make a phone call."

He held out a clipboard and a pen to Kian. "It's time you learned how to do this."

For a split second, Kian made a face, like he couldn't imagine anything less enjoyable than counting and making notations on a sheet of paper. Then his expression changed, like he'd needed to remind himself that everything Bastian asked him to do was important. It was the same look he'd worn when Bastian had banished him to the dish room.

It remained to be seen whether every experiment Bastian tried would turn out like the dish room, but he hoped, like he hadn't hoped in years. He expected all his employees to eventually let him down, some of them spectacularly, most of them by their commitment to mediocrity. Kian was the first who truly gave him hope. Bastian didn't know if the hope was what attracted him in the first place, or if it was what might deepen this attraction into something uncontainable.

If it hadn't been for the hope, he really would have fired Kian the first day, and then fucked him out of his system.

"I just count the boxes, and then write it down?"

"You do more than just count. You *inspect*. You know the menu. You know the specials. You should know the breakdown of plates that we serve every night. More meat on Fridays and Saturdays. Fish on Fridays. The reports that I put up every Monday? Study those. Memorize them. Without that knowledge, this task is impossible."

"Because otherwise I won't know how much fish is enough, and when we need to order more," Kian said, and Bastian felt the familiar flash of recognition resonate through him. He recognized so much of himself in the younger man in front of him. The eagerness, the barely leashed ego, the willingness to work as hard as it took to achieve goals. Those were familiar enough traits, but when reflected back, were apparently irresistible.

"Precisely," Bastian said, and followed Kian deeper into the dairy fridge. Cartons upon cartons of butter, stacked. Lesser stacks of gourmet European butters, purchased to finish certain dishes. Huge jugs of milk and cream. Rows upon rows of eggs.

"The sheet is laid out just like the fridge," Kian observed, his pen making miniscule tick marks alongside each ingredient.

"Did you believe that I'd make my life harder and not easier?" Bastian asked wryly.

Kian glanced up, blue eyes wide even in the dim light. "No, never," he said, and his voice was worshipful.

He didn't want to know what falling off that pedestal would feel like, because it was inevitable that it would hurt. A lot.

Other chefs who came to work at Terroir believed Bastian was the best, but nobody held any old-fashioned ideas about him. They called him the Bastard for a reason. The first time he threw plates, a little of the shine in Kian's eyes would dim. It wasn't going to stop him from throwing them, but it bolstered his resolve to keep his hands off his intern. Things were going to end up complicated enough without deepening that hero worship into something more intimate.

"I remember, always, that nothing is ever perfect," Bastian said gruffly. "That's what we aim for. But the best of us know it's unattainable."

But Kian's attention was already pulled into the inventory, counting wrapped hunks of butter, his fingers quickly flicking away the paper to test their firmness. With anyone else, Bastian might believe his thoroughness was because he was standing in the fridge, observing, but he knew that it wouldn't matter later. Kian knew the bar, and like Bastian himself, was constantly motivated to exceed it.

It wasn't a large space, and Bastian, to his own regret because kitchens tended to be cramped and small, was a large man. It was one of the reasons he'd built his kitchens at Terroir to be expansive and his line more spread out than others—too many years of trying to make himself impossibly smaller. But still, the fridges, while large, weren't designed for two. Even if one was as slender as Kian.

Kian turned to him, pointing to an item on the clipboard, and Bastian realized, a second too late, as he crowded closer, that there was no room behind him to back up. Kian, absorbed in the printout on the clipboard, didn't look up until it was too late, until they were nearly nestled together, right against the shelf holding about a hundred dozen cartons of eggs.

Kian's eyes widened in surprise and he fumbled the clipboard, nearly dropping it. He should have just let it fall, but Bastian reached out and his hand grasped Kian's shoulder.

They froze like that, Kian nearly bent towards him, their gazes locked, and Bastian couldn't help but think, *fuck, hell, shit, this is never going to work*. And Bastian, despite his temper, usually considered himself an optimist.

There was the shock reflected in those blue eyes, and then sparks of heat, lighting them both on fire. It would be so easy to just lean down and discover what that mouth tasted like. Like the bitter coffee Kian liked. Maybe a piece of chocolate that Miles, one of the pastry assistants, had slipped him during this morning's prep. Dark and dangerous, that's how Kian would taste, even though he looked like sunshine, his hair bright even in the dim light.

"Sorry," Kian mumbled, flushing, and objectively Bastian knew he should take his hand off his shoulder, and let him move away, to a respectable distance—at least a distance that didn't have their thighs pressed together, so he couldn't feel the heat of Kian's body next to his. He might be slender, but it was clear to him now that it wasn't just his determination that was strong, he had a body to back that up. His fingers spasmed over a surprisingly firm shoulder, and then slipped down to Kian's bicep.

Kian's eyes watched him the whole way, the wonder in that blue gaze leaving him more breathless than he'd ever admit to anyone. Bastian could only imagine what his own dark eyes looked like, pupils dilated, his fingers gripping Kian's arm like he couldn't bear to let him go.

It wasn't impossible—Bastian was renowned in the culinary world for his legendary determination—but it damn near felt like it.

"Don't be sorry," Bastian said, and immediately regretted it, because that was admitting something he couldn't take back.

It was admitting to something that could never, ever happen between them.

Bastian dropped his hand, and thankfully Kian took a step back, and then another.

"I was . . . I was going to ask why the mascarpone is on the shelf, but not listed here," Kian said, voice high and stunned. Like he couldn't believe what had just happened.

Bastian, unfortunately, could believe it. There'd been a reason he'd been avoiding being alone with Kian.

Unfortunately there was no way to truly train Kian and not end up alone occasionally. Maybe it was time to address the elephant in the room, make it clear that no matter what anyone's personal feelings were, this was professional, and this was *Kian's career*, which somehow had become more important to Bastian than his own need. And that was so momentous that Bastian refused to look any further into it.

"It would be good, wouldn't it?" Bastian asked, trying for casual, ending up nowhere near that tone. "Between us?"

Kian nearly dropped the clipboard again. He looked shocked, and Bastian reminded himself of American sensibilities. Maybe he should have framed the conversation in a subtler way—but then there was the risk that Kian wouldn't understand, and then they'd have to do this again.

"Excuse me?" Kian squeaked.

"It would be good between us," Bastian repeated, this time making sure it wasn't a question, but a statement. Of fact. Because it would be. Nobody was denying that. "It would, and it would happen more than once, and we'd enjoy ourselves. But it can't happen, because we're doing something more important. We're preparing you for a career that I know could be spectacular."

But Kian was still stuck on the first thing Bastian had said. "It would be good if we slept together?"

Bastian shot him a look that was trying very hard to be bored, but sex with Kian wouldn't ever be boring. He was insatiably curious. He would want to discover. He would turn Bastian's world upside down during the expedition, and probably ruin his own in the process.

"Don't you think so?" Bastian asked.

"Uh," Kian said, sounding truly unsure for the first time since his first day.

"This is . . ." Bastian gestured between them, "just an excess of hormones. It won't last. We have more important things to do."

Kian still looked shell-shocked, like Bastian confirming the attraction between them was mutual was enough to blow his mind.

"So you're saying," he finally spoke up, "that it might feel good now, but that it would waste this opportunity."

Bastian nodded sharply. "And be an impossible distraction. You have a future. It would be a crime to waste it."

"And . . . doing that, would be wasting it?" Kian sounded like he didn't quite believe Bastian, and that made sense. He was young. Romantic, no doubt. And Bastian was probably a romantic figure to him. All that hero worship.

"Trading a brilliant career for a few fleeting moments of pleasure?" Bastian didn't bother considering this. "It's not even a question. I just want to make that clear because this . . . hormone surge is going to happen, occasionally, between us. And I want to make sure that we're on the same page."

"Same page," Kian echoed. "Okay. Yes. Same page. I can do that."

"Good," Bastian said, and focused his attention on the clipboard. "Ah, yes, the mascarpone cheese. It's because it was a special request from the pastry chef, René. I'll have to add it to the inventory sheets. Just notate on the side for now."

Later, Bastian felt guilty for springing such an important conversation on Kian unprepared, but they'd needed to clear away any uncertainty and erase the distraction of *maybe, someday,* from the conversation completely. It had been the right thing to do, to bring it up and to pack the attraction away in a box with no lid.

Chapter Four

The echo of the conversation with Chef—*no*, Kian told himself firmly, *you want him, you can call him by his name, at least in your own head*—Bastian lasted for weeks.

It took Kian a long time to sift through the layers of it, even though Bastian had been very clear and extremely forthright. But first there'd been The Moment, which was how Kian thought of it in his head. The Moment had torn away all pretense, forcing Kian to admit that he wanted it all—he wanted everything Bastian had to teach him, and he wanted his hands and mouth all over him, too. The Moment had made it obvious that Bastian felt the same.

And just when the incredulous delight had filtered through him, shockingly sweet, Bastian had proceeded to explain that moments like The Moment would keep happening, but instead of focusing on them, they needed to focus on Kian's career.

Kian wasn't stupid. He didn't believe that Bastian could be a boss and a mentor *and* a boyfriend. Or even a friend with benefits.

Even the thought of Bastian as a friend with benefits made him hot and then cold all over. And it wasn't just the benefits part.

Bastian committed himself in everything he did. He loved and hated passionately, with commitment. They couldn't just casually fuck and then work together in the restaurant the next day, pretending nothing had ever happened.

As the weeks passed, and then a month, and then two, it wasn't like Kian disagreed with Bastian's assessment. It was fundamentally sound.

It still sucked.

It didn't mean that anything changed either. Most days, in fact, during the majority of them, the relationship between him and Bastian was strictly a professional one. Kian kept close, absorbing everything Bastian taught.

Not just Bastian either—one morning when he reported in, Bastian sent him over to Xander, to learn how to make sauces, and to shadow him on the sauté station during dinner service.

"Must think pretty damn highly of you," Xander muttered as he meticulously set up his *mise en place*.

Kian had already whipped out his little notebook and was making notations on how Xander liked things arranged. Every chef liked it slightly different, and while Xander wasn't quite as particular as

Bastian, he still had very definite ideas of how his ingredients should be prepped and set up.

"I'm assuming you know all the mother sauces," Xander said and Kian nodded. That had been a whole semester's worth of classes at the culinary institute. He'd aced that particular course, but he'd learned in the few months since he'd graduated and started working at Terroir that anything he'd learned in school was almost completely useless.

In fact, Bastian had told him more than once to forget everything he'd been taught. The first time he'd said that to Kian, it had been a particularly frustrating and difficult day.

He'd gone back to his little studio apartment, beyond discouraged, which hardly set him apart from anyone else who worked at Terroir. Everyone had a bad day once in awhile, and almost always the reason for that was their illustrious head chef. But Kian believed that what set him apart was that he could shed the frustration and show up the next morning even more determined to learn everything he could from Bastian.

Everyone else slowly grew jaded and bitter, until they started using the Bastard nickname on a regular basis.

Xander was the leader of that particular faction at Terroir. Even though it should have made Kian like him less, he surprisingly didn't.

In spite of the nod, Xander led him through the preparation of each sauce and reduction meticulously, Kian making notes on each one.

When they finished, it was time for family dinner. "Hey," Xander said, pulling him aside before he could join the others at the long table, "Wyatt and Miles and I are getting a house together. There's a fourth bedroom. You interested?"

He actually was. He'd been looking around for a new place because his studio was decrepit and depressing, even though he barely spent any time in it. "Sure. Miles is a pastry assistant, right? The only one René likes?"

"Yeah. He's cool."

Kian agreed with that assessment. He often brought "experiments" in to family dinner, augmenting dinner with some truly delicious pastries and desserts. For that alone, he seemed like a good choice for a roommate.

"I'll send you the ad with the rent and info and stuff," Xander said, shoving his hands in his pockets. "But it's a good deal and a decent enough house, for the price."

"I'm in," Kian said firmly.

For a moment, Xander looked surprised, like he hadn't really expected Kian to agree. And that, Kian realized as they were getting ready for service, made sense because Xander was sort of prickly at the best of times and could be mean at the worst. He didn't make friends easily, but it seemed that he and Kian were actually becoming friends.

At least that was what it felt like until service started and Kian discovered just how unprepared he was to work the line at a high-end establishment like Terroir.

"Two duck, three chicken, four scallop," Bastian called out in a loud voice.

Xander's hands were moving like quicksilver, everywhere at once, checking all his sauté pans, and somehow, impossibly adding more to the stove, even though it felt like it had been full only a moment ago.

Up until now, Kian had been stuck on the simpler appetizers, assembling the salads, and dishing up the soup. He'd been small time and, tonight, he was getting a taste of the big leagues.

"Yes, Chef," Xander barked out, then turned to Kian. "Get those scallop pans going and don't fucking overcook them, not if your life is valuable to you in any way."

"Yes, Chef," Kian said, and tried to calm the trembling in his fingers as he set the pans on the stove and dug the ingredients for the scallop dish out of the refrigerated pull-out drawers underneath the gigantic stovetop.

He knew how to cook scallops, but it was incredibly intimidating to cook them for two of the harshest critics on the planet—Xander and then Bastian.

Still, as the routine tasks took over his hands, they helped. His movements became more certain, and he was fairly confident they were perfectly cooked when he carefully started plating them.

"Wait," Xander said, even though he wasn't even looking in Kian's direction. Did he have eyes in the back of his head somehow? "Those aren't caramelized enough. Chef likes a deep golden brown."

It was not easy to be told he'd screwed up even though he'd given it his very best attempt. "They're cooked through," he insisted stubbornly.

Xander held up his hands. "Your fate."

He'd been confident before, but now he uncertainly slid the plates to the pass-through, ready for the final garnishes and the inspection, which was Bastian's domain.

Bastian started to set a spray of pea greens gently on the top of one scallop when his tweezers paused in the middle of his delicate task. His brows slammed together and when he glanced up, his gaze eviscerated Kian.

"Are these done?" he demanded.

"They're done," Kian promised. Inside he was quaking.

"Caramelize the next batch a little more."

Kian wasn't going to point out that cooking scallops was difficult, but cooking scallops with a gloriously brown sear on them while making sure they were perfectly cooked *while* cooking about ten other things perfectly simultaneously was not easy to do. But he thought it.

After shift he brought this up to Xander while they were in the locker room. "How do you do that?" he asked, because he'd long since learned that there were myriad tricks of the trade that he hadn't learned at the institute, and Xander, if he was in a giving mood, sometimes felt like sharing one or two.

"You think it's impossible right?" Xander asked with a wry smile.

"I think it's really fucking hard," Kian admitted.

Xander's smile widened and deepened, and for the first time, Kian really believed they were becoming friends. Not just co-workers and potential roommates but *friends*.

"That's why they pay us the big bucks," Xander said, stretching his neck.

Kian frowned. "They don't pay us big bucks."

"Yes, well, I guess that's why the Bastard gets paid the big bucks, then. You'll figure it out. It's all about placement of the pan on the stove at different stages of cooking. I'll show you how I do it tomorrow. Right now if I think about scallops, I might vomit."

"Yeah, sure," Kian said. He didn't love how young and naïve he sounded. But that was the job, he figured. He was still learning. Still evolving. Still growing.

And if luck was on his side, that would keep happening, every night, until finally he woke up one day and he was a fantastic chef, ready to be promoted and ready to run his own kitchen.

A month later, he was actually able to sub for Xander, when he had the flu and could not actually stand, and the sauces Kian prepared, though not as subtly brilliant as Xander's, didn't make Chef throw the pans across the kitchen. He cooked pan after pan of scallops flawlessly, leaving Bastian to only raise a single eyebrow as the plates slid over to the pass-through. He took over daily inventory and was meticulous enough that even Bastian couldn't find a thing to complain about.

Slowly, he began shadowing every part of the restaurant, and after the Xander flu incident, Bastian actually encouraged it. It was good to have someone who could step in on a moment's notice and not fuck everything up. Kian was proud of that, and proud of the way he was helping Chef not be so overwhelmed with the incredible amount of daily work that just he was responsible for—never mind everyone else who worked at Terroir.

The days slipped by, eventful in the way that each one seemed very uneventful. Each and every one of them was long. The hours were brutal, but somehow living together helped. Even though Bastian had looked once over the reading glasses that had made their way into more than one of Kian's nightly fantasies, and suggested it was a terrible idea to live with people you worked with, it had been the right choice.

The days didn't seem quite so long when he could come home, flip on the TV, listen to Xander and Wyatt bitch about what shitty thing Chef had said to them tonight, and watch as Miles smiled slow and wide, distributing the pastries he'd snitched from the extras.

It was a good life, and Kian liked it. He might have loved it, if only those Moments could stop happening. They made him yearn for disasters.

Disasters like kissing in the fridges, blowjobs in Bastian's office, Bastian pushing him against one of the stainless steel prep counters late at night and fucking him mercilessly.

Considering that he already knew they'd be disasters, it was surprising that he couldn't push them out of his mind.

His friends teased him mercilessly, because of course they'd picked up on his crush. They didn't call it that, of course, because Kian knew they were secretly horrified since Bastian was their living nightmare. And it wasn't like he didn't say shitty things to Kian sometimes. It wasn't like he didn't make him come to Terroir earlier and stay later than anyone else. It wasn't that he hadn't ever thrown a pot or a dish at some mistake Kian had made. Those incidents happened often enough they weren't even out of the ordinary.

But he also got to see Bastian in a light they didn't.

On the last Sunday of every month, Bastian tested recipes, and from the very first time Kian joined him, it was something special they did together.

This wasn't the first time, but somehow, the miracle of creation never failed to excite him. And sometimes, if Kian was very lucky, Bastian would let down his guard a little, and Kian would catch him staring at him, as he went about his tasks. Something that Bastian would never do when others were around, because Kian knew he was terrified of anyone finding out that the Bastard had *feelings*, even if they were primarily sexual feelings.

"What about the butter?" Kian asked, holding the buttery, lemon-dill reduction out towards where Chef was bent over a plate, tweezers out as he settled the garnishes onto the plate.

They were trying out a new langoustine recipe, and Chef had asked Kian to put together a butter sauce for drizzling. Except that instead of drizzling it, Bastian had moved right onto the garnishes.

"Oh, shit, yeah," Bastian said, glancing up. "Maybe around the edge of the plate?"

When they'd first started working together on Sundays, Bastian definitely hadn't asked Kian's opinion. But slowly, as their time together progressed, he'd begun to ask a question here or there, until, in the last few months, the sessions had started to actually feel collaborative.

Kian looked at the plate Bastian had chosen and knew that sauce ringing the edge of the plate would be a messy proposition at best.

"Let me taste it first," Bastian demanded, and Kian passed over the pot. He dipped a spoon in, licked it clean, and let the flavor of the sauce linger on his palate. Chef tasted a hundred things, every single day, but the recurring thought of, *that should be me*, and the automatic denial was second nature to Kian by now.

"God damn, that's good," Bastian said fervently. "The little spice on the end, that's glorious."

"Thank you, Chef," Kian said formally, but he was smiling. Nothing ever felt better than a compliment from Bastian, mostly because compliments were so scarce, but also because you knew he *meant* them.

Unceremoniously he dumped the langoustine in the trash, sliding the plate down near the rest of their dirty dishes. Dishes Kian would probably end up washing, since Jorge wouldn't be in until later, and he'd have his hands full.

"That sauce needs to be the focal. Which means, a new plate." Bastian prowled over to the shelving unit that held his plate selections, and picked one, then another, and then a third.

They clattered as he deposited them on the counter in front of Kian. "You pick," he said.

This was new. Sometimes Bastian asked his opinion, but he'd never been given control of a decision before. And plate selection was huge. It determined plating and garnish and Bastian had told him a thousand times, those often determined the ultimate success of a dish. Food was visual before it ever hit the taste buds.

Kian examined each one carefully, envisioning in his mind the langoustine, the French beans, the sauce, the garnishes. Only one stood to him as the perfect choice. He glanced up at Bastian, who was watching intently.

"Go on," Bastian said, making a little shooing gesture with his hand, the other tucked up under his armpit. A fierce look of concentration fell over his face as he watched Kian plate the langoustine.

When Kian was finally done, and wiped the plate, Bastian spent a long time looking at it from every angle.

He'd poured the sauce into the bottom of the curved bowl, curled the langoustine in a loose spiral, positioned the beans upright, letting them fan out, and in a final touch, used the eyedropper to dot the surface of the yellowy cream sauce with basil oil.

"You've been paying attention," Bastian said finally.

Kian was almost offended. Was there anyone who assumed he *hadn't* been?

"All it needs," Bastian continued, "is one final touch." He abruptly turned on his heel and headed in the direction of the walk-in fridges. When he came back, he was holding something in his hands. Carefully he leaned down and nestled one of the miniature Anaheim peppers they'd just gotten into one of the langoustine folds.

"Visually, it's right," Bastian said, but he gave a sigh of frustration. "But if any idiot eats that, it'll overwhelm the shellfish and the sauce. What else do we have that's red?"

"What about a single slice of radish?" Kian suggested. "It's a nice vibrant red, but the flavor is fairly neutral."

"Let's try it," Bastian said, and Kian went back to the walk-in, grabbed a radish, then his fish deboning knife, very sharp and very flexible and carved a single, nearly paper-thin slice. The edges were bright red, and the starkness of the white was a good contrast to the yellow and green base. He swapped it for the pepper, and knew it was right when Bastian sighed again, but this time in satisfaction.

He reached over and clapped a hand on Kian's shoulder.

They didn't always touch. Touching always felt a little like Russian roulette, especially in the sacred confines of the Terroir kitchens. But once in a while—Kian was never sure if it was because he'd done something good enough to be rewarded or if Bastian was so impressed he couldn't help himself anymore—he'd reach out like this with a brief clasp of his shoulder.

This time, though, he lingered and Kian's heartbeat accelerated. He couldn't stop it and he couldn't slow it down.

He looked up to see Bastian looking at him, intently. There were a thousand dangerous things brewing in that dark gaze, and Kian trembled.

"You are so . . ." Bastian broke off and dropped his hand, his earlier frustration magnified.

For a moment, Kian considered bringing up the conversation that they didn't talk about. If Bastian was finding it so difficult to stay professional, maybe they could relax the rules a little.

Except that wouldn't work either. If one or both of them ever broke down and touched with more than just friendly, professional intent, the resulting wildfire would be all-consuming. There wouldn't just be a slight bending of the rules, the rules would be entirely incinerated.

There was nothing to say, nothing to be done, because Kian *still* believed Chef was right. He was learning so much, absorbing everything, and if they hadn't had that conversation so long ago, would these Sundays even be happening? Sundays where he'd even begun to establish his own point of view as a chef?

"I'm sorry," Bastian finally said. He sounded wretched—just like Kian felt. "I'd tell you to find another teacher, but I'm horribly territorial and I'd probably end up punching them in the face."

Kian laughed, because he wasn't going to cry. Not in front of Chef Aquino. Six months ago, he might have spent a week in wonderment, that Bastian cared enough about him to be territorial at all. But now, all he felt was a hazy sort of desperation.

How long could they continue like this? Kian's contract with Terroir had been for two years, initially, and he'd intended to stay at least that long, if not longer.

But later that night, as he lay awake in bed, every muscle in his body exhausted but sleep somehow still elusive, he wondered if he could possibly last two years like this.

Something inside him ached, and he was afraid it was his heart. It had been so much easier when he'd believed, like Bastian had hinted at, that their connection was just hormones. But after six months, Kian was afraid that wasn't all it was anymore. He didn't want just to protect Bastian anymore. He wanted to teach Bastian, the way Bastian was teaching him, how to handle the stuff that overwhelmed him. Instead of avoiding it, he wanted to be consumed by the fire between them; he wanted to pull Bastian in with him.

Bastian's own frustration with the arrangement had shown in his face today, but how were they supposed to stop? There was nothing to be done, Kian realized, except to keep going.

Keep learning, keep growing, and keep suffering.

Two months later, one of Miles' pastry videos went viral, and he packed up and moved to LA.

When he watched Miles make himself a drunken mess over his new producer, Kian told himself firmly this was exactly why Bastian had insisted they keep things professional between them. He didn't want to be Miles, and he didn't want to be Miles' new producer either. It was messy and embarrassing and it didn't even matter that they ended up happily together.

Kian told himself firmly that he was thrilled for them, and left it at that.

Four months after that, Wyatt, witnessing the money Miles had made in LA, let himself be lured down there too. He got a job as a private chef for a baseball player, and at this point, Kian was resigned that all his friends were going to abandon him.

As long as Xander stayed, he'd be okay.

Of course, Wyatt leaving meant that Wyatt had to resign from Terroir.

Unfortunately, Kian, who took care of almost all of Bastian's personnel issues now, as well as prepping and subbing as needed on the line during service, couldn't be the one to take Wyatt's resignation letter.

It was going to have to be Bastian, and Bastian wasn't going to be happy about it.

He loved firing people, but people leaving him? *Not good. Abort. Do not pass Go. Do not collect two hundred dollars.*

It would've been weird for Kian to be in the office when Wyatt submitted his resignation but he hovered outside, waiting for the moment when everything went sideways.

He heard murmured voices, and then Bastian's voice edging upwards. Wyatt was still too hard to hear, which meant that he was keeping his own temper, even as Bastian's sneering tone cut right through the glass walls of his office and echoed throughout the whole kitchen.

"Did someone even hire your sloppy ass?" Bastian demanded, and he said it loud enough, Kian could see heads rise across the kitchen. He sighed and leaned back against the wall. This was going just about as badly as he'd imagined it would. The worst part in Kian's opinion was that he knew Bastian didn't mean anything he'd just said. He was so angry because losing Wyatt, who was a fantastic chef with an intuitive touch for meat, was a blow. It didn't excuse the verbal abuse, but at least it helped explain it.

Kian was startled from his studied nonchalance when a crash resonated through the entire kitchen. Almost immediately Wyatt stormed out, his blue eyes narrow and his expression very pissed off. He didn't even acknowledge Kian, who raced past him to discover that *yes,* Bastian had swept the entire contents of his desk onto the floor.

He sighed, and leaned down to pick up a piece of coffee mug that was spinning at his feet.

"I can't believe that fucking bastard quit," Bastian said in a huff, but Kian had known him long enough to know it was all defensive posturing. *I can't believe he left me,* was what Kian heard.

"He needs the money. His grandmother is in a home," Kian said quietly. "And this private chef gig pays really well."

"Private chef," Bastian sneered. "So he's going to go grill plain, tough chicken for some socialite in LA?"

Being Bastian's intern and being friends with Wyatt and Xander was a fine line to walk. He often knew more than he felt comfortable saying to his boss—things that his friends told him in confidence. Like that Xander's new sauce recipe was almost directly lifted from a Tom Colicchio cookbook, or that Wyatt wasn't going to be cooking for a socialite at all, but the only "out" player in professional baseball.

Bastian definitely didn't need to know that there was definitely something going on between the baseball player and Wyatt.

"Probably," Kian said noncommittedly in his most soothing voice. He leaned down and picked up the keyboard, which was missing a few important keys. This was the fourth keyboard they'd been through in the last year, and Kian had started buying extras because he might still need to place online orders for supplies and ingredients the day that Bastian decided to throw a hissy fit. They couldn't run out of artichokes just because Kian didn't have a keyboard.

Kicking a pen, Bastian slumped down into his chair. The anger had passed now, and they'd moved on to guilt.

"I shouldn't have said those things. I just . . . saw red," Bastian said hopelessly.

Kian set the broken keyboard on the chair opposite the desk. He maneuvered around the random detritus on the floor and took a chance by moving closer to Bastian than he normally allowed himself. Even took the risk of placing his hands on Bastian's broad, muscular shoulders, emphasized by the cut of his white chef's coat.

Bastian stared at him, and something inside Kian trembled. They didn't often touch, because even a hand on a shoulder was dangerous, and Kian never initiated contact. But he did today, curling his fingers into the starched cotton of Bastian's jacket, holding him steady as his own pulse accelerated.

"Maybe next time, we can figure out a way for you to only see . . . orange," Kian suggested softly.

"I have a temper," Bastian snapped. "It's not going away." He jerked out of Kian's hands, and the moment broke, like an egg cracking against the edge of a bowl.

It would be nice if Bastian's temper mellowed, but Kian was not laboring under any false impression that it would. Bastian's temper was part of who he was; it was the product of the intense pressure he put on himself and on others to produce perfection every single day. It wasn't ideal, it wasn't always professional, but it wasn't going away.

Still, if Kian could figure out a way to convince him to take a second to *think* before he acted, then maybe the collateral damage would be less. At the very least, Kian would end up needing less keyboards.

Leaning down, Kian began to gather up pieces of the coffee cup and the pens and pencils scattered over the polished concrete floor. Out of the corner of his eye, he watched as Bastian began to pace in the small space, his arms crossed across his chest, like the physical movement might contain what kept trying to escape.

"I just . . . Wyatt . . . he's good," Bastian said, and Kian glanced up to see that he'd stopped pacing and was staring at him, crouched on the floor.

"I know he is," Kian said calmly.

"He knows it too," Bastian muttered, like that made up for the insults he'd just spit in Wyatt's direction.

"Yeah, he does. Which is partly why he's leaving."

Kian had gathered almost all the pens from the desk and was moving onto the paperclips sprinkled across the concrete.

"Here," Bastian said, and Kian looked up from the floor to see the mesh paperclip holder held at eye level. He'd crouched down next to Kian and was also picking up paperclips.

This was by no means the first time Bastian had cleared his desk in a fit of temper, but it was definitely the first time he'd helped Kian clean up the mess.

Kian tipped a handful of paperclips into the container. "Maybe I should get one with a sealed lid," he said, trying to use a bit of humor to distract him from the fact that Bastian was right there next to him, helping him. If he turned his head and leaned a little to the left he'd be pressed right against him.

It might not be an apology, but it was *something*.

Sighing, Bastian pushed back on his heels, observing the mess surrounding them with a cynical expression. "This life is hard."

"Really?" Kian retorted sarcastically. "I had no idea."

Bastian, who could be a sarcastic son of a bitch, ironically hated sarcasm in others, so he ignored Kian's statement. "And this," he gestured between them, "makes me tense."

Like on cue, Kian tensed himself. It was the first time Bastian had overtly referred to the non-relationship between them since that first conversation in the dairy walk-in. He'd come close that Sunday when they'd tested the new langoustine dish—a dish that had carved out a permanent place on the menu, which Kian was still unbearably proud of—but he'd never come out and said it directly.

"It's hard," Kian agreed softly. He didn't really believe that sexual frustration was making Bastian an edgier or more terrible boss than he'd been before. It was a convenient excuse, but Kian still understood what he really meant. There were definitely days, those occasional times when their hands would brush or he'd catch Bastian staring intently, possessively, at him, and he also wanted to throw something.

He'd been at Terroir a year now, and there was a part of him that had fiercely believed that after all this time, something would have happened to shift the status quo, even though they both believed that it was better that nothing ever happened between them.

But Bastian's determination to keep his hands off was forged from steel, and Kian couldn't deny the selflessness attracted him even more.

It grew harder, every day, every week, every month, and still neither of them flinched.

Maybe they never would. That possibility had seemed completely impossible a year ago, but maybe he'd been wrong. After all, it couldn't get much harder than this, could it?

"I'm sorry," Bastian said, so quietly that Kian nearly missed it.

Kian reached out again, and it was perilous, but he covered Bastian's big scarred hand with his own, smaller one. "Don't apologize," he insisted in a hard tone. "Don't you dare apologize."

Bastian's smile was wry. "Even for losing my temper?"

Kian's mom had told him once that when he fell in love, he needed to accept everything about the object of his affection. "You don't have to love everything," she'd said with a laugh, "you don't even have to like everything, but you need to accept who they are because you can't change them."

Kian couldn't believe it had taken him so long to realize, but *of course* he was in love with Bastian. Maybe it was because he'd been trying to keep those feelings locked away, covered with the convenient, much less serious, "hormones" label. But now that he'd realized, it was impossible to deny it was true.

And Bastian—who still shot him yearning looks, who was teaching him every single thing he knew, who seemed to delight in Kian stretching his culinary wings, who denied them the very thing they wanted because it would be better for Kian's future—he *must* love him too.

It should have been a joyous realization, but all it did was fill Kian with frustration.

What was he supposed to do about something he couldn't do anything about?

Nothing, he thought darkly, *I'm going to do nothing. Nothing has changed.*

Chapter Five

Nothing, Bastian reminded himself as he pulled into the valet parking station at the downtown San Francisco hotel, *you will do nothing*.

Kian was next to him, eyes wide as he took in the huge buildings and the crowds of people on the streets around them. He absorbed sights and sounds and flavors like a sponge, regurgitating them in the most unusual ways. Bastian had been sure that with time, his desire would fade, and they could settle into a more normal mentor-student relationship, but he discovered that he was more drawn to Kian than ever. Not just his body or his physical attributes, but his mind—and his heart. He was incomprehensibly loyal, and believed, even after being let down enough times to turn other people bitter, in the best of everyone.

There had been part of him who believed it was a mistake to take Kian on this short trip to the city for the culinary demonstration, but he needed an assistant, and Kian had become essential to him. So he'd booked them two separate rooms, even though the temptation burned in him.

Nobody at Terroir would know what happened this weekend. Nobody would ever know if they didn't use the second room—the only witnesses would be the two of them. But Bastian knew, just as he'd known a year and a half ago, that it still couldn't happen. He was still Kian's mentor, and what a student he was turning out to be.

He could comfortably sub at any station on the line, even somehow, inconceivably, pastry, and he had made Bastian's life both easier and fuller, more complete. When he came home, he didn't feel as alone as he had. Technically he still ate alone, showered alone, went to bed alone, but Kian was a ghost next to him, his faithful shadow, the memory of who he was keeping Bastian company always.

It was still hard, to work together every day, and keep the feelings in the tightly-lidded box. But other than a handful of slips when he'd admitted to Kian just how tough it was, he'd done it because it needed to be done. He'd known at the very beginning that Kian was going to be a special kind of chef, and in the last eighteen months, he'd fulfilled all that promise and more.

Bastian shouldn't feel dissatisfied—he'd accomplished exactly what he'd set out to do, which was keep his hands off Kian, and make sure he learned everything Bastian could teach—but the feeling followed him around anyway.

It reminded him, far too often, that he didn't *need* to be alone when he ate, when he showered, when he slept. That as gratifying as the shadow of Kian was, real flesh and blood would be exponentially more satisfying.

Shaking the thoughts away, Bastian got out of the car, tossing the keys to the approaching valet, and grabbed their bags from the trunk. Kian trailed a few steps behind as they walked into the lobby, eyes wide and growing wider, at the spectacularly massive Dale Chihuly glass chandelier, executed in metallic gold and a progression of bloody reds.

On the drive down, Kian had asked him if he did these sorts of demonstrations often. Bastian had nearly told him that he should already know this, because he'd been working for him for eighteen months already, and he hadn't left the restaurant once. Not a day off in eighteen months.

That's what the old Bastian would have said anyway—with a bark and a bite in his voice. But even though his employees ignored it, he knew he'd grown softer. Less frustrated with things like social niceties. More apt to answer questions about himself, especially when posed to him by Kian.

"No," he'd answered simply. "I hate doing them."

"Then why are you doing this one?" Kian had asked.

"A favor," was all Bastian had said, but he had a feeling that the favor would show himself soon enough and all Kian's questions would be answered.

It turned out the favor was hovering near the enormous carved mahogany desk that doubled as the hotel concierge.

"It is so good to see you, *mon cher*," Luc said, approaching Bastian with open arms.

"This is a surprise," Bastian muttered, managing to duck a little and avoid his embrace full-on, relegating him to a sort of half hug. He deliberately set the bags on the floor, also avoiding Luc attempting any cheek kisses.

He wasn't going to do that. Definitely not with Luc. And somehow, surprisingly, the thought of Kian witnessing it wrenched his stomach.

"They said you wouldn't come but I told them otherwise," Luc announced cheerfully. "Even the great Bastian Aquino can leave the enclave of Napa for a weekend."

There were many times Bastian had been tempted to punch Luc in the face, but none more than right now.

"I gave my word," Bastian ground out, "so naturally, I am here."

"Of course, of course," Luc said. "Shall I show you the setup now or . . ."

Bastian had known Luc would be here. He had fully expected that Luc would want to avoid him as much as Bastian wanted to avoid Luc. However that did not seem to be the case.

"We just arrived. Can we not check in to our rooms first?"

"We?" Luc pointedly looked around Bastian and then saw Kian, who was still transfixed by the Chihuly.

"My assistant and I," Bastian said stiffly.

"Your assistant?" Luc said slyly, looking Kian over from top to bottom.

Bastian had been wrong; this was the moment he wanted to punch Luc more than any other.

"My assistant," Bastian repeated, stressing the *assistant* part. But the knowing look in Luc's eyes was unmistakable.

It was evidence of how pathetic Bastian had become that he almost wished that Luc's sly insinuation was true.

"Well, I'll see you two in the ballroom in a little while. I want to make sure I remembered how you like your *mise* at your station."

When they were finally in the elevator, heading upstairs, Kian turned to Bastian. "Who was that?"

"An old friend," Bastian said, hoping that the closed-book tone of his voice would strongly suggest to Kian to leave it at that.

But one of the things he adored most about the man next to him was his insatiable curiosity. He didn't want to just try one thing with an ingredient, he wanted to cook it a hundred different ways, until he'd discovered the best possible way to prepare it.

He wasn't ever going to leave that tantalizing glimpse into Bastian's past alone.

"Someone you worked with?" Kian asked as Bastian handed him the keycard to his room. "He looked pretty young."

Not as young as you, Bastian thought to himself.

"Someone I mentored a few years back," Bastian said, "when I first opened Terroir."

"Oh," Kian said. "Someone like me."

Someone who is nothing like you.

But Bastian was stupid and said, "Sure." It wasn't accurate, not in any way that mattered, but he believed it might stop the questions, and that was really what he was after.

He never wanted to talk about Luc, and he definitely didn't want to talk about Luc with Kian.

"Oh," Kian said, and the slightly wounded edge in his voice made him immediately want to take it back, but he didn't, because what was he supposed to say? *I don't want to hurt your feelings? Nobody is really like you? Nobody ever, not for me?* Those were things a boyfriend would say, and Bastian wasn't Kian's boyfriend.

Saying them would only make everything worse, and their relationship already felt constantly fraught with the tension of doing absolutely fucking nothing.

"We'll go downstairs in an hour," Bastian said. "So get changed. We'll have to make sure my *mise* is how I like it." It was unspoken that Kian would have to fix it if it was wrong.

Kian nodded, and they both disappeared behind their respective doors. Bastian leaned back against his, head tipped back, eyes closed, wishing that he'd refused to repay Luc's favor by showing up today.

He should have brought Xander, not Kian, though he knew if he had, Xander's semi-abrasive self would have scared away everyone and Kian's wounded puppy dog eyes would have followed him around for a month.

He hadn't really been able to refuse Luc calling in his favor and taking Xander, or another one of the less experienced chefs had never been an option. It was fate that he was stuck here, only one wall away from what he desperately wanted, and he couldn't stop putting his own damn foot in his mouth.

For a moment, he nearly called his mother, but he'd tried very hard not to tell her anything else about Kian. Certainly, she knew something was going on with him, and almost certainly she had guessed it was Bastian's intern shadow, but somehow she'd refrained from pushing him.

Probably because she knew he was too much like his father in ways he didn't like, and as a result, didn't react well to being pushed.

He'd just showered this morning, but he took another one, because the idea of flipping on the television was abhorrent and he was not ready to work—his focus was far too fractured. But the long hot shower quieted his concerns, and he dressed meticulously in his chef whites, like a general donning his armor for battle.

He exited the hotel room, and found Kian waiting for him patiently in the hallway.

"Ready?" Bastian asked, and Kian nodded again, uncharacteristically quiet. Bastian recognized the mood though—before taking shifts at some of the newer-to-him stations on the line, he would often grow silent and introspective, as he prepared for the difficult task at hand. It was a technique that Bastian admired, so he let the silence draw out as they took the elevator downstairs.

The ballroom was filled with chairs, hundreds of them in neat, tidy rows, with a large stage at the front. Luc was standing on the raised platform, directing traffic. Other chefs would be giving demonstrations today, but everyone melted out of the way as Bastian and Kian approached.

"Ah, the illustrious Chef Aquino," Luc said, his voice grating on Bastian in ways that it never had before. Either he'd been protected by a healthy helping of hormones, or Luc had gotten more annoying in the intervening years since he'd left Terroir.

"Where is my *mise*?" Bastian demanded. Kian appeared next to him, no longer the subservient half a step back.

"Right here, Chef," Luc said, gesturing towards the setup in front of them.

Kian got to work immediately, and Bastian suddenly wished that he hadn't brought someone who was so meticulous, that it left nothing for him to do except be engaged in conversation by Luc.

"He is very thorough," Luc said.

Bastian shot him an incredulous look. "Did you forget the way I like things?"

"Oh no," Luc said, shooting Kian another head to toe, scorching look, "I couldn't forget what you like. Especially not when you keep reminding us all."

Bastian wasn't blind; he saw the way Kian's back tensed. He knew what all this talk was about.

"This is not the place, or the time."

He lowered his voice and with the hope Kian wouldn't hear, forced himself to step closer to Luc. His old protégé, his old lover. Someone he'd never really expected to see again. Someone he hadn't cared to see again. Because when he'd told Kian that his future was more important than a few fleeting moments of pleasure, he hadn't been speaking from a place of inexperience.

He'd already done this once, and he'd fucked it all up. He wasn't going to let Kian become another Luc—jaded, bitter, downright nasty with disappointment. It didn't matter that Luc didn't have a shred of the loyalty that Kian held dear.

It didn't matter because Bastian could never stand here and have Kian sneer at him the way Luc was. He could stand a lot of things—uncomfortably hot kitchens, cramped spaces, cooking with not enough prep and not enough help, sixteen-hour days, six days a week—but he couldn't stand that.

"If you brought me here," Bastian continued, in a low, brutal voice, "only to insult me, then I'd be happy to leave and have you perform the demonstration."

Luc gave a sharp nod and turned to check up on some other important task, leaving Bastian to stew.

"An old friend?" Bastian looked up to see that Kian had finished the double check of his *mise* and his eyes were burning with injustice. "You were friends with him?"

There was the undeniable question in his words. *Friends?* Kian was silently asking. *Or more?*

But Bastian was still not prepared to get into it, not right now, not when he was about to give a demonstration for approximately five hundred members of the culinary media.

"Friends," he replied shortly. He couldn't miss the way Kian's expression shuttered, but what else could he say? *I fucked up with him, a way I'm never going to fuck up with you?*

***

The demonstration was thankfully a rather easy dish, actually one of Kian's inventions, the langoustine with dill butter sauce. With ease, despite being in front of five hundred members of a press that would joyfully rip him to pieces, he removed the shell, and carefully sautéed the langoustine. Blanched the beans. Prepared the sauce. Did all of the above with as much grace and skill as he could. Answered questions. Tried to even make a joke or two, which mostly didn't go over, as he wasn't renowned for his humor.

But that was okay, because he caught Kian's expression, where he stood at the side of the dais, and he was smiling. Luc was not, but

Luc seemed to have developed a permanent scowl on his handsome face.

He finished the demonstration to generous applause, and even took a handful of questions, something he normally would not have done.

When it was finally over, he was incredibly relieved and had a headache probably induced from being too nice for too long. Definitely from tolerating Luc's sly looks and endless supply of semi-rude remarks.

Luc had always been too clever for his own good.

Bastian and Kian rode the elevator back upstairs in silence. Luc had extended an invitation to dinner, same as he had with all the other chefs that were in town, but he wouldn't have expected that Bastian would accept.

Instead, he really wanted to take another hot shower, and order in some mediocre room service he could complain to Kian about.

But Kian was young and vibrant and worked too hard, for too many long hours.

He turned to him. "You should go to dinner here. I'm tired. I'm going to order in and probably fall asleep early."

Kian frowned. "You want me to go to dinner with Luc?"

That was the very last thing Bastian wanted. "No, I meant, we're in a beautiful, vibrant city. You should see some of it. Expand your palate."

Maybe if Bastian wasn't feeling quite so stung over all of Luc's insinuations, he might have taken Kian himself, damn the headache. But there were too many people—*let's face it*, Bastian thought to himself, *all the people*—who would assume they were a couple. A much-older gentleman taking his young, delectable boyfriend out for a fancy dinner, all to spoil him.

Maybe another time their opinions might not matter, but they mattered tonight.

"You're not going?" Kian asked flatly.

He shook his head. "Headache."

They reached their floor, and in short order, their rooms. Kian pulled out his key but hesitated, looking at Bastian.

He'd just performed in front of a whole score of media, all willing to rip his head off, but it was the questions in Kian's eyes that terrified the fuck out of him. Bastian whipped out his keycard and escaped into the room before he could ask any of them.

The second shower didn't help nearly as much, as an uncharacteristic ball of guilt settled into the base of his stomach. What made it feel even worse was that he knew, if Kian texted one of his friends, Xander maybe, and accused him of being an unfeeling, abrupt asshole, they would all tell him that he shouldn't expect anything less. He was the Bastard, after all.

The guilt gnawed at him through his room service dinner, which ended up even more mediocre than he'd imagined, and that he just pushed halfheartedly around the plate.

He did drink the wine that accompanied the meal though, and settled back in the bed, television on low, and tried not to think at all.

A firm knock on the door knocked him right out of his unthinking reverie.

His first horrible thought was that it was Luc, here to gloat some more.

His second horrible thought was that it was Kian, here to ask all the questions he hadn't let him earlier.

A glimpse into the peephole confirmed that it was option number two. Kian stood there, nervously shifting from one foot to the other, with a very determined look on his face.

Bastian sighed. They could either do this now, or he was sure he'd be interrogated on the way home and might actually end up crashing and killing them in the process. This way, tonight, seemed marginally safer.

The alcohol he'd drunk burned in his veins as he opened the door, tempting him unbearably. This was just as he'd imagined it happening, wasn't it? The dim light of the hotel room. Kian coming over late at night. Sometimes it felt like there could only be one end to this story.

"Yes?" Bastian asked as Kian let the door close behind him.

"I asked you if Luc had been like me and you said *sure*."

Bastian propped a hip against the credenza. He crossed his arms across his t-shirt-clad chest and wished he was wearing something more substantial than a pair of striped pajama pants that his mother had bought him. "That's not a question."

Kian frowned. "You said we were the *same*, but that isn't true, is it?"

There was an unbearable temptation to tell the whole truth, but that felt incredibly dangerous. Too dangerous, especially in this room, with nobody the wiser to what actually happened in it.

"It's true," Bastian claimed. "He was my protégé. I didn't have an intern then, but he assisted me, when Terroir first opened."

Kian took a step closer, then another, and Bastian nearly stumbled backwards. He hadn't expected Kian to be this aggressive, but there'd been flashes of it lately. Kian touching *him*. Kian approaching *him*. And Bastian knew, with a flash of insight, that this status quo couldn't continue forever, because Kian was changing. He was growing up. He was finding his feet in this world. Sooner or later, he would demand more, and Bastian was not ready for that confrontation. Not even close.

"He wasn't *only* your protégé," Kian said, putting a hand on Bastian's chest. "You slept with him."

For a moment, Bastian considered denying it, but it was useless. Kian already knew the truth. "I did."

A very hard look crossed across Kian's face. "So all that . . . *crap* was because you'd done this before and it hadn't worked out very well for you."

"No . . ." Bastian tried to insert but Kian had been saving up this speech and he intended to unleash it—not even Bastian was going to be able to stop him.

"You pretended like it was *so hard* for you, like it didn't matter that I was *dying* for you," Kian ranted, fingers curling tightly into the fabric of his t-shirt, right above where his heart beat in double time. "You let me think, you let me believe, it was only me. But it wasn't. This is what you do. You do *this*."

"No," Bastian uselessly argued. *There's nobody like you. Definitely not Luc, that fucking disloyal asshole.*

"Why did you even do it? To prove you could? To make yourself feel better about Luc? Because I don't see that working out very well for you," Kian continued, voice growing higher and more hysterical. "I'm not his substitute, I'm not his stand-in, don't you understand? I won't be, I'm not."

Later, Bastian would think back to this moment and envy the solitary certainness of his brain function. He'd only wanted to do one thing—*prove Kian wrong*—no matter what the cost, and that made him do something incredibly stupid and incredibly dangerous.

And probably, Bastian would later think, incredibly inevitable.

He grabbed Kian's wrist and dragged him even closer, until they were hip to hip, chest to chest, and Kian was panting, wordless as they stared into each other's eyes.

This was more than inevitable. It had probably been foretold at the beginning of time—Bastian Aquino was going to meet someone who made him question every ounce of his determination, his resolve, his ego, and who was eventually going to tear his self-control to shreds.

He kissed Kian.

Kian instantaneously melted under him, leaning against his chest and pouring everything into the kiss, even as Bastian selfishly took it all back out. *Mine*, he gloated inwardly, *this is all for me.*

Bastian's hands slid up to his shoulders, to his head and he cradled it in his palms as he did the thing he'd told himself from the first moment that *he would not do.*

The kiss ended in a breathless whimper as Kian pulled back, his eyes as wide and shocked as Bastian had ever seen them. Like he'd just blown every circuit in Kian's body. And he probably had; personally, Bastian felt just as decimated. Like everything he knew about love and attraction and those fucking hormones he liked to blame everything on, was wrong.

"You shouldn't have done that," Kian said, harsh pants against Bastian's cheek.

"I know," Bastian said, and his voice was a surprisingly honest caress. "But I couldn't help it. You . . . you're not like him. You've never been like him. In the most rudimentary ways, yes, you have some similarity. But he is so different, and I was different than I am now, I was selfish and egotistical, and I took whatever I wanted, damn the cost."

Bastian removed his hands carefully and Kian took an unsteady step back. Hesitant, like he wasn't quite ready to let go yet.

Still, Kian was able to crack a little smile, and Bastian thanked God for that. "Selfish and egotistical . . . back then?"

Waving an impatient hand, Bastian had to hold back his own laughter. "You are . . . *god damn* . . . you're my downfall. You know that."

Kian didn't say anything, those blue eyes boring right into Bastian's soul. Like he could read him, and every single thing that was written there, good *and* bad, and somehow he accepted them all.

Nobody had ever done that for him before. Even his own mother sometimes despaired of all his less-than-stellar qualities.

"We're not doing this," Kian said very quietly, and very certainly. "Not like this."

Bastian was afraid to ask what that meant. But secretly, he was afraid he knew.

Not like this, maybe, but some other way, some other day. And Bastian wasn't sure he could turn him down, not after the taste he'd just had.

CHAPTER SIX

THE KISS. THE KISS, as Kian liked to think of it, should have changed something. Before, if you'd asked him what kissing Bastian would change—he unequivocally would have said, "everything."

Of course, he hadn't anticipated what Chef would do on their first day back from San Francisco. He'd called Xander into his office, and Kian had stared frustratingly at the closed blinds and wondered what was happening. There was very little that happened at Terroir anymore that he wasn't intimately familiar with, and Bastian doing this today, after The Kiss, and deliberately not telling him, hurt.

Ten minutes later, Chef announced to the kitchen that they finally had a *sous chef*, and that *sous chef* was Xander.

Kian, who did not typically feel Bastian's need to throw things, wanted to pelt his friend with every eggplant at his prep station, which was a very large pile.

It wasn't that Xander wouldn't make a fantastic *sous* or that he didn't deserve the position, because he definitely would and he definitely did. But the timing of the promotion was infuriating, and Kian knew exactly what he was meant to take away from it: that Bastian was in charge, and that Kian was still an intern or his assistant, or whatever they were calling his position these days.

He wasn't *sous*, and nothing was happening between them, as far as Bastian was concerned.

In spite of The Kiss. Maybe even because of The Kiss? Kian didn't know anymore.

He stayed angry for weeks, and Bastian gave him a wide berth, like he knew Kian's temper, which had never shown itself until now, was prodigious when aroused.

The worst was that he couldn't tell any of his friends about what had happened. Xander took his promotion in stride—more like he'd finally gotten what should have been his forever ago, rather than any sort of exuberant celebration at being promoted. How was Kian supposed to tell him, "by the way, I think Chef promoted you to *sous* because we kissed and he wanted to remind me that nothing else was ever going to happen between us"?

He couldn't. Not ever. At least not while keeping Xander's friendship, which had come to mean more and more to him since first Miles, and then Wyatt, had departed for the brighter lights of Los Angeles.

But as the days passed into weeks and then into months, Xander's promotion didn't change much in the Terroir kitchen. Chef only spent slightly less time on the line, and Xander, who wasn't exactly the greatest leader of men either, didn't seem particularly bothered by this.

Kian continued to sub in at various stations. He continued to be the sole assistant to Bastian during their test kitchen Sundays. He was afraid to ask if Bastian had offered the spot to Xander, and he'd just declined it—but he wanted to believe Chef hadn't wanted to give away his spot to anyone else. Besides, their collaborations were good, sometimes even great. They almost always ended up on the menu, at least as a seasonal special. And they *were* collaborations. They came up with the concepts and recipes together, always, and Bastian had even stopped asking Kian what he thought; he naturally assumed that Kian would offer his opinion when the right moment arrived.

Kian decided Xander not knowing about certain job perks was perfectly fine. He enjoyed them more than Xander ever would. Xander would see being stuck in the kitchen with Bastian on a day he'd normally have the morning and afternoon off, as hell on earth.

Of course, Xander wasn't in love with Bastian.

After they returned to Terroir from San Francisco, and Bastian promoted Xander to *sous*, the moments that made Kian's heart beat feaster and his breath catch happened further and further apart.

Kian knew his own feelings hadn't changed. Suspected that Bastian's hadn't either, but after being confronted with Luc, and almost making a monumental mistake, it made sense for him to pull back.

It sucked, and it frustrated the hell out of Kian, but he *still* wasn't sure pursuing a relationship between them would even be the right thing to do. So he let Bastian pull away, let him redefine their relationship more professionally, and tried very hard to be satisfied with that.

Everything hit the fan when Xander announced to Kian that he'd been offered a new job. Even though he saw evidence of Xander's resentment all the time—and it wasn't like he hadn't ever been angry at Bastian himself—Kian couldn't believe Xander was actually leaving Terroir.

"You're going to take that job, aren't you?" His voice sounded flat, resigned. Maybe three months ago, he would have still believed that with Xander out of the way, Kian might be promoted to *sous*. But lately, Kian had begun to realize that was never going to happen.

Kian was in the spot Bastian wanted him to be in—closest to him, yet so far away, at the very same time.

"Of course I'm going to take it." Xander slammed his knife down on the board. "We're not all like you, in thrall to the Bastard. You wouldn't take another job even if the French Laundry came calling."

First off, Thomas Keller would never try to poach him from Bastian. Second off, Kian couldn't imagine a life where he didn't see Bastian for at least twelve hours a day. It was unthinkable.

The annoying voice in his head, the one he'd been trying to ignore but that kept growing louder and louder during these last few months, told him, *if you left, you could finally figure out how to fall out of love with him.*

Kian didn't really want to fall out of love. There was a somewhat masochistic side of him that enjoyed loving Bastian, despite all the pain that came with it. Moving on would undoubtedly hurt even more, but maybe he'd feel less stagnant. Less like he was running and standing still simultaneously.

"I don't want to work for Thomas Keller," Kian insisted.

"That's exactly the point I'm trying to make," Xander retorted. His temper had cooled, and he just sounded regretful now. Still trying to save Kian, even when Kian didn't want to be saved.

The thing was, Kian hadn't come to Terroir looking for a knight in shining armor. He was capable of making his own decisions—good and bad—and even though Xander hated that he'd fallen in love with Bastian, that had been *his* choice. When Xander had opened the door that day, Kian had walked in wanting a teacher, which he'd gotten in Bastian, and maybe a friend, too. For a long time, Kian had believed he and Xander *were* friends, but now he suddenly wasn't so sure. Weren't friends supposed to be supportive, even when they believed you were making a mistake? But Xander, no matter what happened, or what Kian did or didn't say, couldn't leave this thing with Bastian alone. Even worse, he didn't know the half of it. He didn't even know about The Kiss.

"You're pissed off that I won't listen to your fucking advice," Kian spit out. He'd been chopping carrots for the vegetable medley. It was meaningless prep, especially for him, but he'd been assigned the task because that was what he *did*. He did the stuff there was nobody else for, and he was damn sick of Xander pretending that didn't mean anything.

He continued, barely taking a breath. "Not everyone is you, Xander, and you don't know what's right for everyone. Maybe if you did, you could tell yourself and you wouldn't be so god damned bitter all the time."

Instead of saying anything, Xander just reached over and turned the gas off on the stove where he was currently prepping sauces for the night's service.

"What are you doing?" Kian demanded.

Xander pulled the rug out from under him. "Leaving," he said. "You can tell the Bastard I'm done."

With that single sentence, Xander packed up his knives, pulled his coat from his locker, and despite Kian's incredulous expression, walked out.

He didn't know what he was supposed to tell Chef; *how* he was supposed to tell Chef. Xander and he had plenty of differences—it was difficult to *not* have differences considering how they both liked having the final word on everything—but he'd promoted Xander to *sous*. He'd trusted Xander to have his back.

Kian stood in the doorway of Bastian's office and couldn't help but remember the first time he'd ever stood here, terrified and unsure. That time, Xander had had *his* back, but he didn't anymore. And probably not ever again.

Anger and determination coalesced into a hard, knotty ball inside his stomach.

"What's going on?" Bastian asked absently, sorting through the stack of papers on his desk that Kian had left for him earlier. "Don't tell me Steve's come back to throw a fit."

Steve, one of the brand-new kitchen assistants, had walked out an hour into prep because he didn't feel like he was being treated with respect.

Kian had thought this was ridiculous because as a *newly hired kitchen assistant*, he didn't deserve any respect because he had yet to earn any. Bastian had grumbled, but because Steve's worth had been so minuscule, there hadn't been any tantrums. Kian had been assigned his prep work and that was that.

Xander's departure was going to be a whole different kettle of fish.

"Xander just left." Since coming to work for Bastian, Kian had done some reading on the side about how to deal with difficult personalities in the workplace. Most, if not all, espoused the technique of being direct, but never dramatic.

Bastian still hadn't looked up. "Is he sick? You can make the sauces for tonight. Did he at least finish the soup before he left?"

Kian walked further into the office and shut the door behind him, which mostly got his attention. "He's not sick."

"Not sick?" Bastian looked slightly pained, white lines bracketing his mouth, and that terrifying combination of fear and anger simmering in his eyes. "He quit, didn't he?" he asked flatly.

Kian could only nod.

"God damnit," Bastian bellowed. "Without even a fucking word to me. Did he think he could just walk out and it wouldn't haunt him forever?"

Kian considered telling him to not even bother. If the Hess family had decided on Xander, even Bastian Aquino wasn't going to get them to change their mind and give him back.

"I don't know what he was thinking," Kian said, and that was at least honest.

"How much of Steve's prep do you have left?" Bastian asked. "Maybe I should handle the sauces tonight."

"I've got about half my prep left and then I can finish the soup," Kian offered.

"We'll at least get a temp in to cover the prep tomorrow," Bastian said, rising from his chair and buttoning up his collar. Walking around his desk, he paused next to Kian. "You keep giving me strange looks."

"I keep expecting to have to clean your desk off the floor," Kian said, and he was only half joking.

Bastian sighed. "I saw orange, okay? I saw it, and I'm pissed. But I also think we can get him back."

There was no way Xander was going to come back to Terroir, no matter what Bastian enticed him with, but conceptualizing a plan was at least temporarily delaying Bastian's temper, and Kian wasn't going to spoil that.

"Where is he going?"

For a brief moment, Kian considered telling Bastian he didn't know. Maybe a month after The Kiss, he might have. Maybe even two months after. He'd been pissed for a long time, but now he was just resigned. "Hess. They're opening a farm-to-table restaurant."

"Huh, that's a surprise, I would have expected to hear rumblings," Bastian said, and started to walk past Kian, but at the last moment he stopped. He glanced around, like he was confirming nobody was watching, and then he lifted his hand to Kian's cheek briefly, the fingers brushing against it.

"I'm sorry," he said quietly. "I'm sorry I gave Xander the *sous* job, not when you deserved it."

Kian had been dying for this apology for six months, but even the tender, apologetic look Bastian swiftly shot him wasn't enough.

He wanted more. He wanted Xander's old job. He wanted more than just the fleeting touch of Bastian's fingers on his cheek. He wanted another kiss. He wanted even more than that.

It didn't matter that it was dangerous or that Bastian had said it was impossible. It didn't even matter that a part of Kian believed Bastian was right, because there was another part of him that was actively rebelling. That part wanted more and was not going to be placated with less.

"And you're still going to try to convince him to come back?" Kian said incredulously. He didn't need Xander back; they both knew it. Bastian could promote Kian and the kitchen would probably run *better*, not worse, without Xander.

But Bastian couldn't have looked more surprised than if Kian had been the one to walk out in the middle of prep.

"I don't think you understand," Bastian began, and Kian knew his mental gymnastics so well by this point that he knew exactly what he was going to say. *I don't apologize to anyone, and I'm apologizing to you. You're special, you're important, and you need to stay exactly where I've put you.*

Kian had liked that place, but even at the beginning, it hadn't quite felt like enough, and by now, two years in, Kian was tired of it and *bored*.

"I understand," Kian cut him off. "More than you realize."

Bastian's hand dropped to his side and he flexed it, like he was trying to forget the way Kian had felt under his fingertips. Even if he never forgot, it wouldn't be enough. Kian wanted to weasel his way under his skin, until there was nothing else between them. Until Kian didn't know where he stopped and Bastian began. He loved him. Why had he ever thought this sort of half relationship would ever be enough?

"I guess you do," Bastian said slowly.

"I need to check on the soup," Kian said and walked away.

He wanted to be shocked and incredulous that, in one breath, Bastian would tell him that Kian should have had the job that was Xander's, in the next, tell him he was getting Xander back. But the truth was, Kian wasn't, at all.

He'd known the person Bastian was for a long time now, and he'd loved him anyway. Believing that his mother's advice was solid, he'd loved the good and the bad parts of him, and that wasn't going to change, at least not anytime soon. But he was done tolerating Bastian's shit and he was done giving in.

Most of all, Kian was done being jealous of Luc for having things he never would.

The service passed in a blur of Bastian yelling and far too much work. Kian went home and crashed, passing out on his bed diagonally, with his socks still on. He didn't know where Xander was, and he wasn't sure he even wanted to.

A loud, insistent series of knocks drove him from his warm blankets the next morning, until he finally gave in. He got up, not even bothering to throw a shirt on, and jerked the door open.

He'd half expected a one-night stand of Nate's—their new roommate—or maybe even some kids selling magazines or tubs of cookie dough.

It wasn't a one-night stand of Nate's or a kid. It was Bastian, his aviators and a grumpy look on his face.

"Took you long enough," Bastian grumbled. "Were you dead?"

It was too bad it hadn't been one of those kids. Kian really wanted some cookie dough right about now. He'd scoop it right from the tub, and eat it spoonful by spoonful, unbaked.

Breakfast of champions.

"No." Kian kept his voice neutral. "What are you doing here?"

"I need to talk to Xander," Bastian said, like he couldn't believe Kian had forgotten. He hadn't—not exactly, anyway—he'd just chosen to prioritize other things. Like making it through last night's hellish service and then sleeping.

"I haven't seen him."

"His car's outside," Bastian said impatiently. "Go get him. I'm sure he's sleeping off a hellacious *I just quit Terroir* bender."

Bastian was probably right, but there was something imperious in his tone today that Kian didn't like. He crossed his arms across his chest and let Bastian look at all the bare skin he had on display. Let him look and want. Maybe it would only be a fraction of how much Kian wanted, but that was better than nothing.

"Or I could go drag him out myself," Bastian said, raising an eyebrow.

Kian rolled his eyes. "Fine. Come in and wait in the living room." He held the door open and Bastian followed behind him. Kian couldn't see him but he had a feeling he was eyeing everything, from the mis-matched furniture they'd picked up at Goodwill and IKEA and on the side of the road, sometimes, to the winery posters that Nate had tacked all over the walls.

It wasn't much, it certainly wasn't the sleek, ultra-modern house that Bastian lived in on the top of Mount Veeder. But Bastian knew what he paid his chefs, and even with three of them in this house, they weren't buying multimillion-dollar houses anytime soon. Kian refused to feel ashamed, because he loved the house they lived in. It felt like *home*, not the house Bastian merely existed in between shifts.

"I'll go get Xander," he said shortly, and left Bastian in the living room, while he clearly debated whether to sit on the couch or not.

Fuck his snobbery, Kian thought wretchedly. There was a reason why, in all the many, *many* fantasies he'd had of Bastian, they'd never been at his own house. And today, that really pissed him off.

Tonight, he was going to imagine Bastian blowing him in their bathroom with the chipped tile. Fantasy Bastian's eyes would say everything, but his mouth would be full, wouldn't it?

Taking out his frustration—sexual and otherwise—on Xander's door, he pounded hard on the thin wood, and then even harder when Xander didn't open it.

"Xander, I know you're in there," he said loudly.

"You're wrong," a voice finally croaked on the other side of the door, "Xander isn't here."

Kian remembered that Xander's bedroom door didn't even have a lock, and bracing himself for whatever he might find, decided he was sick of waiting, and just opened it.

"I need to talk to you," he said.

"So talk," Xander said, rolling over in bed, his hair a mess, and his pallor pale, like he'd drunk too much last night. "Clearly nothing is stopping you."

"You walked out last night," Kian said.

"I quit," Xander interrupted him. "I didn't just walk out. I fucking quit. Just in case that wasn't clear."

It had been abundantly clear. Kian had never wanted to punch Xander in the face more than he did right now. And Xander could be annoying and frustrating and infuriating a good portion of the time.

"Believe me, it was clear."

"Okay then," Xander said, and rolled back over, leaving his back to Kian.

It was really difficult to say who Kian was more pissed off at—his friend or his boss. Maybe he should just sic them on each other and let them fight to the death.

"What I keep trying to tell you is that you don't have to. Leave, that is. Chef is here . . . and he wants to talk to you."

"Chef is here?" Xander finally sounded like he was paying attention, Kian thought with satisfaction. "In *our* house?"

"Yes."

"What the fuck," Xander said tiredly.

"I suggest," Kian retorted primly, "that you get cleaned up and get out here before he gets tired of waiting and leaves."

After a long moment, Xander finally listened and slid out of bed, staggering to stay upright.

Kian let the full force of his glare out. And he'd learned from the very best.

"Hurry up," Kian said, and shut the door behind him.

He marched back into the living room, not even a fraction less pissed than he'd been before. He didn't sit down, though Bastian had finally managed to do it, perching on the edge of the couch.

"Is he coming?" Bastian asked shortly.

It was like he didn't know Kian at all. How often had Kian failed to complete a task to his satisfaction? Kian couldn't even remember the last time that had happened. He *always* got his shit done. And constantly questioning if he could, if he was up to it, was really beginning to get to him. Let Bastian question everyone else, the rest of the kitchen that fucked up regularly and couldn't really be counted on. He was Kian, and he was different.

Xander finally emerged, looking slightly less like hell. "What do you want?" he barked at Bastian.

"You quit last night," Bastian said, and despite his own current feelings, Kian was grudgingly impressed at how even his voice sounded.

"I did." Xander also sounded surprisingly even-tempered.

Apparently the only one in this room who wanted to throw something was Kian.

"You're not even going to give me the benefit of a two-week notice?"

Kian barely refrained from rolling his eyes. There was never a two-week notice at Terroir. Only flaming tempers and Bastian's desk in pieces on the floor.

"No," Xander said, still steady.

"Or an opportunity to counter what Damon Hess offered you?"

Xander instantly looked over at Kian, who felt a tiny twinge of shame. Yeah, he'd sold Xander out, but Xander hadn't said where he was going was a secret. And *who* was Damon Hess anyway? That name didn't even sound familiar, and Kian thought he knew all the Hesses in town.

"Not much is a secret," Xander retorted bitterly, which wasn't fair at all. If he'd said it was a secret, Kian would have at least considered not divulging it.

"Kian is worried about you," Bastian said, which was completely untrue. Kian was worried about *himself*. "Worried you're throwing your career away on someone who can't properly support you. You know, he isn't even really a winemaker. He's not a restauranteur. He's playing at growing a garden. But he's not even a Hess—not like you think."

Suddenly, Xander's reticence to tell Kian more yesterday made sense. It wasn't the Hess *family* that was starting this restaurant. It was some far-flung edge of the family, not connected in the same ways at all.

Maybe Kian was more worried about Xander than he'd realized. What was he *thinking*?

"He's exactly what I think," Xander said.

"There's nothing I can offer you that might make you change your mind?" Bastian offered slyly, and Kian gritted his teeth. Here was the job offer that should have been *his*—the second one that Xander had been offered and he hadn't. The first had stung, this one *ached*.

"What," Bastian continued, "if I made you my *chef de cuisine*?"

The *sous chef* was typically the second-in-command of a kitchen, especially if the executive or head chef was on premises, and involved, like Bastian was. If the executive chef was distant, or less involved, there needed to be someone *in* the kitchen who was nominally in charge. And that was the *chef de cuisine*. Kian had never imagined that Bastian would consider taking that step back—or ceding the control of his kitchen to someone else.

To *Xander*.

Yes, it definitely ached, because in some far-flung future, when this inevitably happened, many years distant, Kian had always believed that position was his. Nobody else knew Terroir like he did. Nobody else deserved it like he did. Nobody else had worked as hard.

"You mean the job I've deserved for six months?" Xander demanded. "The one you already should have offered me?"

Xander was . . . wrong. There was no way around it. He was blind to what really happened at Terroir. Blind to anything but his rapidly expanding ego. Kian sighed inwardly.

"I can't apologize for that, Xander," Bastian cut in smoothly. And of course he wouldn't. He didn't apologize to anyone.

Except to you, Kian thought. *Twice*.

"I think I'll take my chances with the 'not real' Hess," Xander said.

"You really mean that," Bastian said, and he sounded surprised. Of course he'd probably believed that this offer would be the one thing that would sway Xander's mind. "Hess said you'd say that, but I couldn't believe it. Couldn't believe you'd turn down *chef de cuisine* to work for a part-time gardener whose restaurant is currently a ramshackle shed without a real kitchen."

Xander frowned. "You went and talked to Damon?"

Bastian stood and began to pace, which Kian knew was a bad sign. "He poached you. In my own fucking restaurant! What else was I supposed to do?"

To salvage his prodigious pride? Kian wasn't sure. At least he understood why Bastian had come here and why he'd offered Xander the job, even though he'd known he wouldn't take it. He'd had to do *something*, so he could feel in control again.

"Fucking *ask me* if I wanted the job. Not my new partner. Not my friend and roommate. *Me*. That's your whole problem. That's why I left. You have to control everything, and it fucking sucks." Kian froze. Xander was notoriously lacking in basic tact, but this was a lot, even for him.

And then it got worse. Xander pointed in Kian's direction. "And that one," he said, "is too nice to ever say anything to your face, but you're a psychotic megalomaniac who desperately needs to be checked."

It was too much. For Bastian's temper. For his ego. For his everything. Kian held his breath as Bastian shot Xander a death glare, and then marched right out of the house.

"You're an idiot," Kian said, which was all he could say. "Are you really going to let someone else, some guy you don't even know, tell Chef Aquino what you want to do?" This was completely unlike Xander, and while Kian was *still* undeniably pissed, that worried him. What was Xander's deal with this Hess person? Was it serious? Because Kian saw reflected back in Xander's eyes some of his own insanity—the determination to follow Bastian everywhere, no matter what happened, no matter what he said, no matter what he did. And that was so unlike Xander, it was sort of terrifying.

"Are we really going to do this? You and me, *really*?"

Kian desperately wanted to pretend that he didn't know what Xander meant. But unlike Xander in this moment, he wasn't stupid and he wasn't unaware of the mistakes he kept making. "I don't know what you mean," he retorted through stiff lips.

"I mean, are you really going to get bent out of shape over my new partner telling Aquino to take a hike when I was going to do that anyway? When you would follow Aquino to the depths of any hell he concocted, just because you're too in love with him to ever tell him no?"

It was such a painfully accurate assessment that Kian felt the wind knocked out of him. He'd done that. He'd done that for *two years*.

"No," he finally said. "No, I guess we're not."

"Okay then," Xander said and he finally sounded pissed. "I'm going back to bed, to contemplate my brief joblessness, and you can go running after Aquino because I know you're dying to."

Xander was right, but he was also wrong. Yes, Kian wanted to go after him, but not to apologize or try to placate him or any of the things that Xander assumed he'd do.

No, he wanted to read him the fucking riot act. *Chef de cuisine, really? Xander?*

Which was exactly what he said when he wrenched open the door of Bastian's car.

Bastian had the nerve to look a tiny bit ashamed. "Get in," he said. "Let's get a coffee."

Kian gave him a look, since he still hadn't put a shirt on, and he was currently in socks, but no shoes.

"We'll go through the drive-through," Bastian amended, leaning back and rubbing his temples. "I didn't sleep last night. I lose too many more good chefs and people are going to talk. They're already fucking talking."

"You care too much about what other people think," Kian said, which was true, but was also an unfortunate symptom of the restaurant business. Everyone had an opinion, and when those opinions were formed by important people, it could make or break a restaurant.

Bastian's glare was expected. He pulled out of their drive in a spray of gravel. "You know it matters."

Kian had heard this story before; too many good chefs would leave a restaurant, and there'd be blood in the water. For patrons, for other chefs, for *critics*.

They'd come in droves, hearing that Terroir's *sous* was gone, to see if the standard of the food had fallen at all.

Kian didn't need to tell Bastian that he would make sure with every fiber of his being that nothing would change, because Bastian was just as committed.

"How did you know it wasn't a Hess restaurant?" Kian asked, changing the subject.

"I know because I know," Bastian said, annoyingly. "Also, because Nathan Hess has been talking to *me* about taking over the bistro at their winery. I'd just about decided to tell him I was interested, but now there's this wrinkle."

"No Xander."

"No Xander," Bastian agreed. "He was an ass, but he was a reliable ass. I still like the bistro concept, I've been wanting to open a second location for awhile now, but I'm not sure I want it on Nathan Hess' property."

"Why not?" Kian asked as Bastian pulled the car into the parking lot of his favorite coffee shop.

Bastian pulled out his phone and dialed. "Yeah, it's me," he said when someone on the other end answered. "Two cappuccinos. Dry. No sugar. Double shots."

Of course this was Bastian's idea of a "drive-through."

"You're insufferable," Kian said as he rolled his eyes.

The smile Bastian shot him was cocky and so sure of himself it made Kian's knees weak. If he hadn't been sitting down, he would have wobbled. As it was, his nipples tightened even in the comfortable warmth of the car, and Bastian, who noticed everything, swept his gaze across his chest.

Kian blushed, and then flushed even redder when a young woman exited the coffee shop, bearing two cups of coffee. Bastian rolled down the window, took the cups, and gave her a twenty-dollar bill.

"Keep the change," he said.

The woman's eyes lingered over him, nearly completely undressed in the passenger seat of the car, and he wondered if he'd hear through the rumor mill next week that Bastian was driving his young hookups around.

It's not like that, but I wish it was, Kian couldn't help but think.

"Drink your coffee," Bastian said brusquely. "We have a long day."

Oh yeah. No Xander. No kitchen assistant.

"I called the temp agency, they're sending over someone, but I'm sure they'll be useless," Bastian grumbled.

"Is the Hess deal why you offered Xander *chef de cuisine*?" Kian asked between sips.

Bastian's expression was locked up so tightly Kian couldn't decipher it. "I offered him *chef de cuisine* because I knew he wouldn't take it."

It shouldn't have made sense, but in a strange, fucked-up sort of way, it did. Bastian had known it was useless, had known that Xander was done with Terroir, but he'd wanted to salvage his pride, to at least make an effort to win him back, even if it was a fool's errand.

"Someday," Kian said seriously, "your pride and your ego are going to get you into big trouble."

Bastian laughed—rich and full and hearty. Kian wanted to lean over and lick the tiny speck of milk foam off his upper lip.

"Someday, huh?" he asked.

"You've done okay for yourself so far," Kian said with a shrug.

"High praise, coming from you," Bastian retorted dryly.

"I learned my expectations from the best." Kian looked over at him. Bastian's hands were clenched on the wheel.

There was silence for a minute. Kian thought he could fill in what Bastian was going to say next. *We can't do this. This is dangerous. This is impossible.*

It was all of those things, and inevitable, too.

Bastian cleared his throat. "I should get you home. Like I said, it's going to be a long day."

It almost didn't matter that Bastian hadn't actually said those things, because he'd thought them, and Kian had known he'd thought them—that was *almost* enough.

"Yeah," he finally said. "I'll need to give the rundown to the new temp."

"Right, yes," Bastian agreed. He started the car and drove them in silence back to Kian's house.

Kian knew he should ask who was going to take over Xander's role as *sous chef*. He should remind Bastian what he'd said just yesterday—that it should have been Kian's job, all along. But he didn't ask, because, he realized as he got out of the car, he was afraid of what he'd do if Bastian said no.

CHAPTER SEVEN

"Chef!"

Bastian looked up from the soup he was stirring. Derek, the new kitchen assistant that Kian had been training, was standing in front of him with a panicked expression on his face.

"What is it?" Bastian asked. He halfheartedly wondered why Kian wasn't taking care of Derek, who liked to freak out over every little thing. Bastian would have fired him weeks ago, but Kian kept insisting he could cure him of his dramatic streak.

But Kian wasn't here, and he definitely wasn't controlling Derek's melodrama, which seemed to be more developed than ever.

Derek wrung his hands, and Bastian suddenly noticed the bright red streaks across his white apron. He didn't think they were prepping beets today, and the color was wrong, anyway. The only thing that was that color was . . .

Bastian dropped the ladle into the pot. He knew he should be fishing it out, but instead he tuned into what Derek was currently stammering about: ". . . and I told him he was going to need to get it stitched, there's blood *everywhere*, and I think Jorge fainted . . ."

"What." Bastian interrupted him flatly. "Who cut themselves?"

Derek had the nerve to look impatient, like Bastian should have been paying attention this whole time. "I told you. Kian cut himself on the Japanese mandolin."

"Oh fuck," Bastian said and skirted around Derek, walking back to the prep stations, where most of the commotion was centered.

Kian was in the middle of a crowd of white-coated chefs, and Bastian caught a glimpse of his pale face. Far too pale.

He knew Kian liked using the Japanese mandolin without gloves because he could get through the prep work faster that way—and he probably cared about speed more than safety because Bastian kept piling more and more shit onto his plate. His stomach lurched sickeningly.

"Get out of the way," he bellowed, and the crowd cleared nearly instantaneously, revealing a mess of bloody towels on the counter, with another, even bloodier, towel currently wrapped around Kian's hand.

"Chef," Kian said, and nobody else might have known him enough to hear the wobble in his voice, but Bastian heard it, because he felt like he lived and died by the various subtle inflections in Kian's voice.

"Let me see," he said, even though he hated to have Kian take pressure off the wound.

One glimpse was all Bastian needed.

Most of the time they didn't really miss Xander, but Bastian did today. Wished, maybe for the first time in his career, that everyone who left Terroir hadn't done so under terrible circumstances, because nobody else was taking care of Kian but him, and he didn't want to leave the restaurant now, two hours before service. But he would.

Pain and shock swam in Kian's big blue eyes, and Bastian knew only half a second before he collapsed, but it was enough that he was able to stagger forward and catch him.

Kian might have grown up in the last two years, but he was still too skinny, and Bastian was able to pick him up easily. He ignored the gaping stares of the rest of the chefs in the kitchen and hoped they wouldn't talk—even as he knew this would be the most discussed Bastard story in the history of Bastard stories.

"We're going to the ER," Bastian said in his most strident voice, even though everything inside him was collapsing into itself. "I'm going to make it back before service, but I need you to finish prep. Everything *must* be ready when I get back. Michel," he called out to the man who'd taken Wyatt's place at the grill, "please make sure the soup is ready. The ladle is probably still floating around in the pot."

Michel looked surprised. But Michel was still new, and hadn't figured out that Kian was what made this whole restaurant run the way it was supposed to.

Bastian didn't remember driving to the emergency room. He didn't remember Kian groaning as he picked him up, didn't remember carrying him through the doors, didn't remember yelling, didn't remember a nurse wheeling out a gurney—it only caught up to him when he sat down in the chair opposite Kian's bed.

He'd woken up after making it to the private room and was giving answers to the nurse for her intake paperwork.

When she finally finished up and said the doctor would be in shortly, Kian turned to Bastian. "You couldn't have sent me with someone else? What about prep? What if we're not back for service?"

"It's fine," Bastian soothed, even though soothing wasn't really in his repertoire. "Prep will be fine." He hoped. "And *I'll* be back for service, but you won't be. I'm going to drop you off at home. You're taking the night off."

Kian pouted, which shouldn't have been adorable, but was, somehow, anyway.

"It wasn't even that bad," Kian insisted, which they both knew was a lie. It had been bad. Bad enough that just thinking of it made Bastian's stomach roll nauseatingly.

"I push you too hard," Bastian muttered to himself, but Kian had heard him and he couldn't take the words back.

Like he hadn't been able to take the kiss back, no matter how much he wished he could. He'd done everything he could to push Kian away, to kill their chemistry, but instead of growing fainter, all it did was grow stronger.

In San Francisco, Kian had been angry because he'd believed Luc's existence meant that he wasn't special after all.

What Kian didn't know, and couldn't ever realize, was that Luc's very existence in Bastian's life was enough to make Kian special. Kian was everything Luc hadn't been: loyal, kind, funny, insanely self-sacrificing, but with enough ego that he respected his own skill. If he hadn't been only twenty-three years old, with a whole brilliant future stretching out in front of him, and also Bastian's student and employee, he'd have believed wholly and completely that Kian was the perfect man for him.

He'd believed that, surely, that sort of bizarrely romantic thinking must have died with the disappointment of Luc, but Kian made him remember exactly why he'd believed it in the first place.

"You push me exactly the right amount," Kian argued. Of course he'd say that. Bastian had brainwashed him into believing that he was the best, with the best judgement. And that definitely wasn't true. What had just happened proved that conclusively.

Celeste was going to be pissed at him. Even more pissed than when she'd discovered he had promoted Xander to *sous*.

"*Merde*," she'd said to Bastian that day. "You are stupider than anyone on the planet."

"I know," he'd said miserably as he sat on her porch during yet another sleepless night. It had been bad enough imagining what kissing Kian would be like, but the reality of it had blown his mind.

His mother would have been thrilled he'd finally stepped over his self-imposed line with Kian, but he couldn't endure her excitement when he couldn't ever do it again.

The doctor walked in then, jerking Bastian's attention back to Kian and his finger.

"It's deep," he finally pronounced, after an examination that had both Kian and Bastian gritting their teeth. Kian because it fucking hurt and Bastian because apparently he couldn't stand to see Kian in pain. "You'll definitely need stitches. Inner *and* outer. We'll give you something for the pain."

"Something strong," Bastian intervened, before Kian could open his mouth and insist he needed to be sharp enough for the evening's service.

Even if he was beginning to wonder differently, Bastian was in charge of both Kian and Terroir and his word was final.

"Something strong," the doctor agreed. "We'll do a local and have him take some pills too."

"Good." Bastian nodded.

"And you are?" the doctor asked, turning towards Bastian. "His boyfriend? Husband?"

Oh god. "His boss," Bastian finally managed to admit between clenched teeth.

"Ah," the doctor said. "And I'm assuming," he waved at Bastian's coat, "he won't be working tonight."

"Definitely not." Bastian shot Kian a look, who surprisingly, didn't argue. Probably because the doctor's examination had hurt a lot, and he knew the stitching would hurt worse.

It wasn't like Kian wasn't incredibly tough—he'd astounded Bastian continually with his mental and physical strength—but clearly he'd reached his limit.

And despite that he'd just told the doctor they weren't involved, Bastian reached out and grasped Kian's good hand with his own. Their palms slid together, Kian's smaller hand fitting into Bastian's much larger one. Glancing down at their hands, Kian smiled softly.

"I'm going to go grab the necessary supplies," the doctor said, and he closed the door behind him. If Bastian wasn't mistaken, he'd been smiling too.

Boss and so much more, Bastian wished he'd had the balls to say. But no matter how strong the pull towards the man in front of him was, he still wasn't convinced it was right to cross the line that he'd built and then reinforced. He'd done it for a reason, and that reason still felt valid, even more so when he looked back over the last two years and realized how accomplished Kian had become.

It should feel more vital than ever, to preserve that professional distance between them, but today made Bastian feel like it was more of a fool's errand than ever.

The doctor returned with the supplies and a nurse, and even though they gave him plenty of pain medication, Bastian still didn't let go of Kian's hand. Bastian could tell he was trying not to rely on him and not squeeze his hand too hard, but he kept tensing and then trying to relax.

Finally, Bastian murmured to him, "Go ahead. It hurts. It's scary. I'm here for you."

The doctor lifted his gaze a moment and shot their hands a single glance, but Bastian didn't care. His boy was in pain, and that was all that mattered.

Finally, it was over, and the doctor removed his gloves, tossing them into the trash can.

"The nurse will be back with your release paperwork," he said. "I'm assuming you'll be driving him home."

"Yes, of course," Bastian said.

"Good," he replied, and after giving Kian some final cleaning instructions, and when to expect the stitches to disintegrate, and what to do if they didn't, he left.

Kian's eyes had grown wide and dazed with the pain medication. He looked down at their hands.

"You didn't need to do this," he said. "It'll make you late for service."

It probably would. But in the last few hours, Bastian had discovered something more important than a service at Terroir. The realization was still blowing his mind.

"This is my fault," Bastian said brusquely, "so *yes*, I should be here."

"Not your fault," Kian said, still staring at their hands. Like he couldn't quite believe it was happening. "You tell us to use the protective gloves, and I don't."

"Yeah, because you're too busy to use them," Bastian said.

Kian smiled. "No, because I like to impress you."

It was almost impossible not to groan in frustration. "Yeah, exactly," Bastian insisted, the edge of his voice growing rough. "I let you do it. I like it when you try to impress me. I'm a terrible boss, and a terrible person."

"No," Kian said dreamily, "you're wonderful and I love you."

It wasn't as if Bastian didn't know. The way Kian looked at him, hot and possessive and adoring, when nobody else was watching made it difficult to deny. But it was one thing to wonder about it, far too late at night when Bastian should be sleeping, and it was another to hear Kian say it.

There were a million things he wanted to say. *I'm too old and too grumpy and too egotistical for you. I'd just ruin you. I'd ruin your future, which is going to be spectacular. I'll only slow you down.*

But most of all, *I love you too.*

But before he could make the choice, the nurse bustled in with the release paperwork, and when they made it to the car, it felt too late. And maybe, Bastian thought morosely, Kian hadn't meant it after all. He was hopped up on drugs. He probably wouldn't even remember this in a few hours.

Bastian *hoped* he wouldn't remember this in a few hours. They hadn't exactly been great at keeping the status quo—the kiss still loomed large, and he thought about it all the time—but Kian's confession might destroy the line forever.

❧ ❧

The kitchen was nearly clean from the night's service—it hadn't been the smoothest dinner they'd ever served at Terroir, but it hadn't been a disaster either—when Bastian's phone rang.

He usually kept his phone in his office when he was on the line, but tonight he'd kept it in his pocket—just in case Kian needed him.

It had stayed quiet all service, but now Kian was calling him.

"What?" he asked quietly, ducking outside, hoping nobody was outside for their post-service cigarette. "Are you okay? Is everything okay?"

Kian laughed, and Bastian still heard the drugs in his voice. "I'm fine. I'm at Damon Hess' with Xander."

Bastian frowned. "You're *what*?"

"I'm at Damon Hess' with Xander," Kian repeated again, like it was no big deal. "But you need to come get me. I think they want to start making out and I'm sort of in the way."

Leaning against the building, Bastian looked up to the sky, wishing and despairing all at once.

"You didn't drive?" he asked, before he remembered that with the meds he was on, driving was a bad idea.

"Silly, Bastian, I can't drive. Xander drove." Bastian's heart skipped a beat. Kian had only ever called him Chef, or Chef Aquino to his face. He'd always imagined that Kian thought of him differently, maybe even by his first name, but hearing it was so much different than just imagining it.

"Give me twenty minutes," Bastian said. It was a monumentally terrible idea. Considering Kian's weakened brain-to-mouth filter and Bastian's own dangerously shaky line between what was right and what he really wanted—this felt like an even worse idea than San Francisco had been.

And San Francisco had been a certifiable disaster.

Still, twenty-four minutes later, Bastian pulled up to Damon's farm. He could see smoke and light coming from the property behind the small ranch-style house and debated whether he should get out of the car or if he should just text Kian to say he'd arrived.

But this was Damon Hess' property, and there was a part of Bastian that wanted to show both him and Xander exactly where Kian's loyalties lay. Just in case they had any insane thoughts about poaching him. Kian was *his*, and there was a barbaric, caveman-esque part of Bastian that wanted everyone to know it.

Even though everyone probably already did. They'd both attempted subtlety, but that wasn't really Kian's strong suit, and it definitely wasn't Bastian's.

He got out of the car, and stripped off his chef jacket, tossing it in the back seat, leaving him just in his white tank. He'd already swapped his working clogs for the sneakers he usually kept in his office.

Detouring around the house, he saw the beginnings of the garden as he had the last time he'd been here. It even looked as if Hess had ripped out even more priceless vines, the vineyards in the back looking thinner than they had before, in the dim light provided by the bonfire.

He could see Hess and Xander, standing close together, and to his own astonishment, he *was* surprised. He didn't generally expect romantic attachments in other people, probably because his own had been so few and far between. But it would help explain why

Xander hadn't even been a little tempted by his counteroffer. He'd known Xander wouldn't take it when he'd offered it, but he hadn't expected Xander to be so sure, so quickly.

But he had, and Damon must be the reason. Bastian supposed he could see the attraction. He was good-looking, if a little brooding for his own tastes. Xander had never been particularly caught up in good-looking men before, but Bastian supposed that was what those people who believed in love at first sight were always nattering on about.

Sometimes you saw someone, and you connected with them despite everything.

Bastian approached the bonfire as he watched the light flickering off the delicate features of Kian's face. Two years in and he still couldn't explain it, couldn't quantify it. Couldn't fucking contain it. He knew the moment Kian saw him because his face lit up, like Bastian's arrival flicked on a lamp inside him.

Bastian was the least humble person he knew, but the way Kian looked at him sometimes was incredibly humbling. He knew he didn't deserve it and wasn't ever capable of deserving it—and Kian knew that, had been witness to so many moments that should have changed his mind, but he'd stayed steadfast and loyal and true, and Bastian couldn't deny it any longer, *in love*.

"You came," Kian said, approaching him, his voice still a little breathless.

"I said I would," Bastian said. "How's the finger?"

"It hurts." Kian made a face, and Bastian chuckled in spite of himself.

"I'm sure it does," he said sympathetically. "Let's get you home."

Kian glanced down at Bastian's hand, and then at his own, the one he hadn't tried to bisect today. He knew what Kian wanted, and the better part of him should have turned away, continued on to the car so Kian wouldn't have a chance.

But Bastian had never pretended to be an angel, and he stayed there, waiting as Kian reached out and took his hand in his own.

There was a million things Bastian could say. One of them definitely was, *I only did that because you were hurting and scared and it made us both feel better.* But he didn't, because even though the circumstances were different, the way Kian's hand curled into his own still made him feel better. Helped cleanse away a little of this wretched day.

Because he's still hurting, Bastian told himself as they walked back to his car, but even he didn't really believe the lie.

Kian had to let go when they reached the car, but as soon as they were back inside, Bastian took a deep breath and placed his hand on the center console, palm up. Eyes wide, Kian glanced at the offered hand, and then back up to Bastian's face.

It was the simplest of touches—it could even be construed as platonic, but there was nothing platonic about the thrill Bastian experienced whenever Kian touched him.

Kian smiled and tucked his hand right back into Bastian's own.

Bastian let out the breath he hadn't realized he was holding. "We should talk about this," he said carefully, even though the last thing he wanted to do was talk and potentially destroy the rest of the ramshackle hut currently trying to contain all his apprehension about this relationship.

Shooting him a very frank look, Kian shifted around in his seat. "If you're going to say that you regret today, that you regret taking me to the emergency room and that you regret holding my hand, even as you're doing it now, you might as well not bother."

"I meant about what you said earlier," Bastian said, and even though his voice was steady, he knew his pulse wasn't, and it was very possible that Kian could even feel how terrified he was in the sudden dampness of his palm.

"What I said earlier?" Kian asked, and even though he'd been so green and innocent when he'd started at Terroir—and in some ways, *still was*—Bastian knew when he was actually clueless and when he was just pretending. He could fool other people, maybe, but not Bastian. Never Bastian.

"You know what you said earlier." It was likely very obvious that he was trying to avoid actually saying the same words Kian had, but then Kian was also pretty damn transparent about his own memory.

"What was it?"

Bastian gnashed his teeth and pulled the car over onto the side of the road. He threw the car into park and turned his full attention onto Kian, who had the faintest smile on his lips.

"Is that it?" Bastian demanded. "You want me to say it?"

Shrugging, Kian glanced down at their intertwined hands again. And Bastian knew exactly the point he was trying to make.

"You can't be in love with me," Bastian said flatly, even though he knew he was, and that this was just plain foolish. "You shouldn't be."

"But I am," Kian said simply. "And I think you're in love with me too."

"We can't do this," Bastian said, and he knew just how desperate he sounded.

"We're already doing it." Kian's voice was gentle, coaxing. "We're doing it right now."

It hurt, maybe even worse than Kian's finger getting sliced up by the Japanese mandolin, but somehow Bastian managed to pull his fingers away from Kian's. Stopping the kiss in San Francisco should have hurt worse, but somehow he managed to feel more now than he had even then.

This is for Kian, Bastian reminded himself. *This is for Kian, even if it doesn't feel like it. Even if it feels like the worst thing on earth. You can do anything, for him.*

Kian stared at him incredulously. "Really? This is what you're going to do? Pretend you don't care about me?"

"I do care about you!" Bastian said, and the pain blooming inside of him made him sound so much angrier than he wanted, than he'd intended. "I'm doing this *because* I care!"

"Then why don't you care about what *I* want?" Kian demanded.

"You don't know what you really want! You don't know what you're giving away." Bastian knew it was a lie when he said it, and fully expected that Kian wouldn't believe it.

But from the way Kian's eyes shuttered, and he turned away, gaze determinedly focused on the dark landscape outside, he thought Bastian believed he was an idiot who didn't know anything and hadn't, in the last two years, thought through the downsides of their relationship at all.

Maybe, Bastian thought brokenly, *that's for the best.*

"Take me home," Kian said, and his voice had dropped about fifty degrees.

For a split second, Bastian wanted to take it back, to plead his forgiveness, but the words were already out there, and Kian already believed them.

It was too late for them, like it had been from the first moment.

It seemed like the right thing to do after dropping Kian off was to drive right past the turnoff to his house and continue down the road to his mother's.

Celeste did not look particularly surprised to see him when she opened the door.

"Rough day?" she asked and handed him a warm mug. "Hot milk," she explained as they headed towards the back porch. "With a touch of brandy."

Bastian took a grateful swallow and nearly burned his tongue. "Ahhh," he exclaimed.

She made a sympathetic noise. "You were five minutes earlier than I thought you'd be."

That was odd, even for his mother. Bastian set the mug aside. "How did you even know I was coming?"

"I follow a few of your chefs on Instagram," Celeste said primly. "More than one of them posted the bloody towels. It wasn't hard to deduce who it was that hurt himself. And that you'd twist yourself into knots when it happened."

Bastian didn't know how to react to Celeste's confession she even *had* an Instagram, never mind that she was following some of his employees. She rolled her eyes at his surprise. "I follow you too, of course, but it's all advertisements for the restaurant. You need to figure out something more personal to put on there. Frankly," she said, making a disappointed *cluck*, "it's very boring, Bastian. I'm surprised you even have followers."

"Uh," Bastian stammered, not very eloquently.

"I even follow your young man. Kian. Very cute. Clever. I can see why you like him."

Even though the mug of milk was probably still close to boiling, Bastian reached for it anyway and took a long gulp. "He's not *my* young man, *maman.*"

Her dark-eyed gaze was penetrating. Under it, he felt eight again, caught again sneaking sweets off the shelf at the corner market with his friends. Except this time the sweet was Kian.

"He could be," she said thoughtfully.

He greatly disliked the point she was trying to make and *hated* that she was right.

"No, no, *no,*" he ground out. "He can't be. I'm his mentor. His boss. It would be inappropriate and an incredible distraction."

Raising an eyebrow, Celeste sipped her own milk. "And it is not now?"

It was something more destructive than mere distraction; she was absolutely right about that.

"Bastian," she continued, reaching out to place a soothing hand on his knee, "you can be so rigid sometimes, and I hate to say it, but that reminds me of your *papa.*"

He couldn't help it; he grimaced.

"*Oui,*" she said, "he wasn't a good man. He was mean and neglectful. Your intensity, your certainty you are always right, those you get from him. But that doesn't make you bad, not like he was."

"Maybe I'm not bad, but I'm certainly not good either," Bastian admitted darkly.

Celeste shrugged, lace ruffles on the sleeve of her nightgown fluttering in the midnight breeze. "You are human. Not bad, not good. But you have tried to do good, staying away from Kian."

"Hasn't done much good." Bastian took another gulp of milk, the brandy burning the way down his throat. He didn't feel like the way forward was any clearer, but like she always did, his *maman* still made him feel better. Or it could've just been the excellent brandy.

"When you came to me two years ago, on his very first day, I told myself, *Celeste, he will not last a month*. But I was wrong. You held back, because for the first time, you care more about someone else than you care about yourself. And that is why you are nothing like your *papa*."

"I want to believe that," Bastian said, his throat suddenly aching. "I want to be better."

"And this young man, he makes you better," Celeste insisted. "I know, I see it."

"So you think I should just . . . give up?" It was both the very best thought and the worst.

"Do I think you should just go to Kian and say, *I was wrong, let us be together?* No. No, you should not. Because you do not get to expect him to drop all *his* concerns and suddenly expect him to be at your beck and call. You know better than that, Bastian."

Was that what he'd expected? That when his desires finally overrode his apprehensions, he'd just crook a finger and Kian would come running, desperate for even the crumbs from his table?

Yes, *maybe.*

The truth hurt.

"See, you have much to talk to him about," Celeste said, sounding very final, as if she'd discovered his solution for him. When Bastian felt just the opposite, unmoored and unsure.

Bastian finished his milk. "I don't even know how to begin." *Especially after tonight*, Bastian thought, *he probably hates me after what I said.*

"That," Celeste said, smiling, "is up to you to figure out, Bastian, darling. I can't solve everything for you. How else would you learn?"

"I said . . . something to him tonight," Bastian confessed. "He's probably not very happy with me right now."

"Then apologize to him," Celeste said.

Bastian stared at his hands. "I guess I do owe him one."

"At least one, I'm sure."

"Actually," Bastian offered, "I think I've apologized to him more than I've ever apologized to anyone before. Except you."

To his horror, Celeste's eyes filled with tears. "Oh, Bastian," she said, rising and wrapping her slim arms around him. "You love him."

Of course he loved Kian. How could he not?

When Bastian woke up the next morning, he felt resolved. He was going to ask to see Kian first thing in his office and he was going to apologize. An apology with no strings attached and no expectations.

But of course, he'd been in love for the better part of two years, with no end in sight, so there were *some* inevitable expectations attached.

He still wasn't sure if he'd been wrong or if he'd been right, but Bastian was beginning to realize that it didn't matter anymore. They couldn't continue this prolonged dance of *not ever*. They'd probably even moved beyond *not now*. They needed to figure out how to move forward into *this might actually be happening*.

Bastian caught a glimpse of Kian's bright hair as he walked out of the locker room and started to hurry over to him, but Kian stopped him with a single, dead-eyed look. He looked awful, white and drawn, shadows under his eyes, like he hadn't slept, and it appeared that the very last person he wanted to talk to was Bastian.

He should have gone over and followed through on the apology. He *knew* that, but for the first time in a very long time, when faced with an uphill battle, he didn't batten down the hatches and keep attacking. He waved the white flag and he turned back around. *Tomorrow*, he told himself, even as he knew that if he didn't do it right now, there was no point in doing it at all.

When Kian came over to him finally, it was mid-morning, and for half a second, Bastian's heart beat a little faster.

"I need the daily assignments," Kian said, in a dry, utterly professional voice that Bastian had never suspected he even owned.

"Right, right, of course," Bastian said, wiping his hands on a towel. They were shaking, and he thrust the towel away awkwardly before snatching it right back. "Let me get them for you."

Maybe what he should have done right then was not just apologize but give Kian the job he deserved—Xander's old job, the *sous chef* job that had been his forever. But he didn't, and he didn't apologize, and as Kian turned and walked away, Bastian believed that this was the very worst.

He'd always believed before that he and Kian had been professional with each other, but professionalism devoid of Kian's sunny smile, the light that shone in his eyes, and those single, brief glances that were more like caresses—it was hell on earth and Bastian was never going to survive it.

Chapter Eight

Kian couldn't believe it. Even after everything that Damon had put Xander through, they'd ended up together. Instead of Xander sulking alone, ranging from furious to distraught that Damon had abandoned him during the opening of their restaurant, they were currently cuddled up together on the couch—like Kian didn't even exist.

Xander probably wouldn't be happy to hear that Kian was especially pissed off that of all the people in the world, *Xander* had ended up blissfully happy and blissfully in love. Prior to meeting Damon, Xander had been bitter and lonely and downright curmudgeonly. While Kian was happy for his best friend, it wasn't supposed to be *Xander* who'd found the love of his life—it was supposed to be Kian.

But then, Kian thought morosely as he tried to avoid watching the happy couple make out, *I've already found the love of my life.*

Every single fucking time Kian believed that he and Bastian had finally managed to find a way through their situation, instead of pointlessly and endlessly spinning their wheels in the exact same damn spot, Bastian would slam on the brakes.

It wasn't like Kian hadn't thought this through. He *had*. He'd spent the last two years, falling deeper and harder, and trying to ignore his feelings, but they weren't going away. The chance they would seemed slimmer than ever. He'd weighed the pros and the cons, and he'd decided that something needed to change. Anything had to be better than the place they were in now. But Bastian wouldn't even have a conversation about it. He said, *nope, it's not happening,* like he was the one who got all the say in their relationship.

As far as Kian was concerned, that was fucking bullshit.

Kian might be young and a little naïve, not as experienced in the culinary arts, but he knew what he wanted. He knew what it might cost, and he was willing to take that chance anyway.

He couldn't sit here anymore. As much as he liked them both, Xander and Damon were sickening together, and every second Kian did nothing, he got angrier.

And he was already really fucking angry.

You don't know what you want! You don't know what you're giving away.

Bastian's words from a month before kept echoing through his head—but he'd been so fucking wrong. Kian knew because Kian wasn't a fucking idiot. It was definitely a risk, but life was a risk, and why should they settle for this hopeless half relationship when they could have more? Possibly without sacrificing a goddamn thing?

Kian stood up suddenly.

"Where you going?" Xander asked lazily, and Kian tried to ignore that Damon was kissing a line up his neck. "You look sort of pissed off." He sounded surprised, like Kian couldn't possibly be pissed off.

Oh, Xander had no fucking clue how pissed off he could be.

"I *am* pissed off," Kian bit off. "And it's none of your fucking business where I'm going."

Xander would almost definitely try to stop him, if he knew, and so Kian wasn't going to tell him. This was something he needed to do for himself.

He grabbed his wallet and his keys and climbed into his tiny little used hatchback.

The drive to Bastian's house didn't take very long. He'd thought when he arrived there would be less anger and more nerves, but as he pulled into the circular driveway, he still felt pretty fucking pissed off.

He banged on the front door, and then again when Bastian didn't come to the door. It seemed unbelievable that he wouldn't be home, because where else could Bastian be?

Picking up another young, naïve kid because he steadfastly refused to touch Kian? He'd never believed that was even a remote possibility. First, it didn't even seem like something Bastian would do, and second, he'd never caught even the tiniest bit of gossip that Bastian was out in Napa, hooking up with random guys.

But where else would he be?

It was so late, the only thing open this late were some of the seedier bars on the outskirts of town. And while Kian had believed at the beginning that Bastian led this incredibly glamorous life, he'd long since learned that Bastian did exactly what all his chefs did: go to the restaurant early and leave late and go straight home after.

He pounded on the door again, not because he really thought Bastian was going to answer, but because he had to get some of this goddamn frustration out somehow.

Maybe Bastian was right after all, Kian thought despairingly, maybe there really was never a right time for them. He'd refused to believe it before—when you felt something this strongly, it needed to be for a reason—but fate was currently, very forcibly, reminding Kian of all the realities that he didn't want to face.

He nearly pulled out his phone and called Bastian. He imagined barking into the phone, demanding to know his whereabouts, the way Bastian did when any of his employees dared to be even five minutes late.

But before he could dial, he heard tires on the gravel turnoff to Bastian's house, then he saw lights.

A moment later, Bastian pulled up, parking his very fancy car right next to Kian's junker.

He got out, and even in the dim light, Kian could see he was frowning.

"What are you doing?" Bastian asked. "Is everything okay?"

It was Bastian's normal MO to ask a series of fast-paced questions. The practice tended to put the other person on edge, and immediately established in any personal encounter who was in charge.

Kian had recognized the technique after being subjected to it hundreds of times, and afterwards, he'd continued to let Bastian do it. Because at Terroir, he *was* in charge, and Kian was supposed to be learning from him.

But they weren't at Terroir now, and Kian had zero intention of letting Bastian just take over the way he always did.

He'd come here to flip the script, and he intended to follow through.

"Where were you?" he challenged right back.

Bastian looked gratifyingly surprised. "Where was I?"

Kian crossed his arms over his chest, and tried, despite his baby-face, to look stern. "Where were you?"

"Uh," Bastian said, pausing on the top step. "I was visiting my mom."

Now Bastian wasn't the only one looking surprised. "Your mom lives here?" Kian asked.

"Yeah, a few miles up that way. Sometimes I visit her when I can't sleep."

That was the opening Kian had been waiting for—not Bastian talking about his mother, but Bastian admitting that he was struggling just as much as Kian was.

"You can't sleep?" Kian questioned as Bastian typed in the code to unlock the front door.

Bastian shot him an incredulous look.

"Me either," Kian admitted, because while he'd intended to control this conversation, honesty was also important. They walked into the foyer, and then into the living room.

Bastian's house was on the extreme end of the open-floor-plan concept. The kitchen sat to the left, with a long counter and barstools set neatly in a row. A long bank of windows, with the terrace that looked out across the valley, let in the only ambient light.

Kian assumed the bedroom lay to the right, but he'd never been in there before. Maybe tonight that would finally change.

"I came here tonight because I'm done not doing anything about it," Kian continued, walking over to the windows. He wondered if anyone could see in, and then decided he didn't give a fuck. If they wanted to watch, let them watch.

"What do you mean?" Bastian sounded guarded and uneasy. Not surprising, considering he was a control freak and Kian had just yanked all his control away.

"I'm done playing around," Kian said, turning around. "We've played around for two years."

Bastian gave a sharp bark of laughter. "Is that what we were doing? I thought I was teaching you to become a great chef."

"You were, you *have*, at least enough that I know what it takes to be one. And I intend to be one." Kian paused, gesturing between them. "What I'm talking about is a little more personal."

Bastian opened his mouth, no doubt to deny that anything personal between them existed, which was a huge fucking lie, and that set Kian's determination on fire.

He was going to keep denying this as long as he could. As long as Kian *let* him.

"Yeah," Kian interrupted. "About that." And he reached behind his head and tugged his t-shirt off. "I told you I'm done fucking around, and that means I'm done fucking around." He tossed the garment onto the arm of the couch.

Bastian laughed again, but it wasn't quite so bitter and it wasn't quite as controlled as before. "What do you think you're doing?"

Toeing off his shoes, Kian kept his gaze steady on Bastian. "You know what I'm doing."

It would have made this a hell of lot more dramatic if he'd been wearing more clothes, but he was wearing enough. He leaned down and tugged his socks off, first one and then the other. They landed next to his t-shirt.

Fists clenched at his side, Bastian looked torn—like he wasn't sure if he should demand Kian put his clothes back on, or join him, instead.

Kian knew exactly which way he wanted Bastian to fall.

He unbuttoned his jeans and then unzipped them, but didn't shuck them quite as quickly, just let them hang on his hip bones. Raising an eyebrow, he shot Bastian a very frank look.

"Are you going to join me?" Kian asked finally when Bastian just kept staring, like he was the angel and the devil, wrapped up in one altogether too-tempting package.

If Bastian continued to emphatically deny it, Kian wasn't sure what else he could do. Could he stand, for an extended period of time, naked in Bastian's living room until he made up his mind?

Fuck yes, he could.

Shoving away the last remnants of modesty, he shoved his jeans past his hips and let them fall to the floor. Bastian continued to stare; Kian wasn't sure he'd even blinked in the last few minutes.

"Are you really going to stand there and tell me you don't want this?" Kian challenged. He tucked a finger under his boxer briefs and saying a quick prayer—probably not to God, who wouldn't approve of this at all, but maybe the Devil instead, because he sure as fuck would—he pulled them down.

He stood there proudly and completely naked and let Bastian just *look*.

For a long, interminable second, Kian wasn't sure what was going to happen. Was he going to end up going back home, heart heavy and the worst case of raging blue balls that he'd ever experienced?

"I don't know why you're doing this," Bastian said and he sounded absolutely wretched. "Put your goddamn clothes back on."

"No," Kian said.

"Goddamn it, you're killing me." Bastian's voice had grown dark and deep, gravelly at the edges, and it seemed impossible, but Kian's cock grew even harder.

He'd never imagined he was much of an exhibitionist, but standing here, naked as the day he was born, and letting Bastian just *look* was an incredible turn-on. Of course, he'd rather if Bastian got his stubborn ass over here and finally touched him, but just this felt like *almost* enough.

"This is me saying to you, I've thought about it. I've considered the pros and the cons," Kian finally said, when the tension and the silence ratcheted even tighter between them. "This is me choosing you."

"Don't I get a say?" Bastian challenged.

Kian had to nod. "Of course you get a say, you can tell me to fuck off, and I'll go home. But I don't think you want to tell me to fuck off, Bastian."

When he said his name, Bastian closed his eyes, praying to someone—or something, maybe?

"No," Kian said tightly, "no, you don't get to close your eyes and not look when you turn me down."

"I'm not turning you down."

"No?" Kian raised an eyebrow and considered his next step. Bastian was so close to breaking—he could feel it, his self-control falling to pieces, but how to get it to crumble the rest of the way? "Then why are you still over there?"

Bastian laughed despairingly. "I don't fucking know."

In that moment, Kian knew. He knew what would break Bastian. Was he willing to play that dirty? *You've already shown up at his house in the middle of the night,* Kian reasoned, *and taken all your clothes off. What's a little further?*

He reached down, and hoping Bastian didn't see his fingers trembling, wrapped them around his cock. Pleasure rocketed through him. It wasn't like Bastian touching him, not exactly, but with his gaze on him, it was different and better than just doing this by himself, in his sad lonely room.

Bastian gasped sharply in the silence stewing between them. Rhythmically, he clenched and unclenched his fists, and Kian was so selfish—he wanted to know what those hands felt like instead of his own.

"I'm so fucking horny," Kian said, "and all I want is you. I don't want to go down to the Tavern and pick someone up. It wouldn't be enough. But if you won't help me, I guess I'll have to help myself."

Letting out a shaky breath, Bastian took a step closer, then another, until he was standing right in front of Kian. His eyes were so dark, Kian thought he could drown in the pupils. His breath was uneven, shaky even, and then Bastian dropped to his knees, and Kian couldn't breathe at all.

How many times had he imagined this? A dozen? A hundred? A thousand?

But Kian had never imagined that it might actually happen. If anything ever happened between them, Kian had always expected that he'd end up fulfilling somewhat of a subservient role, because those were the places they occupied in real life. But this wasn't reality, it was an aching fulfillment torn from the pages of a fantasy.

Kian's hand had frozen on his dick, and Bastian reached up slowly, his eyes never leaving Kian's. "This," he said, as his fingers slowly and carefully removed his own from his cock, "this isn't yours, this is mine. And I didn't say you could touch yourself."

He couldn't help it, he groaned as Bastian's calloused palm closed around him, pumping him so slowly, Kian wanted to cry.

"You came here, and you asked for it," Bastian growled. "You're goddamn gonna get it."

"Then what are you waiting for?" Kian demanded.

Bastian's hand slowed to a crawl, and it shouldn't have been so incandescently hot, to feel each and every ridge and scar and burn, sliding painfully slowly across his cock, but it was.

Still, he'd only dipped his toe into the fire, and it burned so good that he wanted more, he wanted to jump in and be consumed by it.

"More," he insisted. "Goddamn it, Bastian. Don't tease."

Bastian grinned wickedly, and it shot another pulse of heat through Kian. "What, like you teased me earlier?"

"Someone had to do it, or else we'd be stuck at the edge forever," Kian said, his voice so rough. The slow yet confident twist of Bastian's hand was driving him insane.

"Somehow," Bastian said, and he sounded way too cocky, way too sure of himself, "I always thought we'd go over the edge together."

Without another word, he leaned down and slid Kian's cock into his mouth, wrapping around him so tight, he had to bite his lip so he wouldn't yell.

"Oh, god," Kian moaned as Bastian proceeded to suck him so thoroughly, he wasn't sure he'd have any brain cells left when this finally ended.

And it was getting closer, faster, the pleasure spiraling out of control way too quickly. Kian tried to hang on, to prolong the dirty joy of seeing Bastian on the floor, sucking his cock. Nobody else, he knew, would ever see him like this. Fingertips pressed into his thighs and Kian panted, increasingly losing control.

Then Bastian's tongue twisted cleverly across the head and Kian did yell. "God fucking damnit, Bastian," he shrieked as he emptied down Bastian's throat.

For a long moment, neither of them moved. Kian was panting and so was Bastian. He wiped his mouth with the back of his hand and they stared at each other. Maybe Bastian couldn't believe he'd finally touched him; Kian knew *he* couldn't believe it had actually happened. Part of him wanted to reach down and pinch his bare arm, to make sure he wasn't dreaming.

Instead, he reached down and wrapped his fingers around Bastian's arm, tugging him up. *I always thought we'd go over the edge together*, Bastian had said. And even though he'd been obsessing over who had the control before, suddenly it felt important that they were standing as equals, together.

Bastian stared at him for a second, then curled into him, cradling his cheeks between his palms, and kissed him. Kian could taste himself, and even deeper still, the rich dark, cappuccino flavor that he remembered from San Francisco.

They kissed and kissed, like they were trying to make up for lost time, all those times that they'd desperately wanted to do this and hadn't. Bastian's jean-clad legs slid against Kian's bare ones, and he reached around, tugging off his own shirt. Kian gasped loudly into Bastian's mouth as their bare chests collided together. It felt even more intimate somehow, than when Bastian had been sucking his cock.

Kian reached down and thumbed open the button on Bastian's jeans, cupping his palm around his straining erection.

"Fuck," Bastian exhaled after he'd wrenched his mouth off Kian's. "Fuck, if you keep that up . . ."

Kian finished tugging down his jeans, and then shoved his underwear down too, Bastian's cock finally bobbing free of the constraining fabric. It was impressive, and even though Kian had just come, he felt a little frisson of desire just seeing it for the first time.

"Then come," Kian said, wrapping his hand around it. "I've teased you enough today."

Bastian's eyes stared back at him, wide and shocked, and he mumbled, "You can't tease me too much. Not you. Never you."

But he'd clearly been on edge, probably from the moment Kian had stripped his t-shirt off, and so Kian spit on his hand and fit it next to his other one, giving Bastian a steady and tight rhythm as he jerked him off.

It didn't take very long, but then Kian hadn't imagined it would, the very first time. They'd been torturing each other with some form or another of foreplay for the last two years. There was plenty of time to take their time and make it good—and not like this wasn't spectacular already. The novelty of the touch actually really felt like more than enough.

Bastian spilled into Kian's hand with a groan, his eyes fluttering shut. He didn't think he'd ever seen something as beautiful in his life as Bastian giving up control to him, letting Kian pleasure him.

They were going to have to do this all the damn time.

Kian grabbed for his t-shirt and wiped his hand off, and Bastian's cock. He was still staring at him, like he couldn't quite believe this was real, and not a dream he didn't want to wake up from.

"Yeah," Kian finally said, with a smile, "that really happened."

And then, unexpectedly, Bastian grinned too—and it was wide and bright and like nothing Kian had ever seen before. "Yeah," he said, and somehow his grin grew even wider, even brighter, nearly bright enough to blind Kian, "yeah, it really did."

"You sound surprised," Kian said.

"Well, you did just show up here in the middle of the night and take off your clothes." Bastian didn't sound mad, or even conflicted, he just sounded . . . happy. And Kian realized that he hadn't ever really heard him happy before. Not like this.

There was always a deep, contented exhaustion in his voice after a long, successful service. Sometimes Kian saw the joy of creating something unexpected and wonderful, during those test kitchen Sundays. But it had never been like this before.

"I don't regret doing this," Kian said seriously.

Bastian's grin turned conspiratorial, another look that Kian had never imagined he'd see on Bastian's face. "Neither do I." He looked skyward, like he was thanking God or maybe even the Devil. It was hard to say with Bastian. "I probably should, but I don't. I can't. It's been so long coming." He hesitated. "You want something to eat?"

Kian had never turned down food in his life, and definitely not food prepared by Bastian Aquino, in a post-sex haze.

"Sure," he said.

"And then we can do that again, but *better*," Bastian promised as they headed towards the kitchen.

Kian raised an eyebrow. "Better?"

"I mean, that was pretty fucking mind-blowing," Bastian said, "but I think we can do better, don't you?"

Kian had never been so eager to try in his whole life, so he nodded.

"Laundry's just down the hall," he said, "if you wanted to wash your shirt."

Bastian had moved towards the kitchen but hadn't made any move to put clothes on. He was just as powerfully built as Kian had always imagined, staring at him in his loose chef's whites. His thighs and arms looked like they could snap Kian in half, and he sort of wanted Bastian to try.

Kian gathered up his clothes and figured *what the hell*. He'd already stripped in front of him, what was staying naked a little longer?

And, he thought, as he headed down the hallway, it would definitely wrench the tension that still simmered between them a little tighter.

Bastian stood in front of his fridge, staring at the contents, but not really seeing them, as the cold air rushed over the cooling sweat on his body.

Normally, he'd be much more decisive, but the normal structure of his mind had just been entirely decimated by Kian.

The feel of his bare skin under his fingertips, Kian's hand stroking his cock, every single kiss, but most of all, the sheer bliss of giving in and not thinking at all.

At some point, they'd need to sit down and decide what all this meant for them, and definitely at some point, Bastian would need to reciprocate the three little words that Kian had said a few weeks before.

And, he added, he absolutely owed Kian an apology. Or ten.

But he was still enjoying not thinking, so instead, he let himself get lost in the contents of his fridge.

A few minutes passed, and Bastian heard Kian walk into the kitchen behind him.

"Cooking naked, while very sexy," Kian said, "isn't very safe." Bastian turned slightly as Kian tossed him a t-shirt and his pair of briefs.

He'd put his jeans back on, but he was shirtless, and for a second, Bastian wanted to forget all about the food, and instead trace the line of every muscle, every tendon, every inch of skin. He'd wanted this for so long, and it seemed insane to be *cooking* instead of touching, when all they'd done for two years was cook. But, he rationed, they needed to eat. They needed to carb load, probably, because now that Kian was in his bed, Bastian had no intention of leaving it for the next twelve hours.

Tomorrow was supposed to be one of their test kitchen Sundays, but there was no pressing reason not to postpone it until later. They could sleep in. Bastian could make them breakfast and they could even eat it in bed.

But all that energy was going to need to come from somewhere.

Pasta, maybe? Bastian considered, pulling on the clothes Kian had brought him. Rice? He could make a stir-fry. He had chicken, he had lots of vegetables.

The mushrooms in particular were calling to him, and as he plucked them from the shelf, he realized just how dull his normally sharp mental acuity was tonight. He'd make risotto, with roasted wild mushrooms. Carbs and comfort food, all in one.

Kian had settled at one of the barstools and watched as Bastian pulled out the mushrooms, an onion, garlic, butter, and a clear plastic container of stock from the freezer that he dumped into a pot to thaw.

"Risotto?" Kian questioned as Bastian fetched the arborio rice from the pantry. "Are we trying to carb load?"

Bastian peeled the onion and began to dice it finely. "Didn't you hear what I said?" he asked, a hint of a smile tugging at his lips. He couldn't stop smiling, it was obviously a symptom of the Kian disease that had completely overrun his immune system. "I said I thought we could do better. Better is going to require practice."

"And you're a perfectionist," Kian finished for him. His hair was rumpled, and Bastian's fingers itched. He wished he remembered exactly when he'd run them through the golden strands, the feel of them sliding through his fingers. It had all gone so quickly, once

Kian had started taking his clothes off. Bastian's mind had just flipped off, and he'd switched right onto autopilot.

It was a shock he hadn't kissed him the first moment he'd seen him next to his front door, looking frustrated and cutely disgruntled.

"I'm a perfectionist," Bastian agreed. *I made you, didn't I?*

"I think," Kian mused, "that this is the very first time you've ever cooked for me."

Bastian was about to say that Terroir certainly counted, because Kian had eaten lots of things he'd cooked. Hundreds of dishes, probably.

Kian rolled his eyes. "And Terroir doesn't count. That was work. This isn't . . . work."

It was difficult not to notice that Kian didn't define what was going on, just that it wasn't solely professional anymore, and since Bastian was still reeling from their earlier encounter, he thought that was okay for now. They meant something to each other, they'd crossed over that strictly platonic line, and it was fine not to understand what that looked like or was defined as right away.

The one thing Bastian did know was that now that the line had been crossed, he wasn't nearly so restricted in what he could say.

"I wanted to, you know," Bastian said, glancing up. Kian's eyes on him were soft. "I'd lie awake at night and dream of inviting you here, of what I'd serve you, of what we'd do afterwards."

"What's that?" Kian asked, raising an eyebrow.

Bastian shot him a somewhat incredulous look. "Do you need it described to you? Because you didn't seem to need directions earlier."

"I meant," Kian corrected slowly, "what would you serve me?"

"Something simple. Something delicious. Something irresistible."

"Well yes." Kian sounded amused. "I already assumed it would be all those things."

In his mind, Bastian was pulling out the heavy-bottomed pot and setting it on the stove, melting a big fat pat of butter in it, and starting to sauté the onion and garlic. Instead, he was leaning against the counter, his knife forgotten on the cutting board, and staring at the man just across it. He couldn't see his own expression, but he knew it was sappy sweet. If anyone he knew at Terroir could see him right now, they wouldn't believe it.

He'd never acted this way with anyone in his whole life; and that made sense, because in his whole life, he'd never felt this way about anyone.

"I wanted to apologize to you, after we had that . . ." Bastian didn't know what to call it. He didn't want to call it an argument, because that assumed both sides had made their opinion and their feelings known. Instead he'd said something stupid and Kian had been justifiably and understandably pissed at him, and he'd shut him out.

"When you said I couldn't possibly know what I wanted?" Kian's stare challenged Bastian in every way, which was just one of the things he loved about him. That, on top of the apology he'd just given Kian, was definitely something he should also be saying, but he'd never told anyone but his mother that he loved them. Shouldn't the words be given a little more *gravitas* than tossed casually over a kitchen counter while Bastian cooked them dinner?

"I was trying to make you angry so that you'd stop trying to change my mind," Bastian admitted. He picked his knife back up and continued dicing his onion.

"Yeah, I figured that out. Just . . . not right away," Kian said. "I was pretty pissed off at you."

Bastian wanted to roll his eyes—how could Kian have ever believed that he really meant that—but then he remembered what Celeste had said to him. And it uncomfortably echoed what Kian had said to him before, after he'd started stripping all his clothes off.

Of course you get a say, you can tell me to fuck off.

They both knew Bastian was never going to tell Kian to fuck off.

He tossed the onion in, followed by the garlic, stirring around the aromatics with a wooden spoon. "You were within your rights to be pissed off," Bastian said apologetically.

"Does this make me the person you've apologized to most in your whole life?" Kian wondered.

Bastian laughed; he really couldn't help it. "Other than my mother, definitely," he said.

"Not to Luc?" Kian questioned so innocently, Bastian might have actually believed it if he hadn't witnessed just how annoyed Kian had been over his ex-lover.

"I never felt the need to apologize to Luc," Bastian said as he stirred in the rice, letting it toast in the butter, "because the only thing I ever did to him was make the mistake of sleeping with him.

"I meant it, you know. You're nothing like Luc," Bastian continued steadily, even though he was quaking inside. Kian had helped tear some of his walls down, but the foundations were so solidly well-established, it was going to take more than an incredible orgasm to demolish them entirely.

"I believed you," Kian said. "I believed you even more when we came back to Terroir and you promoted Xander."

It was hardly the worst decision Bastian had ever made—though it would probably make the top ten—but Kian kept bringing it up, like it *still* stung. Or maybe he was fishing for the job, still.

It was a risk, but Bastian had to ask, *had* to know. "Is that why you came here? To convince me to give you *sous chef*?"

Kian looked shocked, like he couldn't quite believe the question for a second, and Bastian braced for the worst, and opened his mouth to apologize but shut it again. Kian got up from the barstool, sauntered around the counter, casual but so purposeful, and crowded right into Bastian's space. Putting a hand on Bastian's shoulder, he pulled him in even closer, and kissed him.

It was still new enough, still fresh enough, that each and every kiss felt revelatory. He could do this now, it was allowed, and not only that fact blew his mind, but the passion Kian poured into the kiss finished off the rest of it.

Kian released him and Bastian nearly staggered backwards. He tried grabbing for Kian—because one of those kisses would never be enough—but he'd already gone back to his seat.

"That's why I'm here," Kian said steadily. "I'm not here to get a job. If I want a job, and I deserve a job, we'll talk about it. But it'll be separate from this, and preferably at the restaurant."

Bastian was speechless, and a little flabbergasted that Kian wasn't *more* speechless. "Why not here?" he asked and was embarrassingly aware of how stupid he sounded.

As he shrugged, Kian's tough exterior wavered enough that Bastian could see what the charade was costing him. "Because of *that*," Kian said firmly. "Here is for that, and a whole lot more, I hope, and the restaurant is for work. They need to stay separate."

"I'm glad you think so." And Bastian *was*. He didn't want to be the one to dictate the terms of their relationship, because he'd already done such a shitty job so far—and the perfectionist in him was more than a little humiliated by all that failure.

"Why didn't we do this a year ago?" he asked, checking the mushrooms that were roasting in the oven. Then he walked over to the wine fridge and selected a nice white, opening it with a few economical movements. He deglazed the pan and then pulled down two wine glasses, pouring them each a glass.

"We weren't ready," Kian said, swirling his wine like an expert with the sexiest twist of his fingers. There were a few very good reasons to actually finish dinner. *One*, he'd never actually stopped cooking to have sex before, and doing so now would set a dangerous precedent. *Two*, they were absolutely going to need the energy, and once they went to bed, Bastian had no intention of leaving it anytime soon.

"I was definitely ready," Bastian argued.

Kian rolled his eyes. "I'm not talking about your dick."

Bastian's hand, stirring another ladleful of broth into the risotto, stilled. "If you say that again, you're never going to eat this meal."

"What am I going to eat instead?" Kian asked slyly, the curl of his upper lip nearly irresistible. How had Bastian ever resisted him in the first place? He couldn't even remember; the memories of his willpower obliterated by Kian's skin and his cock and his hands. The naughty gleam in his blue eyes.

"*We*," Bastian argued, "are going to sit down and eat this risotto like civilized people, then we're going to go to bed." He paused. "And then we aren't going to be civilized at all. So behave yourself before I drag you off to the bedroom like a caveman with a particularly tasty carcass."

Kian leaned forward and licked his lips. "Is that a promise?"

CHAPTER NINE

AT TERROIR, A PROMISE was beyond solid, it was ironclad.

In Bastian's kitchen, it turned out that a promise was just as substantial, something that Kian had absolutely been counting on.

He'd long since recovered from his earlier orgasm, and while he might be younger than Bastian, Kian had definitely seen the outline of Bastian's hard cock in his briefs. All it had taken was one very hot kiss, and a little dirty talk, and he was more than ready to go.

Since Kian was too, there seemed very little point in finishing this food exercise.

"Is that a promise?" Kian asked, licking his lips as seductively as he could get away with. Truthfully, he didn't know what the limit even was; or even what they were really doing here. He'd set the most basic of boundaries: sex in this house, work at Terroir. That had felt like the most Bastian was able to tolerate. Kian could tell he was trying, but him pulling down even those boundaries had unmoored the man he loved.

Probably because Bastian fucking adored boundaries.

Bastian set the wooden spoon onto the counter next to the stove and flipped off the gas on the stove.

"Come over here, and see," Bastian challenged.

Kian loved that; they challenged each other like this, just the way they challenged each other in the kitchen. He'd never imagined meeting someone who could face him in every aspect of his life, and then he'd met Bastian and couldn't believe he'd ever find anyone else who fit that particular set of criteria so perfectly, and so effortlessly.

They were perfect for each other. Someday, Kian thought, as he took a lazy sip of wine, eyeing Bastian over the top of his glass, they would talk about that, but for now, this was enough.

This was more than enough.

"You drive me insane," Bastian ground out, and yeah, that was definitely mutual. His biceps bulged in his t-shirt as he clenched his fists around the edge of the marble countertop.

"You sound surprised by this," Kian pointed out. Had he really believed that all he had to do was ask once, and Kian would just fall to his knees?

Probably, yes. Frankly, it was taking a lot of self-control to not do just that. But Kian had come here, tonight, to make a point, and that point had a much wider significance than merely breaking down Bastian's argument against them hooking up.

If he crawled over there now, the very first time Bastian asked, it would only emphasize that Bastian was as in charge here as he was at Terroir, and that wasn't going to work. He couldn't have the upper hand everywhere; as much as Kian loved him, he knew Bastian would become insufferable.

"Surprised that you're secretly a fantastic sexual tease?" Bastian laughed with dry amusement. "It's a good sort of surprise."

No doubt Bastian had figured he was young and therefore inexperienced and couldn't really keep up. He was right about the first two, but Kian had zero intention of fulfilling the last prediction.

"Why don't you come *here*?" Kian said.

"No orders to crawl?"

"If I wanted you on your knees again, I would've asked for that." Kian continued to sip his wine, the alcohol brewing in his stomach alongside a very healthy dose of lust.

He never wanted Bastian to stop looking at him like that—like he was an angel and a god and a very naughty boy who needed to be spanked.

"How about on my feet?" Bastian asked, skirting around the corner, and tugging Kian's barstool so it swiveled around. Kian set his glass on the counter and was very aware his fingers were trembling. He smoothed the fabric down Bastian's shoulders, reveling in the fact that he was *allowed* to touch now, after so much time fighting down the inclination.

Bastian trailed fingers down his thigh to his calf and then lower, to his bare foot. He picked up and tucked Kian's leg around his waist. "I think," he said steadily, even as the heat in his eyes lit them both on fire, "it's time we go to the bedroom. What do you think?"

Kian moved his other leg to mirror the first, gasping as Bastian pulled him tight against him, their dicks, with too many layers of clothing in between, brushing together.

Later, he'd think with triumph that Bastian had *asked* him, not merely demanded or even assumed. He'd *asked*. It was hard to even think straight, not with Bastian looking at him with all that scorching purpose, but it was enough for Kian to tilt his head back and let himself be kissed again.

It was the first kiss Bastian had initiated since their first, and the heat from it scorched Kian, pulling him in so deep that he barely even noticed as Bastian tucked a hand under his ass and lifted him off the barstool.

He carried him all the way to the bedroom, and Kian got a fleeting impression of an impressive bank of floor-to-ceiling windows, covered with dark partly translucent black shades, and a huge bed with a plain navy quilt, before he was deposited on it.

"Do you know, I've never once stopped cooking to have sex?" Bastian asked, breathing heavily, but not, Kian didn't think, from carrying him. Probably from the kiss which had spun out and out until they were both breathless.

Kian wasn't surprised by his confession. "I guess you haven't had really good sex, then," Kian theorized.

Normally, Bastian would no doubt be offended by the suggestion that he was less than brilliant at everything he attempted. But tonight, he just sat back on his heels and contemplated this statement. "I think you might be right," Bastian finally admitted. "What about you?"

"I have a feeling it's about to happen," Kian said, reaching up and pulling back against him. "I want you to fuck me."

Bastian looked surprised. Kian supposed that made sense. He'd been taking charge of every aspect of this encounter, and now it looked like he was giving away control. Kian would have assumed Bastian had more of a progressive opinion of sexual politics, but obviously not.

"What," Kian said, "just because I want your cock in my ass, like I've been fantasizing about for two fucking years, that makes me the weak one? The subservient one?"

For a second, Bastian looked even more shocked. Then he slowly started to smile. "Goddamn it, you are fucking perfect," he said, leaning down and kissing him thoroughly. He broke away only to say, "I would be fucking privileged to fuck you."

"Then what are you waiting for?" Kian asked.

Bastian leaned back again and stripped off his shirt. Kian trembled inside at having so much of Bastian revealed to him. He was powerfully built, with wide shoulders, impressive arms, and a flat, lightly rippled stomach and a trail of dark hair disappearing into his black briefs.

It was Bastian's turn to smile cockily as Kian looked. "Like what you see?" he asked, running a hand lightly up Kian's jean-clad leg. "I think you do," he said, answering his own question as he cupped his cock in his palm. "I think you love it."

"I do," Kian moaned. "Fuck, you're so gorgeous."

"The first time I ever saw you," Bastian said, reaching up to unbutton Kian's jeans, then lowering his zipper, "I wanted to bend you right over the counter you were standing by. Just pull your pants down and tease you until you were begging me for it."

It was scary how similar Kian had felt. He'd gone home that first night and alternating between his determination for Bastian to teach him how to be a great chef had been a truly stupendous orgasm, as he imagined Bastian punishing him for his snarky comment.

Bastian tugged his jeans off, his slow, methodical movements deliberate. Kian bit his lip. "Is that what you want me to do now, beg you for it?"

"Would you?" Bastian asked, the dark edge to his voice sending a thrill right through him.

"Maybe." *Definitely.* Kian met his eyes in the dim room as Bastian pulled his boxer briefs off, still moving in that very slow, very deliberate manner, like there was no need to rush at all. They'd been waiting for two fucking years. That felt like a pretty good reason to Kian. His cock bobbed free, hard and aching.

"Maybe," Kian breathed out unsteadily, "maybe if you did something worth me begging."

Bastian rolled his eyes. "You hold that thought." He leaned over and opened a drawer behind Kian.

"What's that?" Kian asked, trying to see, but the room was too dark.

"You want me to fuck you raw?"

"Oh." Kian told himself that this was already the best sex he'd already had, that it was totally fine and he wasn't disappointed at all that Bastian had already moved past the really spectacular foreplay. But he sort of was. He'd expected better—or at least something different, with the teasing promises he'd been making and the deliberately slow way he'd stripped his clothes off.

"Too quick for you?" Bastian raised an eyebrow. "We'll see what you say when you're begging for my cock."

Kian gasped as Bastian's fingers glided down his thigh, barely brushing against his cock and then his balls, and then found his hole. But instead of immediately inserting a finger, he just stroked around the rim, little teasing touches that had Kian squirming within moments.

He leaned over and his breath barely ghosted over Kian's cock, which twitched against his belly, the wet head rubbing against his skin. "Did you want something?" Bastian asked, sounding very satisfied.

Something that Kian wasn't—at all. "*Yes*," he demanded.

Bastian chuckled, a dark, warm sound, and Kian shivered.

Finally, he slid the tip of his finger inside as he licked a long stripe up Kian's cock. "Yeah," Bastian said as Kian moaned at the fleeting brush of pleasure, "you're definitely going to be begging for me."

Kian almost said something back—something like, *you wish*—but then Bastian's mouth was back on his dick and the finger was moving and pleasure crashed through him.

It went on and on and on: Bastian's mouth barely skimming along the length of his cock, his finger breaching him a little further on each thrust, only to retreat back a second later.

Kian's hands fisted in the sheets and he felt caught in a vise of pleasurable agony, and no matter how he moved, how he shifted, he couldn't escape the inexorable, slow burn of Bastian's hands and his mouth.

He wasn't even particularly against begging, but something about the playful glint in Bastian's eyes made him bite his lip and hold back the cries to do *more, please god, anything*.

"Nothing to say?" Bastian asked, as a second finger teased around the first. "Maybe you don't want this at all."

Kian moaned even though that wasn't really what Bastian wanted. He wanted to know just how desperate Kian was for it—which was frankly ridiculous because he'd been desperate for it for *years*. And all that had changed in that time was that he'd impossibly wanted it even more.

"Enough," he finally gritted out. "I fucking want it."

Bastian's grin lit up the room. "That wasn't really begging."

"Did you really think I would, if you challenged me?"

"Not really, but it was fun to try," Bastian said, his smile somehow growing even brighter. He slid the second finger in and leaned down, wrapping his tongue around the head of Kian's cock, sucking hard.

Spots dotted Kian's vision at the sudden onslaught of bliss sizzling through his veins.

"God, you're so good," Bastian grunted, almost to himself more than Kian. "So goddamn perfect."

"Fuck me already," Kian demanded.

"So bossy." But Bastian slid another finger in with his two and this time it wasn't just Kian who groaned.

A minute later, he slid his fingers out and Kian watched as he ripped open the condom with trembling fingers. And he thought, through a haze of satisfaction, that he'd done that. He'd made Bastian's fingers shake, he wanted him so goddamn much.

"Please," Kian wailed, finally breaking as Bastian's cock brushed his thigh, and then lower, then slipping in an inch.

Kian had only had penetrative sex with one other person, and it had been nothing to write home about. But then, the prep and the foreplay had been nothing like it was with Bastian. And Bastian was definitely in a whole other universe than the other guy.

It was a revelation to feel Bastian slide further and further inside him, until he didn't know where he ended and Bastian began. He slipped in farther and then froze, Bastian's fingers digging into his skin as Kian squirmed against the fullness.

"God, no, stop," Bastian begged, the sound practically wrenched out of him. "I can't . . ."

And it was so good to hear the desperation in his voice, Kian couldn't help it. He pushed back against Bastian's grip, until all of his cock was buried inside him.

"I can't," Bastian repeated, this time his voice a plea.

"Fuck me," Kian demanded. His hand slipped down to grasp his own cock, and they both moaned again.

Bastian was the worst at taking orders—he only gave them at Terroir—but he listened to Kian now, and started to move. Kian's fingers shakily circled his cock, tugging it carefully because he felt right on the edge, and he knew as soon as he came, Bastian was done for. They'd both needed this for so long, and their earlier orgasms had barely taken the edge off all that wanting.

His thrusts picked up speed and then he hit a spot inside that had Kian seeing not just stars but the whole goddamn galaxy. He was right on the precipice, he just needed a little more, and he wanted Bastian to be the one to give it to him.

"Kiss me," Kian commanded.

Bastian froze, like he was surprised by the sudden demand, and then his face softened. He leaned down, and the kiss was softer, and sweeter than Kian had expected. He'd braced for the hot rush of a sloppy, wet hungry kiss, something like what their bodies were already doing, but the tenderness of it unwound him until he was gasping into Bastian's mouth, come spurting between them, clenching around Bastian until he too, gasped and came.

For a long moment, neither of them moved, or spoke. Most of Bastian's weight was still back on his elbows, but Kian liked that he was covering him, enveloping him. He'd wondered forever what this might feel like, and now that he'd felt it, he didn't know what he'd do if he lost it.

Before, there was always that fleeting, niggling worry in the back of his mind—that he'd dreamt all those moments, a whole chain of them, that led up to this one. That San Francisco was the product of a tired, fantasizing mind. That he'd imagined all those hot, dirty looks. That the times he'd caught Bastian staring at his ass had been all a mistake.

He hadn't been wrong. It wasn't only him that had suffered in silence, wanting but never taking.

But now that they'd both taken—and no matter who'd taken the cock, Kian believed they'd definitely taken each other, Bastian's currently awestruck expression was evidence enough of that—what were they going to do?

It was easy enough to banter and flirt in Bastian's kitchen. But what about the Terroir kitchen? It was so easy to say, *oh that stays at home*, but could it? Was it even possible?

Kian felt a shiver of something real and concrete enter into the little golden bubble he'd been living in since Bastian had finally touched him for the first time.

How the fuck were they going to do this?

It was like the moment hit Bastian at the exact same time, because it was then that he retreated, carefully sliding out of Kian and purposefully looking away to dispose of the condom. He grabbed a tissue from the box on the beside table and wiped Kian and then his own torso. He disposed of that, and then there was nothing to do but look at each other and wonder.

What are we going to do?

Bastian sat down on the side of the bed and rested his elbows on his knees. He still hadn't looked at Kian.

There was a part of Kian that wanted to shamelessly beg now. *Don't say you regret it.*

Clearly he didn't, not really, anyway. You couldn't regret something you were such an enthusiastic participant in. But the chances of him saying it were too real for Kian to wait for the words.

Instead, he spoke first. "I thought you were going to make me dinner?" Kian asked.

Bastian's glance his direction was swift and amused. "Don't say you wish I'd done that instead."

"I don't," Kian said steadily. "But now I'm starving."

It wasn't really a solution, to get half dressed again and go back to the kitchen, but Kian knew that was the place *he* retreated to when he felt lost, and he had a hunch Bastian was the same.

"Then I'll make you dinner," Bastian said, reaching for his shirt and tugging it on. "Come, get dressed. I'm hungry too."

When Kian came back to the kitchen and resumed his spot on the barstool, Bastian had the gas on the stove back on, and he was poking at the mushrooms in the oven.

"Salvageable?" Kian asked.

"Not really," Bastian grumbled and grabbed the pan bare, not even bothering with a towel, and dumped out the contents into the trash. He looked up and then smiled, which surprised Kian because nothing bothered Bastian more than good food wasted. "But it was totally worth it."

"Of course it was." Like after waiting so long, the sex *wouldn't* be crazy hot. He'd known it had to be; he'd needed it to be. And it had still eclipsed even his wildest dreams.

"Get over here," Bastian grumbled. "You're completely capable of prepping these mushrooms while I try to salvage the risotto."

Kian thought it was the height of the fantasy to sit here, watching as Bastian made him dinner with his own hands, crafting the flavors just for the two of them. But it turned out that he'd been wrong.

The real fantasy? The fantasy that bled into real life until Kian didn't know where one ended and the other began?

It was standing hip to hip with Bastian in his kitchen, preparing dinner *with* him.

Maybe, Kian thought as he chopped the mushrooms into chunks, dropping them onto a fresh sheet pan, it was because this felt like something a couple might do together. Because his deepest, most closely held fantasy, the one he wasn't sure he'd ever be able to confess to Bastian was just that: living as an established couple. Fighting, loving, working—doing it all together.

They'd just taken the very first step towards that, but there were a hundred roadblocks and those were just the ones he'd thought of. In the end, it might not be possible, but Kian knew now that he could at least say he'd tried.

And tonight, that was enough.

Bastian finished the risotto, Kian pulled the mushrooms from the oven, and together, they plated.

Nothing fancy like at Terroir, but aesthetics were still important. They dished up the pale risotto in dark brown enameled bowls, Kian arranged the mushrooms over the top and then Bastian grabbed a bottle of basil oil, drizzling that over everything.

Kian picked up one of the bowls as Bastian grabbed spoons, hesitating over the silverware choice. "Forks maybe?" he asked.

"Bring both," Kian suggested, and hesitated, because he didn't know where to go. Were they eating in the kitchen? The living room? It was far too cold to eat on the table on the terrace. And Bastian was fairly fastidious—Kian couldn't imagine he'd ever want to eat in bed.

In the end, Bastian surprised him by balancing his bowl and the silverware in one hand, and gently placing the other on the small of Kian's back and leading him to the couch.

Kian played it safe and sat on one end, curling his bare legs underneath him.

Glancing over at Bastian, he was surprised to see a hurt flash through the other man's eyes.

"Do I smell bad or something?" Bastian asked.

Hardly. He smelled spicy and dark and wonderful, like bergamot and rosemary with the slightest hint of espresso and chocolate. Kian wanted to bury his nose into his neck and not move, but the last thing he wanted was to make Bastian uncomfortable with his clinginess.

He shook his head.

"Then why are you all the way over there?" Bastian asked.

Kian knew exactly how to sit, where to go, what to do, when they were at Terroir. He knew better than to ever touch Bastian, always leaving a buffer between them.

But this wasn't Terroir, so he slid a little closer. Bastian made a frustrated noise and reached out, crowding Kian against him with the arm he'd slung over the back of the couch. He reached up and stroked the back of Kian's head with his fingers, absently toying with the strands of his hair. "This is better, isn't it?"

Bastian had astonished him more than once tonight, but this was the biggest surprise of all. That Bastian Aquino, head chef of Terroir and not-so-affectionately known by his staff as the Bastard, was a cuddler.

"What?" Bastian questioned, a smile crinkling the corners of his eyes. "I wasn't allowed before."

"You didn't allow yourself," Kian grumbled, barely able to hide his own smile as he scooped up a bite of risotto and mushrooms.

"Still, I'm going to take advantage of it now," Bastian said, eating deftly with only one hand as he balanced the bowl in his lap. "If you don't have any objections."

Kian laughed because all of a sudden he felt a little teary and more than a little overemotional, and he absolutely was not going to bawl his eyes out on Bastian's couch over a little cuddling. "Just don't tell me tomorrow you've changed your mind."

Bastian's gaze was steady and soft. "You must not know me very well. I'm rather . . . intractable when I've set my mind to something."

"I might be familiar with that particular tendency," Kian said, sniffing.

"Eat your food," Bastian said. "Then we'll go to bed."

It was after noon the next day when Kian let himself in the house with his key. He'd definitely hoped that Xander would already be gone, or might be at Damon's, but no, he was right there, at the kitchen table with his laptop and a huge mug of coffee.

"You're back," Xander said steadily, not looking up from what he was typing. "There's coffee on and I brought some bread from the restaurant."

Kian set his keys on the counter and grabbed a mug from the cupboard. He was definitely a little sore this morning, muscles used in places that felt like they'd only ever gotten occasional use. When he looked up from pouring his coffee, Xander was watching him.

"So, it finally happened," Xander said conversationally. Like he hadn't been arguing against it happening for the full two years they'd known each other. "Or maybe you just braided each other's hair and told ghost stories."

It really wasn't any of Xander's business but Xander was also his best friend. Kian hesitated.

"*Please*, like I would tell anyone," Xander added as he rolled his eyes.

"You're right," Kian conceded. "You're not exactly the person I'd go to for hot gossip. And for the record, no, we didn't braid each other's hair or tell ghost stories."

A smile flitted across Xander's features. "I didn't think so. Wouldn't have pegged Aquino as that type."

"And me?" Kian asked as he sat down next to his friend. He tried not to worry if Xander was going to see the fairly obvious marks on his neck or if he was going to mention them. It wasn't like he and Damon weren't always practically fucking on their couch, when they had an empty house of Damon's they could screw in.

"You're the type, but I can see that's not all you were up to," Xander said in a shockingly judgement-free tone. He tilted his head, as if to see the marks in a slightly better light. "Aquino is thorough, I guess."

Kian fought against the blush, but it rose across his cheeks anyway. "Very," he admitted.

This morning, as Kian had finally pulled on his clothes for the trip home, Bastian lazing on the bed, watching like a great big tabby, he'd said, "I think I got a little carried away last night."

There was so much to remember, that it had taken Kian a minute to remember that after eating, they'd ended up making out on the couch, Kian perched in Bastian's lap, mindlessly rubbing against each other as Bastian had kissed and bit up the sensitive tendon just behind his ear.

"It's fine," Kian had said, brushing away his concern. "I'll just make sure to wear my coat buttoned all the way up."

But from his own glance in the rearview mirror this morning and the buried astonishment in Xander's gaze as he looked at the marks, that probably wasn't going to cut it.

"As long as you're happy," Xander said.

Kian had not been expecting such full acceptance of his developing relationship with Bastian. "No more concerned lectures?"

Xander sighed and set his elbows on the edge of the table. "I know that sometimes I've been a shitty friend," he admitted, "but I was worried. I was afraid he'd take advantage, I was worried he'd use you up and throw you away, but none of that happened. Instead you fucking pined after each other for *years*. Those are feelings with power. Who am I to argue with that?"

"Yourself?" Kian asked, raising an eyebrow.

Xander laughed.

"Okay, that's fair," he said, then hesitated. "It's only because I'm a friend, and I care about you that I'm asking. You're okay? Everything is okay?"

"I'm good. Really good." He suddenly laughed. The realization that the last sixteen or so hours had actually happened was just now hitting him. "I can't believe that actually worked."

"What did you do?" Xander sounded amused now. "You sure seemed pissed off, heading off last night."

"I was. I was furious. Just . . . fucking tired of him getting to dictate the terms of what we were. So I showed up at his house and just started taking my clothes off."

Xander choked on his coffee. "You did *what*," he said when he finally managed to take a breath.

"He wasn't *listening*," Kian argued. "What else do you do with someone who won't listen to you?"

"Not take my damn clothes off," Xander said, still laughing.

"Hey, don't judge. It worked." Kian flushed. "Really, really well."

Xander shook his head. "Apparently. Just . . . be careful. Be honest with each other. I know Aquino isn't easy to deal with, but god knows you've figured out the right way to do it. And for the love of god, ask him for my job. You're already doing the work without getting the credit or the salary."

Kian really didn't want to confess that in the last two years, he'd gotten enough raises that he'd been making more as Bastian's special "intern" than the *sous chef* at Terroir. Bastian had made sure he knew his contributions to the restaurant were appropriately valued, even if he didn't always say it in words.

But then that was Bastian, and Xander was right, Kian had figured out the best way to deal with him.

As for the credit, it would be nice, but anyone who was already in the Terroir kitchen knew to listen to Kian when he asked for something. He got a wide berth, respect, and he realized, the chafing he'd begun to feel in the last few months hadn't been over his position in the restaurant—it had been the rut he and Bastian had fallen into.

Now that they'd resolved that, Kian thought maybe he wouldn't feel so stagnant. He was only twenty-three. He still had a lot to learn. He'd become *sous* eventually, and at some point, maybe he'd even leave Terroir. But for now, he didn't feel like rushing the process. He was content right where he was.

Chapter Ten

After his shower, Kian had tried various methods to hide the blooming bruises on his neck, but he finally gave up because the neck kerchief looked incredibly contrived, borrowing one of Xander's chili pepper bandanas didn't seem right, and the makeup called more attention to them than it hid.

He was just going to have to go in and hope everyone was too busy working to examine Kian's neck—and if they did, they wouldn't connect it to Chef's unexpectedly good mood.

Because that was exactly what Kian expected to walk into when he finally arrived at Terroir: Bastian not yelling and quite possibly spreading encouragement and good cheer wherever he went.

Of course when he walked in, what he heard was Bastian verbally destroying the hopes of the new young kitchen assistant.

"This is fucking garbage," Bastian yelled, the gravelly edge of it echoing in Kian's memories from the night before. "You want to just take the trash and dump it on a plate and serve it to our guests?"

"No, Chef. I'll fix it." Derek sounded a tiny bit teary, but also resolute, which was a fucking relief. Kian wasn't going to have to coax him out of the bathroom for service—at least not this time.

Kian forced himself to take his time putting his stuff in his locker, making sure his coat was fully buttoned, not that it would do much to hide the bruises on his neck, before walking out into the prep stations.

The last thing Kian had expected to be greeted with after the night before was a glare, but Bastian definitely glared. It was almost certainly residual from Bastian's encounter with Derek, but no matter what little white lie he told himself, it still stung.

"You'd better fix it," Bastian growled, and then turned towards Kian. "I've started the soup, but you need to finish it, and you need to monitor the hell out of Derek's prep. He's a fucking mess."

Bastian was all business as they walked towards the massive bank of burners, where the gigantic pot of soup was bubbling away in the corner. "It's a take on a *posole*," he said. "You know how I like that to be finished."

"Yes, Chef," Kian said, and ignored the thrum of arousal he felt when he said the words. He remembered this morning, crawling down Bastian's body and sliding his cock into his mouth. Bastian's hot gaze on his face, on his mouth, as he'd sucked him off. It was hard to even believe that man even existed in the brisk, tough, blank-faced Bastian in front of him now. Kian wouldn't have believed it, but he'd experienced it.

Kian had been the one to say he wanted things to stay the same at Terroir, and there was definitely a part of him that was undeniably glad they had. Terroir was like a support system, always there, always morphing but still strong and stable underneath the culinary experimentation, and Bastian was absolutely an extension of his own restaurant.

But another part of him wanted to see just a sign, even the faintest hint of a smile, some sort of reassurance that everything that had happened wasn't just in Kian's head.

Maybe he'd dreamt the whole thing after all.

He'd believe it, except for the chain of bruises currently dotting his neck.

"When you're done with the soup, I'd like to see you in my office," Bastian said, surprising the hell out of Kian. "If you're not too busy managing Derek."

Kian didn't think he'd imagined the sudden thaw in Bastian's dark eyes. "I shouldn't be."

"Then, I'll see you in a bit," Bastian said, and walked back to his office.

Sighing, Kian went to check the soup and then to go find Derek, who had better not have retreated to the bathroom again.

The blinds were up on Bastian's glass walls when Kian approached his office, so he didn't think Bastian had asked to see him for anything non-Terroir related.

Last night had been a revelation, a reveal of all the soft, sexy inner parts of Bastian, but Kian knew, as surely as the sun setting and rising, that he wouldn't reveal any of that in the heart of his empire.

Kian didn't even want him to. Those parts were for Kian and Kian alone to enjoy.

He knocked on the glass and Bastian glanced up from his computer monitor.

"Oh, that was quick," Bastian said.

Kian fought back against the urge to apologize and explain that he had done everything to a quality level Bastian would approve of. He didn't need to apologize *or* explain. Bastian trusted him, he believed that, so instead of answering, he merely took the seat.

A year ago, he'd used the corporate credit card Bastian had given him to buy more comfortable chairs for the office, and Bastian had given him a look when he'd brought them in but he hadn't said a word. Kian figured that he was willing to sit here and take whatever shit came out of Bastian's mouth, but he didn't need to do that *and* be uncomfortable at the same damn time.

"Xander has been gone three months," Bastian said. "I think it's high time I promoted someone to *sous* chef, and I can't think of anyone more qualified or that deserves it more than you do."

Kian couldn't help himself. He gaped.

Of course, the moment Kian decided he was perfectly fine not being promoted to *sous*, Bastian decided that the time was finally right.

But Bastian wasn't even done. "But the more I thought about it," he continued, "I realized that if I want to partner with Nathan Hess, I'll be relying on you more and more. And that's why I want to offer you the *chef de cuisine* position."

Kian shot to his feet. "You want to do *what*?"

"Don't tell me you're surprised by this," Bastian said, leaning back in his chair and crossing his arms over his chest. "You've wanted this."

He wasn't going to apologize for being ambitious. Yes, he'd wanted it. Specifically he'd wanted Xander's job, the *sous* chef job, but only if he was qualified for it and Bastian believed that he'd earned it.

While he desperately wanted to find some sort of equal footing with Bastian, he wasn't stupid enough to believe that extended to culinary knowledge, experience, or Terroir.

"Of course I want the job," Kian said. "I'm just not sure I wanted it like this."

"Like how?" Bastian challenged.

Kian rolled his eyes. He wasn't going to say it, but they were both thinking it. Last night had been momentous. He didn't want Bastian to ruin it by making him think he'd gotten the job because he was good in bed, not good in the kitchen.

"I told you when Xander quit," Bastian added, his voice softening, "I told you that I should have promoted you instead."

He'd been so fed up—angry and frustrated—when Bastian had confessed that particular tidbit, but later he'd thought about it. And he wasn't sure he really agreed with Bastian, which was blowing his mind.

"I knew this kitchen better than Xander did, but he had five more years of experience than I did—that means he had more than *double* the experience I do. That's not insignificant," Kian pointed out.

Bastian made a frustrated sound. "Would it be too much to ask for you to just say, *thank you, Chef,* and take the goddamned job?"

Yes, it probably would, and if Bastian had only wanted a sycophant in his kitchen and in his bed, Kian wouldn't be here right now. He definitely wouldn't have been curled up with Bastian the night before. Bastian wanted someone to challenge him. Someone to call him out on his bullshit.

But he also really wanted this job. He'd wanted it before he'd even known what it was, and long before Bastian had ever offered it to Xander. If Bastian thought he was ready, maybe Kian should defer to him. After all, he was always claiming to know everything.

"I'll take it," Kian said after a long moment. "But I think your timing continues to suck."

First the Xander promotion right after they'd gotten back from San Francisco and now this. It was only two instances, but it felt like a pattern of their personal lives influencing the decisions Bastian was making in the restaurant. That didn't only feel wrong, it felt completely unlike the Bastian that Kian believed he knew.

Bastian laughed, and it broke up the tension that had built up between them. "I'll give you that," he said, and even though he didn't offer another apology in words, the tone was there, in his voice. "I'm not very good at this. I'm rather . . . inexperienced, if you'd believe it."

Not sexually, clearly, but with being in a relationship with someone he cared about? Kian could see that. "Just tell me this has nothing to do with last night." Kian dropped his voice towards the end, as the door was still open. He didn't think anyone would eavesdrop, but this industry was also cutthroat and god knew what people would do to get ahead.

There were absolutely people in the world who might find out about last night and believe that Kian had only done it to get this promotion, and Bastian had let it happen because that was his right as Kian's superior.

Those people were fucked up, but they existed, and while Kian might be naïve, he wasn't *that* naïve.

"Of course it doesn't," Bastian said. "Do you really think I would promote you because of *that*?"

Kian shrugged, because the timing remained suspicious.

"I know . . . I know it looks like that," Bastian allowed. He looked reluctant to continue, but he did anyway, like this was worth enduring the discomfort of the remaining confession. "I have a bad habit of reacting poorly when I lose control. I lost control in San Francisco. I never meant for . . . *that* to happen. Not with you. I'd told you we couldn't, and I had fully intended to keep that promise, but you get under my skin, past my defenses, and what you said that night—it struck something inside me. I knew what Luc's presence made you feel, and I didn't want you to feel that anymore. But that didn't change anything about our situation. I still believed it shouldn't happen, but how could I tell you with words when words were clearly meaningless? Promoting Xander was a reminder to you, but mostly to myself, that even if I favored you, the hierarchy of the kitchen was still important. There were still vital reasons not to cross the line again. Yes, you have less experience than Xander did, but we work better together than he and I did, and that's essential in a *sous*. Which is why I told you that it should have been you instead, not him."

It wasn't an explanation that Kian had ever expected to hear. It didn't take the sting entirely away from that day—it had happened and nothing could change that, or the way he'd felt at the time—but hearing Bastian's reasons helped. He hadn't done it to be an asshole.

He'd done it, like he'd done so much, because he had been trying to do what he believed was the right thing.

Kian nodded. "And today?"

"If I explain everything, am I going to lose my essential mystery?" Bastian wondered archly.

"If you explain everything, I might actually want to take this job, and then we can celebrate later. Properly." Kian grinned.

Bastian returned the smile, definitely lighter at the edges, and it was a forcible reminder that while Bastian's hair might be threaded with gray, he wasn't really old. He'd just shouldered an incalculable burden with an incredible amount of accompanying pressure at a too-young age.

"I'd hate to take away the possibility of a celebration," he said gravely. "Fine. I offered you the job today, not because of what happened last night, but because I realized I was holding you back. I was holding you with me. Not because I didn't think you were ready, but because I didn't want to let you go. That wasn't right. When our relationship changed, I realized that was what kept stopping me from giving you this job you deserved. And if you deserve *sous*, then there's no reason you can't be *chef de cuisine*. I'm not disappearing. I'm not going to turn into Emeril or Mario and be unavailable. But I do want to take this opportunity with Nathan Hess, and I need you to take charge of things if I do."

"Okay," Kian said, feeling unsteady and unmoored. *Chef de cuisine* at a Michelin-starred restaurant at twenty-three years of age. It was practically unheard of.

"I became *sous* when I was twenty-three," Bastian said. "And I know it was the making of me as a chef. I believe you can do this."

The steady look of unflinching belief in Bastian's eyes helped to steady Kian. He *did* believe in him; he wouldn't have given Kian this promotion otherwise. Not with his life's work, Terroir, hanging in the balance.

"Thank you, Chef," Kian said. "I intend to make you proud." He rose to his feet. "I need to check on the prep for the evening's service."

"Of course." Bastian stood too, and hesitated. It was so different from this morning when Kian had left Bastian's doorstep, and they'd kissed goodbye, their embrace turning heated as soon as their lips met. It was the only time they'd ever done that, but strangely, it felt odd not to repeat it now.

And from the way Bastian paused, the sudden nervous energy in his hands, Kian knew he felt the exact same way.

"I'll make the announcement at family dinner," Bastian said. Kian ducked his head in agreement, and then walked out the door before he did something monumentally stupid like try to kiss him.

After promoting Kian, it was readily apparent to Bastian that there was nobody even remotely suited in the kitchen to promote as *sous*—and Bastian wasn't cruel enough to expect him to succeed without the proper tools he'd need, and that included a trusted and competent second-in-command.

Two days after the promotion, a resume crossed his desk that caught his attention. A fellow student with Kian at the Academy. He'd worked at Michael Mina since graduation but was looking to move back to the Valley. Bastian checked the references, even spoke to Michael himself, and decided this was the best *congratulations, you're promoted* present he could find.

Other than giving Kian a truly spectacular blowjob the night before. Kian had claimed breathlessly that he'd never come so hard in his life, but then Bastian had bent him over the counter and fucked him like he'd wanted to do so long ago, the first time they'd ever met, and he'd come again, even harder the second time.

Bastian hadn't lied when he'd told Kian that he'd believed he could succeed. He *could*—he had all the tools, most of the skill, and definitely the drive required. Watching him as he directed the line during service, Bastian was struck again by how much Kian reminded him of himself at that age. Ferocious and determined to achieve that success only because he'd truly earned it.

But Terroir was a large establishment, with the capacity for large crowds, and Kian was going to need a *sous* chef he trusted. That wasn't an easy thing to find, but someone he already knew? Someone he'd gone to school with? That was a very good start.

The first sign of a problem came when the new hire walked in, and instead of looking pleased, Kian frowned.

"Mark?" he questioned. "What are you doing here?"

Bastian did not frequently rethink his decisions, but he couldn't help but feel, looking at Kian's displeased expression, that maybe he should have included Kian on the hiring process to find Kian's *sous* chef. Which felt appallingly obvious, once Bastian thought it.

Merde.

"I've been hired here," Mark said smoothly, looking over at Bastian. "I'm your new *sous*."

Kian's eyebrows slammed together and the gaze he directed Bastian's direction was decidedly frosty. "I see," was all he said. "Welcome to Terroir."

Between getting Mark's orientation done, and getting him up to speed prior to service, there was no time for Bastian to pull Kian aside to try to explain.

The additional time was also helpful, because after watching him during the service, Bastian felt like Mark could actually be a decent addition to the team. He wasn't quite quick enough yet, but he was careful, and had clearly learned some good habits at Michael Mina. Maybe Kian would come around once he saw Mark's possibilities.

No, Bastian reminded himself resolutely, *he would come around.* Because Bastian had no intention of getting rid of Mark just because of a small personality conflict. He'd endured Xander's sneers for years, and even that godawful ridiculous nickname, and he'd done it because Xander was a fantastic chef, and he'd wanted him in his kitchen.

It was too suspicious to be continually taking the same car to and from the restaurant, so Kian and he had driven separately this time. *This is good*, Bastian thought as he drove home after service, *an extra ten minutes to get my head on straight.*

Bastian knew Kian had every intention of cornering him to discuss Mark. He'd been terse and brief all service, and he'd barely looked in Bastian's direction. None of those little quick glances that felt like a caress—something to connect them when they couldn't touch.

He pulled into the driveway, saw that Kian's little hatchback was already parked, and braced himself for the forthcoming and unavoidable argument.

It had been almost a week since Kian had shown up, determined not to be turned down, and it had been one of the best weeks of Bastian's life. Still, in the back of his mind, he'd been bracing for the moment when something happened to mar all that uninterrupted perfection. He'd known it was inevitable because they were both two very opinionated, driven individuals and Kian's new promotion, while not giving him equal footing with Bastian, gave him a decided step up from where he'd been before. From the way Kian had taken over in the kitchen, he knew it too, and no doubt he had every intention of exercising that newfound power now.

"What the hell, Bastian," Kian spit out from almost the second Bastian opened the car door and stepped out. He'd given Kian the keycode to the house a few days ago, but he'd chosen not to use it tonight, and instead had lain in wait for Bastian outside.

"I take it you don't approve of Mark as a choice of *sous*," Bastian said, and hated how tired he sounded. He knew everyone believed he enjoyed a fight, but he actually dreaded them. He dreaded their prelude, he dreaded the actual yelling, and he absolutely dreaded the aftermath.

He knew they would get through this, because Kian was a reasonable person who wanted the best for Terroir, just the same as Bastian did, but he was also unexpectedly stubborn, when allowed the freedom to be.

It was sexy as hell when they were flirting or during foreplay or even in the middle of sex. It was not sexy as hell now. Now, all it meant was a conversation that should have been easier, wasn't. Bastian knew he shouldn't, but he resented Kian for it.

"Of course I don't fucking approve," Kian spit out, words tumbling over themselves. "How could I possibly approve when you never asked me?"

"Is that the problem? That you were not consulted?" Bastian typed in the entry code to the front door himself and walked in. Kian shut the door behind him harder than he needed to. Forcing himself not to jump at the sudden bang that echoed through the house, Bastian set his keys and wallet on the counter and walked over to his wine rack. Picking out a nice pinot noir, he opened the bottle with careful, slow movements and poured himself a glass. Didn't pour one for Kian because he hadn't asked, and Bastian wasn't feeling particularly generous at the moment.

The whole time, Kian kept up a long monologue about why Bastian had fucked him over.

"There are a lot of problems with this. First, your fucking overbearing motives. You put me in charge of the kitchen, but then you keep interfering, you *hire new staff* without even asking, without even letting me interview them first. You always think you know what's best for everyone, like a chess master setting out his pieces, and it fucking pisses me off. And then, you had to hire *him*." Kian said the word like it was bitter and poisonous, and Bastian tuned back in. Maybe he would finally hear what the real issue behind Mark's hire was.

Other than that you did it without his permission and without even asking him, Bastian's guilty conscience proclaimed loudly and very clearly.

"What is your issue with Mark?" Bastian asked and was more than a little proud of how even his voice was. Some of what Kian had said stung, but it was also *true*, so he tried to let it go. "I know you went to school with him."

"He's a fucking suck-up, piece-of-shit, copycat asshole," Kian said bitterly. "Two years ago he wanted in my pants, probably to try to steal anything he could to get ahead of me. He would have, but he didn't even realize I was smarter than he was and could figure out what he wanted in a second flat. He's a snake, plain and simple, and I don't want him in my kitchen."

Bastian took a long sip of wine. "*My* kitchen," he corrected softly, firmly.

Kian flushed a bright shade of puce. He didn't say anything else.

"I'm sorry you don't like him," Bastian finally said. "I'm sorry you didn't get along before. I'm sorry he was shitty to you in school. I certainly hope that he thinks better of trying to get in your pants now—because he'll find that I do not like to share. But based on his performance tonight, I do think he could earn his place at Terroir. I want you to give him the chance to do that."

"Why?" Kian asked, and he sounded even angrier now than he had ranting about Mark.

"Because sometimes we don't personally like someone but they're good enough at what they do that we tolerate their shittiness as a person. And also because sometimes we're an idiot at eighteen, but we grow up," Bastian said. "He did good work. He has good references. Let's give him a chance."

Kian frowned. "He was just on good behavior tonight because you were there."

"And tomorrow, and during subsequent evenings, *you* will be there. As *chef de cuisine,* you are my representative. It's up to you to make sure he stays in line. If he doesn't, then you know what to do with him."

Kian's face grew harder around the edges than Bastian had ever seen it before. "Yes," he said shortly, "I take out the trash."

"Eventually, yes. *If* he proves that he can't handle Terroir." He tipped the wine in Kian's direction. "Would you like some?"

"I really want to hate you right now," Kian grumbled, and instead of answering, Bastian pulled out another glass and poured, generously. Kian had earned this wine today, though Bastian wasn't going to be the one to tell him that.

"But you don't," Bastian said, smiling.

Kian smiled, thawing a little. "I really don't, even when I do. How does that work?"

"God, I wish I knew," Bastian said, and reached for him. "I am sorry that I didn't consult you ahead of time. But I can't say that if I had, and you'd told me all that, I wouldn't have hired him anyway."

"Because he had good references and did well tonight?" Kian slipped out of his grasp, eyeing Bastian coolly over his glass of wine.

"Yes," Bastian said honestly. If he couldn't be honest, this relationship would never get off the ground. Just because they loved each other didn't mean that they could truly accept each other, and if Kian couldn't accept that he'd do anything for Terroir to succeed, then this wasn't going to work.

"So, that thing you said when you gave me this job," Kian said steadily, "you meant that."

"Did you want me to give you a free pass on Mark, and get to do whatever you wanted with him just because we're sleeping together?" Bastian questioned. "Because I had the impression that you wanted to keep Terroir at Terroir and sex at home."

"I do." Kian looked very unsure all of a sudden. "I was going to say, I wanted you to trust me, but then I realized that trust has to go both ways, doesn't it? You want me to trust you, here."

"While I'm trusting *you* with Terroir, which is the most precious thing in the world to me." *Almost the most precious*, Bastian mentally corrected. He still hadn't returned Kian's three little words from the emergency room, but then Kian had yet to say them while not on drugs. They were still figuring all of this out. It was too soon to tell Kian that he'd become just about as important to him as the restaurant and the career he'd built from scratch with blood and lots and lots of sweat.

"Oh," Kian said, and his eyes lit up, like he suddenly understood. "*Oh*."

This time Kian was the one who moved closer to Bastian, reaching up and putting a hand on his neck, his shoulders. "Sweetheart, we're figuring this out. I don't know how the fuck to do this," Bastian confessed quietly. "I don't know how to love you and love my restaurant."

Well, maybe he *was* doing this right now.

Kian's mouth formed a small *o* of surprise. "You love me?"

"Did you ever doubt that I did?" Bastian stroked up and down Kian's arms, bare as he was wearing just a t-shirt he'd thrown on after service.

"Noooooo, not exactly," Kian hesitated. "Maybe a little bit. Tonight."

Bastian had felt the doubt, the coldness radiating from him, and maybe that was why he'd finally let those words slip out. His subconscious had known better than he did just how thin the ice they were walking on was.

"I wanted to make the words more special," Bastian confessed. "I always want to do right by you. Even when you think I'm fucking up, I'm still trying to do right by you. I didn't think there was anyone at Terroir who deserved to be your *sous* and I went looking for one. For you. Only for you. All for you."

Kian's lip trembled. "You love me that much?"

"More," Bastian chuckled, leaning down to brush a kiss on his lips. "So much more. If I loved you less, I could have resisted you. If I had loved you less, I wouldn't have ever hired you to begin with. Less is not really a problem here, trust me."

Kian melted into the kiss, and for a second, Bastian let himself be consumed by the fire that blazed between them. He was still shocked by how hot they always burned, and how quickly it always seemed to burn out of control.

But it was Kian who broke away, panting. "I do trust you. I do." He hesitated, and Bastian's heart became a manic thing, pumping away wildly as he watched Kian wet his bottom lip. "I meant what I said, when I told you in the hospital. I love you too. I've loved you for a long time."

Bastian's heart was still thumping hard as he pulled Kian flush against him. Somehow, he was still too far away, still not as close as Bastian needed him to be. "*Mon cher*, I've loved you for far too long," he murmured against Kian's lips, "I need a shower. Join me and let me show you how long."

Chapter Eleven

It wasn't that Kian didn't theoretically agree with Bastian's suggestion that he give Mark a try at *sous*. He'd made good points, and Kian was not only willing to approach his new position in charge of the kitchen at Terroir with logic, he *wanted* to.

Bastian finally telling him he loved him too certainly didn't hurt either.

When Kian walked into the Terroir kitchen the next day, flipping on lights as he went, he was determined to fulfill Bastian's belief in his potential. It started like so many days at Terroir, with Kian receiving shipments, logging them in, and making sure that the huge walk-in fridges were ruthlessly organized and that any item that was even slightly questionable had been disposed of.

Mark came in on time, which was really ten minutes early, and that filled Kian with additional optimism. He'd been notorious for barely ever making it to class on time, and Kian had hoped that Michael Mina had broken that particular bad habit.

"Johnson," Kian acknowledged his arrival as he walked in from the locker room. "Do you want to go over prep assignments?"

Mark nodded, but his face contorted into a frustrated little grimace. Kian told himself that this was normal, prep was hell, and frankly they had a very green kitchen assistant who also happened to be a drama queen. Mark would have picked that up right away, and also probably knew Kian was going to ask him to watch Derek closely—just as Bastian had asked Kian to do. It was exactly the kind of expression Xander might have made, but of course, he wouldn't have ever done it to Bastian's face, he would have waited until he was gone first.

Mark, Kian acknowledged, was still a little stupid, but a little stupid was better than a lot stupid. He could work with that.

"Derek, you need to watch him. I want to see a perfect dice. I know he's capable of it, he just gets lazy and sloppy, and that isn't how we do things here," Kian said as they hauled out crates of vegetables out of the walk-in.

"I'm surprised Aquino permitted it," Mark said. Kian told himself firmly to ignore the little twisty jab in his words.

"*Chef* Aquino," Kian said, emphasizing his title, "isn't the villain he's painted to be. He's tough, he has exacting standards, but he's willing to work with people to meet them. But Derek knows he's on borrowed time, so if he gets sloppy, you let me know and I'll deal with it."

Glancing at Kian up and then down again, Mark chuckled under his breath. And yes, Kian was a decidedly less intimidating figure than Bastian was, but that didn't matter. Kian had learned from the best. He could eviscerate anyone without lifting a finger.

"All of this?" Mark asked as Kian hauled the last of the eggplants out. "That's a lot of work."

"Terroir is a larger restaurant than Michael Mina," Kian said shortly. "You'd better get on it."

All in all, not the greatest start to their working career together, Kian considered as he grabbed his own veggies to start the daily soup special, but it also hadn't been the worst. Mark was suspicious and a little intractable, but Kian still believed he could win his respect. He had always been a good chef, but from Bastian's mentorship, he could run this restaurant exactly as it needed to be run.

He didn't intend to have quite as firm of a hand as Bastian had—he believed that he could get results without any of the yelling or the worst of the insults. But the way Kian got there mattered far less than the end result. He knew that was all Bastian cared about.

As Kian's knife flew through the carrots he was prepping for the soup, it was a habit to watch out of the corner of his eye for Bastian—forgetting that Bastian was meeting with Nathan Hess today, and wouldn't be in until much later. If at all, Bastian had added absently.

Kian wasn't dumb enough to take his tone at face value. This was, undeniably, a test. A test Kian intended to ace. Even without Mark, Kian knew he was still at a disadvantage. Bastian might have promoted him, but a part of Kian knew he wasn't really ready, and that meant he needed to work twice as hard to prove himself.

He took an hour and took his time on the soup, believing that the prep was underway by Mark. Kian had a feeling he wouldn't appreciate being checked on every ten minutes anyway. None of the work he was doing was particularly difficult, except maybe dealing with Derek, and Kian had left a detailed list of what needed done.

He also had a pretty solid idea of how long it should take to complete the list he'd compiled, so he was surprised—and not in a good way—when he detoured through the prep station to find that after an hour, Mark and Derek had barely made a dent in the crates of vegetables spread out over the counter. If he looked at the list, he would guess they'd barely completed a quarter of the prep, when they should really be more than halfway done.

And even worse, instead of working with purpose and speed, they were taking their sweet-ass time and gossiping like two old ladies.

"He came in with this whole *chain* of bruises down his neck. And I know there's no boyfriend," Derek said, completely fulfilling Kian's worst impression of him. "So who gave them to him? I'd like to know."

"You don't think it was Aquino, do you?" Mark said, and there was that sly tone that Kian remembered so well from their culinary academy days.

"Excuse me," Kian said in the firmest Bastian impression he could manage.

Mark didn't look the tiniest bit embarrassed at being caught gossiping about Kian *or* the illustrious head chef of Terroir. Derek, however, did Kian the favor of at least blushing at his sudden appearance.

"Why is this not all done, already?" Kian asked. "You should be a lot further along by now. We have a lot to do. There're stocks to get ready. Sauces to start. And you guys are still fucking prepping."

"Derek here was just giving me the big scoop," Mark said, and glanced right at Kian's neck. Thankfully in the last week, the bruises Bastian had kissed into his skin had already faded considerably. This morning he'd looked in the mirror and been a little disappointed to see them slowly disappear, but now he was undeniably glad. Mark *could not* find out that Bastian had been the one to leave them. Kian wasn't sure what he'd do with the knowledge, but it wouldn't be good; Kian knew that much.

"Derek's *job*," Kian emphasized, "is to help you with the prep work of the day, not gossip." He didn't reiterate what Mark's job was because Mark fucking knew what his job was. He was just pushing Kian, seeing what he could get away with, and he had to know, Kian *needed* him to believe, that Kian was going to push back.

But the way to earn Mark's respect wasn't to call him out in front of Derek. It was to show Mark that Kian was in charge, and that he wasn't going to tolerate any bullshit on shift.

"Just to make sure that's very clear," Kian continued, "Derek, I'd like you to go help Jorge in the dish room. I'll finish assisting Mark with prep."

Of course, Kian had other things to do, but with his presence to stifle any further laziness, he knew they could finish blowing through the rest of the list.

"Yeah," Mark said indulgently, after Derek had already departed, "maybe you could slice my eggplants for me. On the Japanese mandolin, right?"

Kian gritted his teeth. So he'd heard that story too, had he?

"Correct, and I'd be happy to," was all Kian said. Maybe if he didn't engage Mark, then eventually he'd lose interest in pursuing whatever story he'd concocted in his head.

Of course, it just so happened to be a *true* story, but Mark couldn't ever figure that out.

Kian whipped through the eggplants, being careful and also not putting the gloves on, because he didn't want to give Mark any more reasons to believe the story he'd heard was the truth. His finger had long since healed, leaving only a thin, nearly invisible scar.

The rest of the chefs piled in for the service, and Kian directed them as necessary—but they'd all been at Terroir long enough that they knew exactly what to do, and how to do it. And Kian, to his own surprise, realized that he'd been telling them what to do a lot longer than his official promotion. Maybe, Kian thought as they sat down to family dinner, Bastian was right. Maybe he did in fact deserve this position. But no matter how many times he told himself that, he still felt over his head.

He wished he could've confided in Bastian and talked it through with him—wasn't that what you did with a partner?—but the thought of admitting any weakness to Bastian was terrifying. He was relentless and inexorable. Weakness was denied until it didn't exist. Mistakes happened once and only once. Kian had become very good at sticking to Bastian's personal rules, but he'd never been this far out of his depth before.

Kian put himself on the pass-through, adding garnish and inspecting each plate as they left the kitchen, and assigned Mark to one of the three sauté stations on the enormous stove. Sauté was easily the most grueling station, other than the grill, but Wyatt's replacement was so good that Kian wasn't going to tempt fate by testing Mark there.

As he started calling out orders for starters, Kian watched Mark at his station. He was just learning the recipes, so it was not surprising that his movements weren't as confident or as innate. Or as quick, Kian thought as the starters went out, and more entrée orders poured in.

It was still early, and they were by no means at capacity yet, though Michelle, the front of house manager, had dropped by during family meal to grab a bite and to tell Kian they were totally booked up tonight. Which meant that as busy as it seemed now, this was still quiet compared to how many orders they were going to have in an hour.

"Keeping up?" Kian asked, keeping his tone light as he swung by Mark at his sauté station.

"Yes, Chef," Mark said in a strained voice.

He was only just keeping up, but that was still keeping up, so Kian let it go. And then Mark sent some scallops up to the pass that were definitely not quite done.

Overdone scallops were a criminal offense in the Terroir kitchen, usually causing Bastian to throw the plate, or worse, a whole stack of plates. Underdone, that was just a rookie mistake, but Mark and Kian had been working in professional kitchens for exactly the same time. Just as Kian was too experienced to make a rookie mistake—Mark should have been as well.

Kian dumped the dish in the trash can and set the plate onto the stainless steel counter with a click that resonated through the kitchen, despite that there was the normal loud chatter that accompanied every service.

"Chef?" Michel, Wyatt's replacement on the grill, asked, the expression on his face hopeful that the offender wasn't him, while he clearly believed that it wasn't.

"Are we trying to poison our guests?" Kian asked, raising his voice just enough to cut through the normal kitchen noise. "Are we trying to make them ill? Five hundred bucks for a night of food poisoning doesn't sound like a very good tradeoff."

Everyone stilled, and Kian continued. "Those scallops were raw, Johnson. Make them again and make them *right* this time."

"I plated the wrong pan," Mark said mulishly, pushing another towards Kian.

But it had been a good minute and a half since Kian had first spied the nearly raw scallops. Ninety additional seconds for a pan of perfectly cooked scallops would mean that this batch was now *overcooked*. He glanced down at the plate, not taking it, just looking. And he could tell, without even touching a single fingertip to them, that they would be tough and nearly inedible.

"You plated the wrong one again, Johnson," Kian said. "These are overdone. Start over."

Bastian would have been throwing things by now, and Kian told himself he was proud that his voice was steady, but still calm. Relentless, because perfection was a difficult journey yet a possible one. They were here at Terroir to achieve perfection. It didn't even matter that Kian loved Bastian and never wanted to serve a plate that wasn't perfect in his restaurant; he would have striven for that no matter what his personal feelings were.

But he knew, the hard realization lodging in his gut, that he could not let him down. Not now. Especially now.

"But, Chef," Mark dared to argue, "I have . . ." and he signaled to the six other pans he had on the stove in various states of cooking.

Kian knew the glint in his eyes was dangerous, and for the first time Mark seemed at least partially chastened. "Are you telling me that you are unable to handle your station?"

"No, Chef," Mark finally said.

"Then get me another plate of fucking scallops. And tomorrow, we'll have a one-on-one lesson on how to cook them properly so this doesn't ever happen again."

It was a lot for a chef like Mark to swallow; he had his ego, like they all did. But he'd also fucked up and knew it, and so he turned back to the stove and began another pan of scallops.

Michelle, watching the entire exchange, gave him a smile, just reassuring enough, but not patronizing. She'd worked for Bastian too long to ever do that.

Two minutes later he handed her the plate, after checking it carefully himself. The scallops were cooked perfectly. Kian couldn't have done any better himself.

And that, Kian told himself later, as the kitchen was being scrubbed down, and he was sitting in Bastian's office, feeling like half-an-imposter in the big leather chair behind the desk, was why he couldn't just give up on Mark. He *knew* better. He had potential. He had all the tools needed to succeed. Bastian was right. He just needed . . . fine tuning. Kian wasn't sure he was the right person for the job, but he'd made it through tonight, hadn't he?

He also hadn't yelled once, and that, too, felt like an accomplishment.

Mark poked his head in the open doorway. "Chef," he said, and the challenging note in his voice was not entirely gone, but it was diminished. Enough that Kian couldn't help but still feel optimistic about this working out.

"Is it done?" Kian asked.

Nodding, Mark didn't move. Kian waited for him to speak, because clearly something was on his mind.

"Michael Mina was a lot smaller," Mark said, repeating his excuse from the morning.

"And Terroir is not," Kian responded back smoothly. "You need to up your game. I expect your best effort tomorrow."

"Derek was right," Mark mumbled, as he turned, "you've turned into a copy of that bastard."

Clearly he hadn't meant for Kian to hear him, but he also hadn't really gone out of his way to muffle his voice enough. Kian's temper spiked, because not only wasn't he a copy of Bastian, it was the sort of comment that only a few weeks ago would have been something he'd have taken as a compliment.

And now, with the sneer of Mark's voice still ripe in the air, he couldn't anymore, and that really, *really* pissed him off.

When he heard another set of footsteps outside the door, he didn't even look up. "I'll be there in a moment to lock up," Kian bit out sharply. He wasn't in the mood to talk to Mark anymore today—and he wasn't stupid enough to think he could actually tell Bastian about what had happened.

"I already locked up."

Kian glanced up in surprise because that wasn't Mark's voice at all.

"It's still weird for me to see you in that chair," Bastian said softly. "Sorry, I didn't mean to surprise you."

It was undeniable that he was in a bad mood, and Kian's gut reaction was to demand to know why he was here. Was he here to check up on him after his first shift as *chef de cuisine* without Bastian there as support?

"You didn't." Kian sighed, and sat back. "It was just a long day."

Bastian sat down on one of the opposite chairs, and he was right, it *was* weird to see him like this, their normal roles reversed. "Michelle texted me and said it was a good service."

It was impossible not to hope that Michelle, who'd witnessed the entire scallop incident, hadn't told him that part of it. But whether Bastian knew about it or not, he didn't say another word.

"I thought you could use a hot bath and a little food," Bastian said. "And maybe a drive home."

He was really tired but he raised a questioning eyebrow anyway. "Do you think leaving my car here is a good idea?"

"I really don't give a fuck, you're worn out. Let me drive you back." Bastian stood, like Kian's agreement was a given.

Of course Bastian didn't give a fuck if Kian's car was seen here overnight. It wouldn't be his reputation that would be compromised. He'd probably get high fives and the subtle admiration of everyone for finding a cute young guy to fuck. The gossip would assume that Kian had slept his way to the top, instead of the truth—that he'd worked his ass off.

If Bastian couldn't think that through, then Kian wasn't going to help him along.

Finally, he seemed to get it when Kian didn't move. "You're afraid people are going to talk."

"People are already talking. People have been talking for two years." Kian paused. "I don't want to give them any evidence that they're right." He didn't want to mention that Derek—already on his last chance at Terroir—had been gossiping or how intently Mark had been listening, but he would if Bastian pressed him.

"How about we park your car on the other side of the building? Where we get the deliveries?" Bastian suggested. "Michel is scheduled to receive the few we're getting tomorrow, and he'll keep his mouth shut."

Kian would have agreed with him only yesterday but after catching Derek today, it was hard to trust anyone. Before today, he'd believed he had Derek's full support and his respect because he'd personally saved Derek's overdramatic ass more than once.

"I'm just going to follow you back," Kian said, standing up. Today's service had driven home the fact that he was in a far more precarious position than he'd believed, and he didn't want Bastian trying to convince him otherwise.

"If you insist," Bastian said as he followed him towards the locker room. "But you have the morning off, tomorrow, yes?"

Kian grabbed his coat and his bag. "You know I do."

He flipped on the after-hours lights, and they exited the restaurant into the cool night air, the already-locked door closing behind them.

"I made brunch reservations for us tomorrow," Bastian said as Kian stopped at his car door.

"You did what?"

Bastian shrugged, but his shoulders looked tight, and maybe he needed the hot bath as much as Kian did, after a long day dealing with Nathan Hess. Not anyone's favorite person.

"You said sex at home, work at Terroir, but..." Bastian hesitated, and Kian couldn't remember him ever looking so uneasy, so unsure of himself. "But I don't want our options to be only limited to that."

Kian supposed there were places they could go where they wouldn't necessarily be recognized, but he very much doubted that Bastian had made brunch reservations at one of them. He would have called up one of his many friends, who'd offhandedly mention the incident to another friend, or even worse, they'd been seen by someone who knew them.

Bastian shoved his hands into the pockets of his jeans, looking frustrated. "This isn't just fucking to me. I don't want to be your dirty secret."

"And you think I do?" Kian questioned. "You think that's how I think about this? After two years of waiting, and wishing that we could do something about how we felt, you think I'm only here for *sex*?"

There was a part of Kian, vocal but somewhat drowned out by the overwhelming exhaustion he felt, that told him they needed to talk about this when he wasn't already in such a bad mood.

The problem was that the conversation had already started and from the way Bastian's expression had tightened, Kian knew he wasn't just going to leave it.

"Listen," Kian said before Bastian could say something else—probably something he'd regret later—"I'm worn out, I had a fucking long day. I'd like to take you up on the food and hot bath idea, but I don't want to fight about this. Not now."

Bastian surprised the hell out of him by laughing. "Are you trying to avoid a fight?"

"Aren't you?"

"Yes. No. I don't really fucking know. I just know I don't want this to be a secret. Not forever, anyway." Bastian looked confused, and *sounded* confused, which probably confused him even more.

Kian reached up and slid a hand around Bastian's neck, tugging him down closer. Bastian leaned in, like he'd only been waiting for the invitation. "Not forever," he agreed. "But you *just* promoted me to *chef de cuisine* at twenty-three fucking years old. Let's give it a little time."

Sighing, Bastian leaned in, resting his forehead against Kian's. "You're right. I'll change the reservation. We'll go someplace else."

"Thank you," Kian murmured. "I know it sucks, I know this isn't . . . normal."

Bastian's grip tightened on Kian's hips. "I don't give a fuck what's normal. I love you. I just want to do right by you. Always."

Kian reached up and kissed him then. It was just a quick little brush of his lips against Bastian's, but that still felt like risking it. The parking lot was empty, but anyone driving by right now would see all the evidence they needed. "Let's go home," he said, reaching for his door handle. "Someone pretty amazing promised me a hot bath and some food, and I'm starving."

Bastian's smile was warm and sweet. "For the food or for something else?"

Kian risked another quick peck, this time to Bastian's cheek. "Can't I be hungry for both?"

"Go," Bastian said, chuckling with amusement, "before I decide that this parking lot is private enough for what I have in mind."

❧ ☙

Kian didn't know if Bastian had deliberately lured him to his house with only a promise of a bath, but once he'd suggested it, Kian wanted it. They'd spent more than a few late nights tucked up together in Bastian's oversized tub and it was already a favorite spot of his.

"Food first or bath?" Bastian called out as Kian let himself in the front door of his house.

"Food," Kian said, walking into the kitchen. They tended to get distracted in the bath and he had a feeling that an orgasm would be enough to finish him off completely for the evening.

"I figured," Bastian said. He was sautéing some ingredients in a pan, and there was already a pot of water bubbling on the stove. "Pasta?"

"Works for me." Kian slid onto one of the barstools. "This doesn't really get old, you know."

Bastian looked up, and the boyish smile on his face made Kian's heart contract. "Me cooking for you? Why wouldn't I? You're the one who worked hard in the kitchen today. I only had the longest fucking meeting in the history of meetings."

"That bad, huh?" Kian asked.

"I knew Nathan Hess was difficult," Bastian admitted. "But he makes me look like a fucking saint, and that's a problem."

"What was the meeting about today?"

"We were supposed to be finalizing the contract, but instead he threw me and my lawyer for a loop. Demanded a percentage of profits as well as a monthly rent. Seemed to think I was doing him a favor, instead of the other way around."

"You know Xander's boyfriend is his son, right?" Kian said.

"I am well aware." Bastian's voice was testy as he added a pint of cherry tomatoes to the pan. "I am not going to ask *Xander* to intercede on my behalf."

Kian stole a tomato from the pan, quicker than Bastian could bat his fingers away with his metal tongs. "I didn't think he should," he said. "I'm just saying that maybe it would be easier to do this without Hess. Xander says he made Damon's life a living hell. Do you really want to make that your problem too?"

Whatever Bastian answered, it was clear how he felt from the expression on his face. He grunted noncommittally as he used his tongs to check the pasta.

"Get the plates," was all he actually said, which Kian thought made it rather obvious.

They were sitting side by side on the barstools, eating their late night pasta in silence, when Bastian brought it up again. "I'm hoping my lawyer can convince his lawyer that he's fucking insane," Bastian said but he didn't exactly sound confident. "If he thinks I'm paying a dime from my profits, he'd have to be."

"Why don't you just do this without him?" Kian asked. "You don't *need* him, not really."

"No," Bastian sighed, pushing the food around his plate. A bad sign all around, because like everything Bastian made, it was delicious. "But it would be easier. He already has the facility, the kitchen. It needs some updating, but that would only take a few weeks. Staff wouldn't be difficult. Menu wouldn't either. It's . . . a lot, honestly, building from the ground up. I was trying to avoid it. Maybe it's unavoidable."

There was a part of Kian—a part he'd been trying very hard to ignore these past weeks—that wanted to tell Bastian that this clearly wasn't the right time to do this, and that even if it meant a demotion, it was okay to give up the proposed partnership with Hess. It was the same voice that wouldn't stop whispering at him that he was ill-prepared and not experienced enough to run Terroir nearly by himself.

Kian ignored the voice. "Maybe it is," he said, trying to inject as much cheer into his voice as he could, despite his exhaustion.

"Let's take a bath," Bastian said. "It seems we both had trying days. I'd frankly like to forget mine as soon as possible."

That was the most direct reference Bastian had made to the scallop incident yet—nearly like he wished Kian would tell him, but despite that hunch, Kian had no intention of saying a word. Bastian had tasked him with running Terroir, had given him Mark, and despite Kian's concern, believed in him completely.

There was no way Kian was going to tell him that he was over his head and that Mark was a nightmare, possibly developing into something even worse. It just looked bad, he told himself as Bastian took care of the dishes and Kian walked to the bathroom, because he was so tired. Everything would be better in the morning.

He flipped on the hot water and plugged the drain, perching on the edge of the tub. He stripped off his t-shirt, toeing off his socks.

Bastian appeared in the doorway and pulled a small lighter out of his pocket, flicking it on and lighting the vanilla-scented candles scattered around the tub. They were new, Kian realized, and he hadn't even noticed, he was so god damned worn out.

"I told you," Bastian said quietly, placing his hands on Kian's bare shoulders, "I want to take care of you."

Kian had never been particularly interested in being taken care of before, but he was too tired to fight it.

He looked up, and nodded slowly. "Okay," he said.

"Then what are you waiting for?" Bastian asked, gesturing to the rapidly filling tub. "In you go."

"You're not joining me?" Kian frowned, slipping his jeans and then his underwear down over his hips, leaving them in a pile with the rest of his clothes.

"Sweetheart, you're dead on your feet. I've been there, so I know how you feel. Get in."

Kian did as he requested, sliding into the water, sighing at how perfect the temperature was—just a shade cooler than too hot to stand.

Reaching up, Bastian flipped the lights off, and then to Kian's surprise, Bastian turned back with a few little bottles and drizzled one in the water. The scent of chamomile and vanilla filled his nostrils and he sank back against the tub edge, his head tipping back. He could fall asleep right now, just like this.

"I'd say you work too hard, but . . . I'm still me," Bastian said, his voice a dark rumble.

"And I'm still me," Kian retorted with only a little heat, "and I wouldn't stop even if you asked me to."

"I don't want you to stop, I just want to make it a little easier when you do," Bastian murmured. He leaned against the tub deck, wetting a washcloth and reaching out for Kian's leg.

Never in a million years would Kian have imagined that Bastian would take such a subservient role, or would bend that everlastingly proud back to wash him, but he was doing it now, hands careful and firm on his skin.

It was inevitable, because Kian would have to be dead to not be aroused by the feeling of Bastian's hands on him. Lazy arousal unwound through him, the scent of the steam surrounding them lulling him to a dreamy state where even his cock thickening under the water wasn't something to be worried about.

He felt his blood quicken when finally Bastian closed his fingers around it, giving it a gentle but purposeful stroke. "Is this okay?" Bastian murmured, the dim light of the candles shadowing the stunning angles of his face.

Kian found he couldn't even reply, could only nod as Bastian continued to stroke his cock, fingers wringing the pleasure from him with a measured, even touch. His orgasm took him by surprise, but Bastian must have realized it was coming, because he was ready with the wet washcloth, and as the aftershocks faded, Kian slumped back against the lip of the tub.

"Feel any better? Bastian asked.

He was in a warm, cozy tunnel, so far away, so out of it, that he thought he'd answered, but maybe he didn't at all. Maybe he fell asleep in the tub, and maybe Bastian lifted him out, as gentle as he'd ever been with anything in his whole life, dried him off, and took him to bed.

Maybe, because in the morning, Kian still wasn't sure how he got underneath Bastian's soft, silky sheets.

Chapter Twelve

"When I said that we needed to go somewhere for brunch where we wouldn't be recognized, I wasn't anticipating *this*," Kian hissed under his breath as they settled into the booth, the vinyl squeaking underneath them.

"You told me it was important to you that nobody would see us together," Bastian said. "I can guarantee that this is the last place anyone would expect me to go for brunch."

Kian still looked disbelieving. "Okay," Bastian continued, drumming his fingers on the table, "I can be a little bit of a snob."

"A little?"

Bastian rolled his eyes. "I am not going to apologize for my high standards." He looked around, taking in the cheap fixtures, the tired, haggard waitresses, and the wailing baby three tables over. "But what's important to you is important to me."

"I just keep expecting you to run out of here, screaming," Kian teased. He reached over the table and grasped Bastian's hand in his own smaller one, his thumb rubbing one of his burn scars.

"We haven't even ordered yet," Bastian said, and figured this was as good a time as any to examine the laminated menu card the waitress had set in front of him only a few moments before. It was still damp from being wiped down—from what, Bastian wasn't sure he wanted to know.

"Unlike you, I've been here before. Many times," Kian said, not even bothering to glance at his own menu. "You don't seem surprised by this."

"You were in school. You were on an intern salary for the first six months. This place is cheap and open twenty-four hours. I might be a snob, but I'm not an idiot," Bastian said. He paused. "Fruit Loop pancakes? Cinnamon roll pancakes?"

Kian laughed. "Those will definitely be too sweet for you."

"How do you know I don't have a secret sweet tooth?" Bastian said, pouting a little. Maybe he had been interested in the cinnamon roll pancakes, if only because he was curious what they'd be like.

"You don't have a secret anything, not from me," Kian said, "though I admit that you're sweeter than I thought you'd be."

"What, you believed I'd be throwing plates at home? Yelling at the TV?"

Kian looked thoughtful as he stirred some of that awful fake creamer into his coffee. "Actually no. I just think you have a soft side that most people don't get to see."

It was hard, but Bastian ordered himself not to blush. He knew what this was really about—the bath he'd given Kian last night. At the time it had felt right, to take care of him like that, but he also had no intentions of discussing it.

"I think it's nice," Kian continued and Bastian gave him full bravery points for actually taking a sip of the sludge they called coffee here. "Don't get me wrong, I really like it."

"I'd be worried if you didn't." Bastian told himself not to get defensive, but it still lingered in the edges of his voice.

"Hey, hey," Kian said, reaching for his hand again. "I'm trying to say thank you, you surprised me, in a super nice way, and I'm doing a bad job of it."

"You'd had a really hard day, some of which was my fault. What was I supposed to do? Tell you to suck it up?"

Kian's smile was luminous. "You'd tell just about anyone else that."

"Exactly." Bastian sipped his ice water, and tried not to grimace at the metallic taste. "You're not like everyone else."

The waitress appeared at their table, breaking the moment. "Are you ready to order?" she asked.

"Yes," Kian answered, before Bastian could argue that he'd barely glanced at the menu. "We'll both have the grand slam breakfast.

Scrambled eggs. Bacon, extra crispy. Hash browns, well done. Sour-dough toast. Butter on the side."

Just when Bastian thought Kian was done surprising him, he'd go and do something like that. Anyone else ordering for him would have gotten a full-on Bastard glare, but Kian had said he'd been here lots of times—maybe he knew better. Bastian would give him the benefit of the doubt.

"And an order of the cinnamon roll pancakes," Bastian added smoothly.

When the waitress left, Kian shot him a look of disbelief. "They looked okay," Bastian defended.

"My advice at someplace like this is to keep it simple. It's hard for them to fuck up eggs and hash browns," Kian suggested. "But I guess you do have more of a sweet tooth than I thought."

"I usually indulge it with really good dark chocolate truffles," Bastian admitted with a wry smile, "and I will torture you sexually for hours if you admit it to anyone, but they looked pretty good in the picture."

Kian raised his eyebrow. "It's probably all marketing and a really good food stylist," Bastian said.

"Seems legit." He did not seem convinced. "But I'm definitely interested in this sexual torture thing."

"It isn't as fun as it sounds." Bastian tried to keep his voice serious, but instead the tone came out all growly sex. It wasn't his fault; in a moment of self-sacrifice aided by a healthy helping of guilt, he'd gotten Kian off but hadn't had any release himself. And this morning, there hadn't been time because he'd promised Kian brunch before his shift started.

"Yeah, I don't buy that for a moment," Kian said. "So, let's get this straight. The famous Bastian Aquino has a secret soft side and a secret dessert kink. I like it."

Bastian shrugged. "If I can't tell you those things, then who else?" Maybe Kian really hadn't believed that he'd never told anyone but his mother that he loved them before. Because Kian seemed more surprised than he'd ever expected.

"Let me guess, Luc doesn't know about either of those," Kian said.

There was nothing Bastian regretted more than ever letting Kian know about the existence of his ex. If Luc could even be considered that, because of course he hadn't known about either.

Luc had gotten the hard-as-nails Bastian who, at that stage of his life, had wanted to believe that his softer underbelly didn't exist at all. His father had died only a year or so before, launching Bastian into a desperate, overly ambitious race to out-work even his own entirely absent father.

That hadn't been Luc's fault, but he'd never had access to any of the softness Bastian hid like it was shameful. The only person he'd ever been tempted to uncover it for was sitting in front of him.

"Luc got the Terroir version of me, and not much else," Bastian admitted. "So I guess I do owe him something of an apology, after all."

"Or not," Kian said with a grin. "He was enough of an ass when we met. Decent payback."

"I doubt he would feel that way."

"Frankly, I don't give a shit how he feels," Kian said.

It was this hard, nearly bloodthirsty attitude hiding beside the sweet, kind smiles that had ultimately convinced Bastian that Kian could handle Terroir, including a *sous* chef who didn't really like him.

"How did Mark do last night?" Bastian asked. Michelle had texted him some updates, but he'd really been hoping that Kian would tell him his own version of events. He'd anticipated not even needing to ask, but Kian had been very close-lipped about service the night before.

"He was fine," Kian said in a closed-off voice, making it clear he had no interest in discussing Mark.

It was totally fine that Kian wasn't telling him, Bastian told himself. He wanted to handle it on his own; and technically he wasn't obligated to tell Bastian anything, since he'd handled the incident with the scallops himself.

Maybe with a few less broken plates than Bastian himself would have, but that was also okay. Kian wasn't his carbon copy; he might not need to throw things to get his point across.

"Michael Mina is a lot smaller of a restaurant," Bastian offered, despite Kian's clear directive that he didn't want to talk about Mark.

"I know that," Kian said shortly and Bastian swore inwardly, because why the fuck hadn't he just left it alone? Because it wasn't in his nature to leave things alone, he thought shortly, it was in his nature to pry.

It was in his nature to control everything; even the man he loved.

"He'll adjust," Bastian said, aware of just how lame and unlike himself he sounded. When he'd headed the kitchen at Terroir, adjustment was instantaneous, or bad things happened.

He knew Kian didn't feel that way; Derek was evidence enough of that. Bastian had allowed Kian to coax him along because he hadn't felt like dealing with yet another new employee, but any other time, he would have been long gone, likely in a shower of pottery shards.

Kian looked startled. "I wasn't anticipating him doing anything else," he said.

"Right, right, of course," Bastian said, and searched for another topic they could discuss that didn't have anything to do with Terroir. But Terroir had been their primary discussion point for so long that Bastian floundered.

The waitress arriving with their plates saved him.

The food didn't look . . . terrible. Bastian was willing to admit at least that.

The bacon seemed adequately crispy when he tapped it with the tines of his fork, and even the eggs seemed moderately fluffy. The hash browns looked like a deep-fried slab of potato, which was not something Bastian usually found appealing. The toast was dry and too pale, but Kian slid over the caddy of packaged jams anyway.

The pancakes were sitting at the edge of the table, the white ropes of frosting in danger of sliding unceremoniously off the top of the brown speckled pile.

"I'm currently thinking everyone who works for me should get a raise so nobody has to suffer through this," Bastian said.

"Oh, stop being such a snob," Kian said fondly, and Bastian was so glad he'd moved past the subject of Mark that he scooped up a pile of eggs onto his fork and took a bite.

Ignoring the slick of fake margarine, they actually had a decent flavor—they were definitely real eggs and not egg substitute which Bastian had been secretly afraid of.

"See, it's not going to kill you," Kian said, gesturing with his bacon. "It's just breakfast."

"This isn't really breakfast; it's breakfast-adjacent," Bastian sniffed, but he was eating the rest of his eggs, and even took a bite of bacon, letting the sharp saltiness linger on his palate.

Then he watched with horror as Kian reached for the bottle of ketchup the waitress had deposited on their table and proceeded to coat his hash browns in a thick layer of red goop.

"I don't think I know you at all," Bastian said, eyeing his plate dubiously.

"It's just ketchup, it's not poison," Kian said with a little giggle.

"We're going to have to agree to disagree on that," Bastian said with a shudder.

But Kian's gaze was fond as he met Bastian's frown. "You really are the worst, sometimes."

"I'm here and I'm actually eating this food," Bastian protested. He took another bite of eggs and bacon, and eyed the pancakes out of the corner of his eye again. If he tried them, he was going to save them for last, because the unrelenting sugar was going to be overwhelming.

"Under duress," Kian pointed out, waving his fork. "You've even managed to insult ketchup."

"I'm not sure what else I was supposed to do with it."

Kian shoveled a big bite of deep-fried potato into his mouth and smiled as he chewed. "Eat it," he said, once he'd swallowed. "Try it. I thought you were an adventurous cook."

He'd already finished his eggs. He only had a bite or two left of the bacon. He supposed that if he was going to try the hash browns he should prepare them as directed. "Fine," he said, reaching for the ketchup bottle, squeezing a very tiny amount on the edge of the slab. "How is that?"

Kian shook his head. "You need to be diner trained," he said with a laugh.

Bastian shot the offending bottle a withering glare. Any human would have run before this, but the bottle wasn't smart enough to figure out that it had ended up on the Bastard's shit list.

"I was trained at Le Cordon Bleu in Paris," Bastian argued. "What else would you suggest?"

Kian rolled his eyes. "In a *diner*. When you order hash browns you always get them well done and you always smother them in ketchup. It's the only way."

"*Merde*," Bastian muttered and squeezed out some more of the slop onto his plate. It was a really fucking good thing that nobody he knew would ever be caught dead in a place like this.

"There you go," Kian said, sounding very satisfied. "Now eat up, darling."

"I think you're enjoying this," Bastian grumbled.

"Oh, I am."

"I thought you loved me," Bastian argued. "Why would you want to torture me?"

"This was *your* idea," Kian said with a laugh. "And I do love you, even more, if you'd believe it."

"I think you're laughing at me," Bastian said as he continued to poke with his fork at the hash browns.

"You're just so damn cute," Kian pointed out. "Just eat the damn things."

"I feel like a Michelin inspector is going to pop out of this faux woodwork and revoke my stars," Bastian said, but he scooped up a healthy bite and finally put it in his mouth.

Initially, he was tempted to actually spit out the food in his mouth. Overcooked potato, somehow raw yet burned around the edges, smothered in that fake margarine, so slick and oily, Bastian nearly choked. And over the top of all of that, the bland acidity of the ketchup. Then he chewed again, and swallowed. Took another bite. Chewed that one and swallowed again.

Kian was outright laughing now.

"Trash!" he echoed Bastian's voice. "This is trash!"

Bastian glared but kept eating. He ate the whole slab in record time and shoved the plate away. "I think you've ruined me."

Kian's glance felt like a caress on his cheek. "Then we're ruined together. Exactly as it should be, as far as I'm concerned."

"I suppose I should put aside my snobbery and try these too," Bastian finally said with a sigh, pointing at the pancakes.

Kian just nodded, looking on with unabashed interest. "I've been waiting. Maybe you could even give Chef René a few helpful tips." Chef René had been trained in Paris under the masters of French pastry and even considered Christina Tosi, of Milk Bar fame, an imposter.

"If I told Chef René, he'd probably fall over dead," Bastian said with a rumbling laugh. Despite the oddness of the cuisine, this was one of the best mornings he had in a very long time. Definitely the most fun, because fun hadn't really been something in his vocabulary until he'd met Kian.

"He does eat a lot of butter," Kian replied very seriously, his eyes twinkling.

Bastian cut into the stack of pancakes, making sure to get some of the melting frosting onto the wedge of pancake on his fork. He put it in his mouth and promptly spat it back out, the first thing he'd been unable to stomach since they'd arrived.

"Oh my god," Kian said, and he was laughing so hard, he nearly fell out of the booth. "Were they that bad?"

"Worse," Bastian said with disdain, wiping his mouth with his napkin. "I feel violated."

"Well, I think that's our cue to leave," Kian said with a little hiccup. "I'll go pay the check?"

Bastian grabbed for the receipt the waitress had left but Kian was too quick. "I invited you here," he insisted, which was maybe something he shouldn't be bragging about right now.

"And I think this is something I can pay for," Kian said with a quick roll of his eyes. "I'll meet you outside at the car."

Even days later, Kian couldn't believe that Bastian had really taken him at his word and brought them to the one brunch restaurant he was sure they wouldn't be recognized.

Bastian's expression of wonder, followed by the one of ultimate disgust, had already been filed away in Kian's vault of special memories. They were still figuring out how a relationship worked between them, and he wasn't naïve enough to believe that a relationship fraught with as many difficulties as their own, was guaranteed to survive forever.

But if it ended, he'd still have all those memories to warm him later. There would be good, mixed in with the heartbreak, and that was what Kian was determined to take from this.

"Chef, that's smelling a little . . . burned," Mark offered, his voice for once somewhat deferential.

"It's supposed to be," Kian said, jiggling the sauté pan with a practiced movement.

"What are you working on?" his *sous* asked. They were nearly done with prep for the day, and Kian had ducked out of his official responsibilities a tiny bit early to work on a recipe he'd been toying with in his mind. Something that echoed the hash browns he and Bastian both unexpectedly loved.

"Spin on *tortilla Española*, with a little bit of a *patatas bravas* twist," Kian said, referring to the Spanish potato dishes. "Might be a possibility for a new vegetarian entrée."

"Yeah, like Aquino would ever let you put a dish on the menu," Mark muttered under his breath.

Kian was afraid of the day he'd finally decide it was okay to say his bullshit to his face. For a second, he considered informing Mark that Kian was either directly or partly responsible for about half the Terroir menu, but ultimately he decided it wasn't worth it.

The bare facts were unappealing to him; to Mark it didn't matter if he was wrong, he'd already formed his opinions and it was going to take a lot more than a single sentence to change his mind.

"For a French-inspired restaurant, you guys do some weird shit," Mark said, louder this time, so clearly Kian was meant to respond to this comment.

"Adapt or die," Kian said succinctly, which was one of Bastian's favorite sayings. He slid a thin metal spatula under his potato cake and lifted it slightly, checking its crispness.

"You're literally becoming his clone," Mark huffed. "I'd never have imagined you'd end up here, parroting him instead of developing your own point of view."

Kian rolled his eyes. "What do you call this? You *just* said we were doing some weird shit. How do you know that isn't my point of view?"

"Good point." Mark leaned against the edge of the stove. Kian belligerently hoped his coat would catch on fire.

"I like to filter unexpected dishes through a French perspective," was all Kian said. *None of this is going to change his mind,* Kian reminded himself, but it was hard. He didn't enjoy being disliked—though in reality, who really did? Maybe Bastian. Except that even that long-held belief was slowly fading away in the face of his sweeter, softer side.

Maybe Bastian didn't enjoy being disliked after all. Maybe he just tolerated it because that was the cost of running a restaurant like Terroir.

"Maybe you just want to filter *yourself* through Aquino's perspective," Mark said, waggling his eyebrows in a grotesque re-enactment of what he thought might be going on between them.

Kian barely held back a shudder. "You are fucking crazy," he said succinctly. "Bastian isn't a *filter*."

He only realized his mistake that would probably be his undoing when an unholy light lit up Mark's face.

"Oh, it's *Bastian* now, is it?" Mark said, his eyebrows working double time now. Kian glared. He hoped he'd get an eyebrow cramp—if that was even a thing, and Kian believed it *should* be.

One of the reasons why Kian had hated Mark so much at culinary academy was the way he could scent the blood in the water, and when he did, he'd pounce harder and faster. It wasn't like Kian hadn't learned to be tough during his two-plus-year stint at Terroir, but Mark was a different animal.

He had all the pieces. He probably wasn't going to put them together quite right, but in the end, that wasn't going to matter. The right way—*we've been in love with each other forever*—wasn't nearly as interesting as the story Mark would no doubt concoct.

"You're just jealous that we're friendly," Kian tried to deflect, but it was a bad excuse.

"Yeah, *real* friendly," Mark said, his sly insinuation unexpectedly painful. "I wondered how you managed to convince Aquino to make you *chef de cuisine* at twenty-fucking-three. Now I know. You did it on your knees."

"I did it on my two feet, *Chef*," Kian retorted tightly. "And this conversation is over."

It had only been a five-minute conversation, but it had eroded away any headway Kian had been making to establish himself from a position that Mark might, in some faraway, possible future, respect.

He'd wanted to believe that Kian was under-qualified and out of his depth, but before he'd only had gossip. Now he had ammunition to back it all up.

Dinner service was a tense disaster.

Kian gave himself a pep talk prior with a reminder that he didn't want to be the irrational asshole Bastian could be sometimes. He didn't want to yell or throw things or generally be a dick. The problem with that strategy was it assumed you already had your underlings' respect, and while Kian might have had *most* of the kitchen behind him, he didn't have it all.

He threw his first plate at 7:31 PM and instantly felt sick with guilt. Mark had deliberately goaded him into it by mishearing on purpose the orders and the instructions Kian was shouting out over the regular kitchen noise.

"I thought you said four scallops," Mark said, his tone genuinely apologetic, but Kian knew better. Mark didn't have bad hearing and he definitely wasn't stupid; he was trying to push Kian past his breaking point.

Unfortunately, he was succeeding.

"I said *five* scallops," Kian ground out, his voice rising despite every effort to prevent it. "Are you fucking deaf tonight?"

"Not at all, Chef," Mark said.

"Then get another fucking pan going," Kian yelled. "And apologize to everyone else because they have to figure out how to fucking hold the rest of the dish. Times *four*."

And when a minute later, Kian asked for the scallops, Mark shot him a bewildered look. "You already have the four up there. What do you mean?"

The tense air in the kitchen shattered when Kian swept the bare plate, no scallops to be found, off the counter and to the floor, where it exploded in a thousand tiny white shards of porcelain.

He'd always believed that it must have made Bastian feel better—after all, if it didn't, if you only felt *worse* afterwards, why the fuck would you continue to do it?

Kian couldn't answer that question, because he definitely didn't feel any better. Somehow he felt even fucking worse, and like he was slowly beginning to lose his grip on his self-control. He'd broken a plate today; what was next? Mark's nose?

When service finally ended, he hid out in Bastian's office again, burying his pounding head between his hands, and wondering how the hell everything could have devolved so quickly. The kitchen was a tense, fraying mess, and everyone was clearly affected. There'd been other issues tonight, at other stations—stations that Kian would have depended on a hundred percent before tonight—and at the head of everything, he felt like the very worst offender.

He couldn't tell Bastian how quickly everything had fallen apart. Bastian had trusted him with his restaurant and believed in him completely. How could he go to him, the man he loved and the man he respected more than any other, and confess that he'd fucked it all up?

He couldn't. He knew he couldn't.

Michel had been the one to approach him, not Mark, even when that was clearly outlined as Mark's job. "Kitchen's cleaned, boss," Michel said, voice gentle and quiet as he stood in the doorway.

It was the first time Michel had ever used that particular nick-name, he'd always used the respectful and traditional "Chef" title with Kian, like he appreciated how difficult it was for Kian to fill the shoes Bastian had passed down.

Kian told himself it didn't mean anything, Michel still respected him, but the thought felt empty. *He* felt empty.

He'd thought being the boss would feel more like it had before, when he'd been doing a lot of the same things, but with Bastian's tacit permission. But it didn't, and now it was hard not to face the fact that a lot of the kitchen staff weren't as completely behind him as he'd thought.

Probably they'd thought the same thing Kian did—that he wasn't really qualified for this job, and maybe even knowing what they did about the close working relationship between him and Bastian, they'd made the exact same assumption Mark had.

"Thanks," was all he said shortly.

He knew Bastian would be waiting for him at his home, for their *food followed by sex* evening tradition, but Kian wasn't sure he could even face him tonight.

It was a cop-out, and Bastian would know that, but he texted him anyway, begging off. **Hard day today and I'm tired. Going home and passing out.**

To his surprise, when he drove home, Xander's car was in the driveway, and he was actually sitting on their beat-up couch in the living room when he walked in.

"You look like shit," Xander said. "Is that why you're not at Bastian's?"

Kian collapsed onto the couch and bit his lip as hard as he dared, praying the pain would keep the tears at bay.

He couldn't cry, and he definitely couldn't cry in front of Xander. His phone buzzed in his pocket and he ignored it. It was probably Bastian, and the very last person he wanted to talk to right now was him.

"You're home early," Kian said dully, eyes on the TV, even though he wasn't really watching it.

"Seriously, you don't have any clue when I get home," Xander pointed out. "You haven't been here in weeks. Not since you finally got into Bastian's pants."

Kian clamped his lips tighter together.

"Though, I know how hard being in a relationship is when you work crazy hours," Xander continued, like he didn't even realize Kian was right on the edge of breaking down. "You've got to make time while you can. But that doesn't explain why you're here, not there." He glanced over at Kian, and he realized his mistake. Xander knew.

"I threw a plate today," Kian said slowly. "Maybe Mark is right. Maybe I am becoming Bastian."

"I can't believe I'm saying this, but maybe the Bastard isn't all bad. He has a few redeemable qualities. Ones you have too. If you threw something today, it was because you were at the end of your rope. I know what that feels like." Xander paused. "Feel like talking about it?"

Did he want to talk about it? Kian wasn't really sure he did, but he thought he should.

"I feel like raiding Nate's good wine stash," Kian muttered.

Xander stood up and gestured towards the closet Nate, a sommelier and their fellow roommate, was always threatening to lock. "Pick your poison," he said.

Kian stood up too, and walked over to the closet, opening the door. He almost pulled out a pinot noir that he knew was really good, but the last time he'd drunk pinot had been with Bastian, and he didn't want to think about Bastian right now.

Instead he chose a cabernet and walked to the kitchen to grab the opener.

"So, what happened today?" Xander asked as Kian opened the bottle with a few quick, efficient movements.

They didn't really have wine glasses, so Kian pulled two mugs from the cabinet and poured a few healthy glugs of wine into each, handing one to Xander.

"Do you remember anything about a guy from culinary school who'd made my life a living hell?" Kian asked, figuring they were going to need to go back to the beginning.

"Yeah, Bart? Was that his name?"

Kian took a long gulp of wine. Nate was probably going to kill them for stealing this particular bottle, because the wine was full and rich on his tongue. "Mark, actually. Two weeks ago, Bastian hired him as my *sous*."

Xander looked stunned. "I'm sorry, I thought you just said *Bastian* hired your *sous*."

Kian shot him a wry look. "Don't worry, he's already apologized for that one."

"And he should still be apologizing," Xander said. "Jesus fucking Christ."

"Yeah, I'm not sure you're wrong." Kian looked down at the wine in his mug. "He's got control issues, which you know better than anyone."

"At first, I thought it would be gratifying and a little bit funny to watch Aquino's control issues go head-to-head with Damon's dad. Now I'm not so sure," Xander said, as he opened the patio door off the kitchen, and they stepped outside, settling down at the old, worn-out picnic table they'd dragged into their backyard one day.

"It's not gratifying or funny?" Kian asked.

"No, it's fucking insane and it makes me worry about you. What happens when this falls through, because we all know it will, and Bastian goes back to Terroir? You're demoted? Mark takes your job? I don't fucking know. I don't know how you're handling all this. I'd be a wreck."

"How do you know I'm not a wreck?" Kian asked quietly, staring out in the dark night.

"Are you?" Xander sounded startled.

"I don't know. Maybe. I should be able to handle Mark. I should. But he keeps getting under my skin, and I gave him some fucking good ammunition today."

Xander had always been the smartest guy Kian knew. He figured it out in under ten seconds. "Oh Jesus, he found out you and Bastian were sleeping together. You didn't tell him, did you?"

"Of course I didn't fucking tell him," Kian said bitterly. "I'm not an idiot. I told Bastian we needed to keep it quiet. I don't want anyone to know."

"Listen, everyone's favorite gossip subject has always been Bastian. That's not your fault. You slid into his orbit and *poof*, it happened. You got that job at a really young age. People are gonna talk about it."

"It's like Mark looks at me, and he *sees* me, the me inside that's quaking and afraid and fucking terrified. And he calls me on it. Constantly."

"Easy solution. Fire him and hire someone you actually like. Or promote Michel. I've always liked that guy."

"Bastian thinks he's too quiet. Too contained." Two things Bastian could never understand. "And I can't."

Xander scrubbed a hand over his stubble. "Fucking hell. He told you not to."

There was a part of Kian that didn't want to sell Bastian out to Xander. But Xander was his best friend, and Xander had always wanted the best for *him*. Not for Terroir, but for *him*. For all the talk of his soft side, Bastian hadn't done that, and Kian didn't believe he ever would. He needed to be okay with that, and aside from Mark, he *was*. But Mark was the wrinkle that was fucking everything up.

"If it helps," Kian muttered into his wine, "he made a few very good points."

"It doesn't." Xander sounded annoyed. "He's supposed to be creating an environment where you can succeed, not dragging you down by putting you in a bad spot."

"I don't think he sees it that way," Kian said with a heavy sigh.

"So what are you going to do?" Xander asked finally.

Kian tipped the rest of the liquid in his mug into his mouth. It helped, a little. "I don't know."

"I'm guessing you have no intention of telling him how tough Mark is making things."

"How can I? Xander, he told me he believes that I can do this. He trusts me, completely. How can I go to him and say, *I can't*? You know how Bastian would take that. It would ruin everything."

Kian couldn't actually bring himself to say it would not only ruin his future at Terroir, but their relationship. But he *knew* it would. Bastian might not exactly have him up on a pedestal but he *did*. He believed that Kian could do anything he set his mind to. He believed in his superiority over puny little insects like Mark. How could Kian say, *you were wrong* while preserving the things Bastian loved about him?

Plain and simple, he just couldn't.

"So you're going to go back tomorrow and just . . . keep throwing plates?" Xander asked skeptically. "And hope that eventually Mark gets sick of dodging them and quits?"

Kian couldn't tell him that he hadn't even thought that far ahead. "Yeah, sure," he said.

Xander laughed humorlessly. "You are so fucked. I . . . I wish there was something I could do. You know, right, that if you ever leave Terroir, you can always work for me?"

Truthfully, Kian had never even considered it. He'd never considered what would happen to make him leave Terroir—by choice or not.

"Yeah, of course. Thanks."

Xander stood up and put a reassuring hand on Kian's shoulder. "Just remember that, okay? I've got to go, Damon's picking me up."

Kian watched him go inside. He didn't move. Working for Xander wouldn't be that bad, he assumed. Xander would be a good boss. But he wasn't Bastian. Nobody was Bastian, except Bastian himself.

Chapter Thirteen

Kian would have told him *if something was wrong.*

Kian wouldn't lie to him by omission.

Kian still trusted him.

Bastian repeated these three things over and over as he paced through his kitchen. He wouldn't let himself look over at the dining room, where he'd actually set the table for their evening meal. Kian had really enjoyed the bath he'd had the other night, so Bastian had decided that putting out his nice dishes and buying a few additional candles wouldn't be too much.

But then Kian had texted and claimed to be too tired to come by. It was the first night he hadn't come over since their relationship had begun. Bastian's first instinct was to, of course, believe him. After all, he knew better than anyone how exhausting managing the reins of Terroir was, night after night—and he was used to doing it.

But after a few minutes, doubt had started to creep in. He'd texted Michelle, and asked her how the night had gone, something he'd really tried not to do. Everything he found out about Terroir, he wanted to find out from Kian.

The annoying niggling worry he was hiding something still bothered Bastian.

Michelle's reply hadn't reassured him. She'd been deliberately vague, giving no details, merely telling him everything was fine.

It immediately made Bastian believe that nothing was fine.

For five interminable minutes he resisted the urge to drive down to Terroir and make sure it was still standing.

He was lucky to have lasted five minutes, he told himself as he drove down the hill towards the restaurant. After he parked in his normal spot and got out of the car, he looked over the lot and it was quiet and empty, everything as it should be. He typed in his code at the door and walked inside.

He wasn't entirely sure what he'd been anticipating finding here. Stainless steel gleamed in the dim light of the emergency lights, and he ran a hand along one prep counter. It was weird, not knowing what had happened on it today, depending instead on little snippets of what other people told him. They weren't ever detailed enough for his comfort.

That, Bastian knew, was the main problem. He wanted to be here every night. He wanted to watch it all, his control freak side comforted by knowledge that nothing happened he wasn't aware of.

Taking over as *chef de cuisine* at the restaurant was a huge job—Bastian wasn't going to discount the enormous effort that Kian had put forth to reach that position and to maintain it. But sitting back and trying not to strangle Nathan Hess? Letting someone else, even someone else as beloved as Kian, step forward and run his restaurant? It felt impossible sometimes.

"Just because it's not easy doesn't mean it's not right," Bastian said out loud, the words echoing through the empty room.

But he'd been followed around by an unassailable belief that his chosen path was the right one for the last twenty years. Not once had he ever felt even a tiniest bit of uncertainty, and now he was plagued by it. Surely that meant something? But what it was, Bastian didn't know, and that was even worse.

Pulling his phone from his pocket, Bastian weighed it in his hand for a long moment. Finally, he dialed the number he'd selected.

His mother picked up on the fourth ring, just when he was afraid she'd gone to sleep already.

"Bastian," she exclaimed, "is everything alright?"

He didn't know what to say. Was everything alright? It sure didn't fucking feel like it.

"I just drove down to the restaurant in the middle of the night, to make sure it was still standing. And I resent Kian for knowing what happened tonight when I don't." Bastian figured this would answer the question much better than he could.

"You're there, at the restaurant now?" his mother asked.

"Yeah."

"Hang on for a few minutes," Celeste ordered. "I'm coming down there."

It was late, the roads were dark, and a little bit slick from the rain they'd had earlier in the Valley. He opened his mouth to tell her that she shouldn't, but she interrupted him.

"Bastian, I am still your mother," she said and hung up the phone.

Bastian went into his office, flipping on his computer but instead of doing any actual work, merely stared mindlessly at the screen, waiting for her to show up.

The knock on the back door came much sooner than he'd anticipated. Jumping up, he made his way to the door and opened it.

Celeste had a scarf tied around her head and made her leggings and wrap sweater look like high-end fashion, like she wasn't his mother at all but a retired model.

"Goodness," she said as he opened the door wider, "it is empty in here during off-hours."

Bastian frowned, and she placed a hand on his arm. "Let's go upstairs," she said. "I wouldn't turn down a nice nightcap, if you could find one."

They took one of the service elevators and he led Celeste to the bar, settling her in one of the high stools before ducking behind the bar.

"Any preference?" he asked.

"Something that will loosen your tongue," Celeste said primly.

"I called you, didn't I?" Bastian argued as he set out glasses, and pulled ingredients from one of the under-counter fridges.

"That means you know you *should* tell me what's bothering you, not that you actually will."

Deftly, Bastian peeled an orange, rubbing the edges of each glass with the oils. He dropped a piece of peel in, added a few dashes of bitters, and then poured in a measure of cognac into each glass. A brandied cherry completed each drink, and he placed one in front of Celeste, and the other at the place next to her.

"I'd be concerned your bartenders will be upset, as I'm sure they account for every orange, for every ounce of alcohol," Celeste offered as he sat down, "but it's difficult to imagine anyone being upset with you and actually daring to express it."

"You'll need to meet Kian," Bastian said ruefully. "As for the drinks, you're not wrong, but I'll leave them a note."

"The man you love," Celeste said. "Yes, I would very much like to meet him."

It was foolish but Bastian spluttered anyway. Of course he loved Kian, but he hadn't anticipated his mother calling him out on his feelings. Was he so obvious? Or maybe he was just obvious to her.

Celeste took a sip and hummed approvingly. "Very good," she said, "but then I would not expect any less. As for you being in love with Kian, of course you are. You gave him the most precious part of you."

He was quiet for a long moment. He took a drink, but the alcohol didn't help. "I see the best version of myself reflected in his eyes. But I don't *want* to be that version. I don't want it. I want to love him, but I don't want that." He was all too aware of how miserable he sounded. "I thought this deal with Hess would feel differently, like I was growing and changing and adapting. Learning how to let go. But I don't want to let go."

Her laugh startled him. "Oh, darling, you are your father's son."

It was impossible to hear that pronouncement and not tense from the very ends of his hair to the tips of his toes.

"He was an asshole, *vraiment*," Celeste continued, her words doing nothing to alleviate Bastian's edginess, "but some of the things that made me hate him, make me love you more. You're both stubborn to a fault, and feel intensely, both your likes and dislikes. You do nothing by half measures. That dedication is why we are sitting here now, at your beautiful restaurant."

"I know all that," Bastian said, though he hadn't quite come to terms with some of it. Anything remotely familiar to his father was abhorrent and to be rejected, always, no matter what his *maman* claimed.

"Of course you can't let go. The best version of yourself isn't a man who does, it's a man who *doesn't*."

That was a concept that had somehow never occurred to Bastian. "A man who *doesn't*?"

"You've convinced yourself that to be better, to be a partner worthy of your Kian, you need to let go." Celeste shook her head. "Your greatest asset is your ability to *never* let go. I would guess that is one of the reasons he loves you."

"I can't, I can't just come back here, and upset the structure," Bastian argued. "Kian would hate me for doing that. For dividing the loyalty he's trying to earn."

"Why would you being here divide his loyalty? Would he manage things differently than you? Give different direction?"

It wasn't difficult at all to shake his head. He'd trained Kian meticulously himself, and if Kian had ever given him a moment of concern about the direction of his management at Terroir, Bastian never would have promoted him in the first place. He trusted *Kian* implicitly, but he worried that the trust was not reciprocated.

"Then, why can you not be here during service?" Celeste asked simply. "You don't need to completely absent yourself. You've made yourself miserable, trying to deny something that is part of who you are."

"*Oui*, I am so stupid," Bastian murmured. Every inch of carpet, every ladle, every chair, every cocktail on the menu, bottle of wine in the cellar, onion in the storeroom—they were all an extension of who he was. He was nothing without Terroir and Terroir was nothing without him.

Celeste placed a hand on his arm. "You are a man. It is to be expected."

Bastian laughed, the tone rough with emotion. "You're too good to me."

"My lot in life," she said sweetly. "As is Kian's. He knows what you are, Bastian, better than anyone else. He worked for you for years. He knows what you are, what you need. He has never fought against that."

"Once," Bastian said ruefully. "Once, and he was right. Right while being wrong at the same time."

Celeste raised an eyebrow. "Do I wish to know what happened?"

This time Bastian's laugh felt less torn out of him, and more a product of genuine amusement. "No. No. Definitely not."

"You are a good son, and a good man. I hate to see you doubt that."

"I've done some . . . sometimes I'm not good. I can be cruel," Bastian admitted, finishing his drink in one gulp.

"Your chosen profession, that is cruel though, sometimes?"

"Sometimes," Bastian acknowledged. She wasn't wrong. The fine dining kitchen was a place of exacting standards, and sometimes a very thick skin was needed to deal with the cutthroat atmosphere and unrelenting perfectionism.

His own behavior wasn't always ideal, but Celeste did have a point. He knew he could be better, but she was right; his greatest advantage was that he never wanted to let go of anything.

It was why he hated it when employees left, even when there was a good reason for them to move on. It was why he'd refused to promote Kian, even when he deserved it. It was why staying home during service these last few weeks had nearly killed him—even though he'd been willing to try for Kian.

Clearly he'd been approaching this situation entirely the wrong way.

"Do you feel better?" Celeste asked.

Scrubbing a hand over his face, Bastian thought for a long minute. Truthfully, a little of the panic he'd been feeling had died the moment he'd walked into the kitchen. It wasn't all gone, but it had calmed considerably.

The only thing still bothering him was the text that Kian had sent him, and the niggling feeling that he was actually hiding something.

"Much," Bastian said. "Finish your drink and I'll drive you back home."

"But," Celeste tried to interrupt but Bastian shot her a hard, uncompromising look.

"Yes, you're my mother, but it's late, and I'm not letting you drive home without me. I'll send someone with your car tomorrow."

While he waited for his mother, he pulled out his phone and finally replied back to Kian's text. **I know you're tired, but I'd like to see you.**

Glancing back at the words, it was impossible to deny there wasn't an inherent demand in them, similar to how Bastian moved through life, expecting all barriers to melt away or be conquered. But he was reminded of his mother's words as they walked to his car.

He knows what you are, Bastian, better than anyone else.

After he dropped Celeste off at her home, giving her a quick kiss on her soft cheek, he checked his phone, and to his surprise, Kian had actually replied.

Out on the back deck was all he'd said, which Bastian assumed was an invitation of sorts.

The house was dark when he pulled up to it, and Bastian realized as he got out of the car that he'd barely ever been here. He was Kian's boyfriend and he'd made him come to him almost every time. Yes, he wanted to avoid Xander and their other roommate, who was apparently a sommelier, but even when he'd tried to make their relationship feel equal, inequalities kept cropping up.

Kian was sitting on the back porch, a mug in his hands. When Bastian approached, he didn't think he was being too paranoid to believe that Kian didn't look exactly thrilled to see him. Maybe he should have given Kian the space he'd clearly been wanting. But Bastian was so terrified that a night of space might lead to even more space, not less.

"I'm sorry," was the first thing he said when he sat down.

Kian looked surprised. "For what?"

Bastian drummed his fingers on the table. "For being myself?"

"I knew what I was getting into when I took my clothes off the first time," Kian laughed.

He leaned over, bumping shoulders with Kian, and glanced down into his mug. There were clearly dregs of wine in it. Bastian raised an eyebrow.

"It was a night," Kian finally confessed. "Nothing I can't handle. But a night nonetheless."

It was impossible not to wonder when Bastian's first instinct had shifted from tough-as-nails to apologetic. Because he'd nearly been about to apologize *again*, and that wasn't his fault. Not really. Well, he conceded, it might have been, because he'd been the one to hire Mark.

"Do you want to talk about it?" Bastian asked carefully. Not apologizing, necessarily, but trying to be supportive—the way a normal boyfriend might be. He wasn't ever going to be a normal boyfriend, but Kian was right. He'd known what he was getting into when he'd made his feelings clear.

"Honestly?" Kian asked wryly. "No, not really."

It was exactly what Bastian had feared. He tried not to react, but Kian knew him well, and could probably see how afraid he was.

"I already know you didn't burn the place down," he said, trying to make it lighthearted.

He must have failed because Kian looked startled. "You went to Terroir?"

"Not because of you. Because of me. I guess I was also having a bad night. Bad week, actually."

Kian frowned. "Do *you* want to talk about it?"

"It's not anything to do with you. I said you'd made me the happiest I'd ever been, and I meant it," Bastian said, reaching out and brushing a kiss across Kian's lips. "I love you. But letting go of the restaurant is hard for me. Impossible, actually."

"You make it sound like something really terrible," Kian said with amusement, "but I already knew that."

"That's why I went. I . . . missed it. I missed knowing everything that happened."

"I know I'd miss it so I can hardly blame you for missing it. You *created* it," Kian said simply.

"Would you be okay if I came by? Not to undermine your authority. Not to take away your decisions. To just . . . be there. Would that be okay?"

Kian laughed. "It's your god damned restaurant, Bastian."

"Yeah, but." Bastian took a deep breath. "I'm trying to keep things separate."

"You told me way back at the beginning this was going to be messy."

"I was right," Bastian said. "And I'd still do it, every time."

Kian stood up, a gleam in his eyes that always boded well for Bastian and offered a hand. "Do you want to go make things messier?"

Remembering his words from earlier, Bastian hesitated. "I thought you were tired."

"I think I'm getting a second wind," Kian said, grinning. "Come on, we've got an empty house. Let's use it."

Kian didn't know exactly what had driven him to his house tonight—but even though he couldn't identify what it was didn't mean that he couldn't understand it.

Even when he wasn't sure he could face Bastian, he'd still missed him, still craved his touch.

He reached out and took Bastian's hand, the rough scars from too many cuts and burns now so familiar to him. All it took was the feel of their palms sliding together, the nearly innocent gesture a reminder of the not-so-innocent nights they'd spent wrapped up in each other.

"You're sure there's nobody here?" Bastian asked as Kian pulled him through the sliding door.

"Xander and Nate both know we're together," Kian said, trying not to roll his eyes. Bastian wasn't all that concerned about keeping their relationship a secret, so Kian didn't get why he'd even care if they heard them. It wasn't like Kian hadn't had to lie awake some nights, listening to one or both of them have sex in their respective rooms.

"Yeah, I know," Bastian admitted. "You trust them, that's enough for me. But I wanted . . ." A look of uncertainty that Kian had never seen crossed Bastian's face. "I want you to fuck me."

Bastian had hinted once or twice that he shared Kian's versatile interest, but he'd never expressed a desire for Kian to fuck him before. It didn't surprise Kian that he wouldn't want anyone around if that was really what he wanted. Bastian would equate it with a loss of control, with the resulting vulnerability.

"Okay," Kian said, and squeezed Bastian's hand reassuringly. He knew better than anyone else how difficult typical and utterly normal relationship milestones were for him sometimes. He'd assumed they would come easier, once Bastian had insisted he take over Terroir, because Kian had always believed that the restaurant represented all of Bastian's control in one brick-and-mortar structure. But maybe that wasn't entirely true, because Kian had never seen the shadowy fear that he saw in Bastian's eyes tonight—or his clear need to relinquish control while he fought against it at the same time.

"I'm not good at this," Bastian murmured.

"At trusting someone else or being fucked?" Kian asked archly. "Because you keep saying that, and I keep not believing you."

Bastian cracked a tiny smile. "Are you going to lecture me again about sexual politics? Because I'm not going to lie, that was hot the last time you did it."

"Probably because I was half naked while I did," Kian said, and hated how all it took for his breath to catch was a few words. Bastian, for all his hang-ups and control issues and occasionally dickish behavior, was the key to every lock inside him.

"I can arrange that." He hesitated. "Where's your bedroom?"

It hit Kian then that this was only the second time Bastian had ever been in his house, and that they'd never even kissed inside it. Their entire relationship had played out in the starkly luxurious confines of Bastian's house. He'd never dried off after a shower with one of Kian's threadbare towels. He'd never seen his bare bones room, with its mattress that lay on the floor. He could have upgraded—he had some money saved—but it had never seemed important. He was barely ever home, and then he and Bastian had taken their relationship past mere pining, and then he'd never been home at all.

For all his vaunted internal boasting that their relationship was more equal than ever, it wasn't, was it?

"This way," Kian said, walking Bastian down the hall, opening the door to his bedroom. He wasn't worried it would be a mess; you'd have to live in a room for it to be a mess, but he'd barely even been in here the last few weeks.

"Save your breath," Kian said wryly, "there's no real compliment to be found, but that's okay."

Bastian raised an eyebrow. "It is?"

"This is just a place I sleep. And not even that, lately."

"But not tonight," Bastian said, reaching out and pulling Kian to him. "My house is a soulless box and I've never felt that as acutely as I did tonight."

Fuck it, Kian thought. "I don't care where we are, I just want to be with you," he admitted, and afraid of what Bastian might—or might not—say in return, kissed him.

They'd shared so many different kinds of kisses: undeniably passionate, sweet and tender, filthy and lustful. But none of them had ever felt like this one had, an echo of what Kian had just gone out on a limb to claim; kissing Bastian felt like coming home.

The kiss deepened and lengthened, drawing out like a golden thread that Kian didn't want to break. Maybe instead of fucking, they could just make out all night, their hands moving restlessly over each other, swallowing their mutual groans.

But Bastian had admitted to wanting something that he never had before, and Kian wouldn't be a very good lover if he selfishly ignored that. So he tugged Bastian closer to the bed, and finally pushed him down on it, climbing on top of him and fitting their mouths back together.

Even if he was trying to be generous, it was impossible not to take some pleasure for himself, he thought as he rubbed his hardening cock against Bastian's thigh. It wasn't like he had a lot of experience to compare this to, but with Bastian, everything always felt like the first time, but *better*.

The novelty hadn't worn off, not in the least. If anything their desire for each other had only increased once they'd let it free of the restraints, and everything was *better* because they'd begun to learn each other.

Kian stripped off his t-shirt and wiggled out of his shorts without even climbing off Bastian. He hadn't realized he was so flexible, but it turned out that needing to be naked ASAP made all sorts of things possible that never had been before. Bastian lifted his head and pulled his own t-shirt off, leaving Kian rutting helplessly against Bastian's jean-clad crotch, with only his briefs as a barrier.

"Fuck," Bastian whined helplessly, "you feel so fucking good."

Kian already felt on the edge—the kissing and the touching felt goddamn perfect, it was impossible not to be—but to fulfill Bastian's request, he'd need to find some sort of self-control. And get on with it, because he knew his own wasn't nearly as ironclad as Bastian's.

Leaning over, he sorted through the crap in the drawer of his bedside table. Bastian's hands skated up his sides, fingers tickling the sensitive skin, and his mouth found a nipple, making Kian's concentration waver. He needed a condom and some lube, and he needed to stop trembling so he could find them and do this properly.

Bastian had always deserved his best, and that was never more true than this moment.

Finally, he managed to put his hands on what he needed, barely managing to shut the drawer, before Bastian had them flipped over, lips coasting down his chest and towards the straining cock in his briefs.

If Bastian put his mouth on him . . . it didn't matter how much Kian wanted to keep his composure, it would be completely gone. There was something insane, still, about seeing his cock between Bastian's lips, and the wicked way he used his tongue coupled with that mind-blowing sight always unwound him desperately fast.

He needed to stay focused. Kian reached down, his hand skimming over Bastian's skull, to the close-cropped dark hair, sprinkled with silver. The silver at his temples was still one of the sexiest things in the world to Kian. He squeezed his eyes shut—that was not something he needed to think about right now. Instead he inserted a reminder of how, the last time Nate had brought someone home, they'd sounded like a drunk rooster.

It helped, and he was able to regain focus, hands reaching down to tug on Bastian's shoulders. "Not now," he said even though there was definitely a part of him that wanted it—desperately.

It was too simplistic to say tonight was supposed to be about Bastian, because it felt like a lot of their nights had been about Bastian. But then, a lot of their nights had been about Kian too. They were a self-centered, mostly egotistical pair of chefs who believed they were more like gods than men. It wasn't a surprise that their sexual escapades often took on an indulgent, worshipful side.

Kian pushed Bastian onto his back, and quickly divested him of shoes, socks, and pants. His fingers trembled over his briefs, finally reaching up for the waistband to also pull them down.

"I want this," Bastian said, and though his voice was gruff and deep and he was in as much of a sexual thrall as Kian, he still wanted to reassure him.

That was the Bastian Kian knew and loved—the one that so many others had never been privileged enough to see. Once, Xander had told him that there must be more to the man, for Kian to be so wild about him, and Kian had merely said yes, that was true. Hadn't gone into detail and hadn't wanted to. What he experienced, what he saw that nobody else did, that was for him and his eyes alone. It might be selfish, but he wasn't going to share it.

"Then I'm going to give it to you," Kian said lowly, slicking up his fingers as Bastian spread his legs.

Bastian was tight and tense, and Kian took longer, certainly longer than Bastian would have liked, considering how he swore and begged, loosening him up. First just rubbing around the taint and his hole, not teasing exactly, but not giving him anything Bastian wanted either. Finally, he slid in a single finger, coaxing it in deeper, searching for the spot that would make Bastian swear even louder.

He'd promised Bastian they were alone, with the unspoken vow that nobody would hear him scream, and he had every intention of fulfilling it.

"Come on," Bastian begged in a high-pitched whine. "I'm not made of fucking glass."

He wasn't, but he was still precious, and Kian could tell that he hadn't done this in awhile. He wasn't going to rush him.

"Remember when you said you weren't sure you'd had good sex before," Kian said in a breathless rush.

"I hadn't." Bastian's eyes were dark and intense on his face. "I have now."

Kian slid in another finger next to the first, pushing them both up against his prostate. Bastian yelped, his entire body bowing in pleasure on the bed.

"It always will be, with me," Kian swore. "I wanna make it good for you, every time."

"You fucking blow my mind," Bastian said. "Every time." His voice shook, and Kian took advantage of his sudden relaxation to slide in a third finger, pumping them carefully but with purpose.

He'd wanted this for so long—figuratively and literally. He'd dreamt about being deep under Bastian's skin, so far in that Bastian didn't know he was even there, Kian was simply a part of who he was. An inseparable, impossibly necessary piece, and without him, Bastian would be like a clock without one of its gears.

With shaking hands, Kian opened the condom, and finally managed to slide it on, slicking himself up after. He took a deep breath, and felt, not for the first time this evening, that once they took this step, nothing would be the same after.

He was okay with that—much more than okay, if he was being honest with himself—but he needed Bastian to be, even though he'd been the one to ask for it.

"Please," Bastian finally said, as Kian smoothed a hand down his thigh. "*Please.*"

Kian pushed in slowly, steadily, inexorably. Bastian's cock jumped on his muscled stomach as Kian's cock slid home, Bastian's eyes never leaving Kian's.

He'd always known that being inside Bastian would be over-whelming, but it was so much more than he'd ever thought. Bot-toming out finally, he thought joyfully, *I'm here now, I'm never leaving.*

"I wanted you like this. Forever." Bastian's voice was guttural and deep, wrecked with pleasure. He wrapped his hand around his cock, and Kian's hips stuttered as he clamped down around him.

Kian prayed he was close, because he didn't think he could last either. It was the most overwhelmingly intense experience he'd ever had in bed, and it didn't seem to end, just went on and on as he continued thrusting, pleasure sizzling through his nerve endings. He realized he was actually whimpering, as he desperately tried to hang on.

But Bastian seemed determined to wring his orgasm out of him, just the way he'd tried to wring every last ounce of determination out of him during their last two years at Terroir. He was stroking his own cock in earnest now, face contorted, and Kian dug his fingers into Bastian's hips, holding on for the ride.

Bastian tipped over the edge with an actual yell, splattering his chest with come, and Kian followed only a second later, as the con-tractions practically pulled the orgasm right out of him.

Kian slipped out and collapsed next to him, Bastian wrapping an arm around him, his expression sleepy and blissful.

"Thank you," he said.

Bastian rarely apologized—he'd already admitted to Kian that he was the only person he'd ever apologized to, barring his own mother—but an expression of gratitude? That was completely unheard of.

"You're welcome." Kian paused. "I do love you, you know."

Bastian's expression was relaxed as he rolled over, facing Kian. "I love you too. Even when I'm not good at this."

"I don't know if anybody is," Kian admitted.

"You seem to be." Bastian's tone was contemplative, like he hadn't figured out yet how that could be.

"I just hide it really well," Kian admitted. "Most of the time I have no idea what the fuck I'm doing. I just know I love you, and I start there. The rest? It is what it is."

"It is what it is," Bastian repeated, a wrinkle appearing in his dark brows, like he was trying to puzzle out what that really meant. But, Kian thought, it meant what he'd said it meant. You just had to figure it out, one step at a time, and he'd always hoped, they'd do that *together*.

Maybe that's what Bastian really coming over tonight was about, Kian thought as he finally sat up and went to the bathroom to grab them a damp towel to wipe down with. Maybe Bastian was finally figuring out that doing things together was better than struggling in vain alone.

He'd missed seeing him every night at Terroir, and even though the evenings after service were always wonderful, it was like losing an arm, the phantom feeling following you even though it was already gone.

Kian had been clear that he wanted a separation of their work and personal lives, but he hadn't ever said that he wanted Bastian to remove himself.

Maybe, he thought as he settled into Bastian's arms to finally go to sleep, Bastian had finally discovered he felt the same way.

Chapter Fourteen

Mark was dumb, but he wasn't stupid. The next day during family dinner, Kian offhandedly mentioned to the staff that they might see Bastian a little more. "He's working on the menu for the new restaurant," Kian had said, even though Bastian hadn't been entirely clear about what he'd be doing. Still, the announcement bought Kian what he wanted, which was a reprieve from Mark on his bullshit.

He might push Kian when Bastian wasn't around, but the threat of him suddenly appearing made him take a step back.

A week passed, with Bastian dropping by nearly every day, usually during prep, almost always staying for family dinner. Most days he left when service began, though once or twice he'd actually retreated to his office, and when Kian walked by, it was obvious he was doing work on his computer.

The kitchen definitely ran better with more of Bastian's presence, which rankled Kian a little bit, even though he tried to tamp down the feelings of inadequacy. Bastian was a figure of monumental proportions, and he'd spent twenty years developing a fearsome reputation to augment it.

He had his Michelin stars, he had a temper, and he had an insane commitment to perfection that nobody, even Kian, could match. That, Kian kept telling himself, was *fine*. He was good. They were doing better than ever. Despite Bastian's clearly uncomfortable feelings about hanging around Xander, and to a lesser extent, Nate, he'd even made the effort to spend some time with Kian at his house.

Everything felt good, if not great, but Kian couldn't seem to shake the sensation of impending doom.

At first, he'd assumed it was because he felt guilty at hiding just how shitty Mark was from Bastian. Then, when Mark, no doubt terrified of Bastian and his inexorable retribution, had taken a step back from his normally shitty attitude, Kian justified that the problem had fixed itself and there was no need to confess that it had ever existed.

That wasn't entirely true, but it was true enough that Kian knew that couldn't be the issue that kept him up nights, long after Bastian had fallen asleep beside him.

Something was going to go wrong, and because of the pressure cooker nature of their jobs and their tempers, it was inevitably going to be a huge fucking mess.

Bastian continued to battle with Nathan Hess on every point of the contract they still hadn't signed. A week in, as Kian was preparing to leave for Terroir, Bastian leaned against the bathroom counter and said, "I'm not going to be in today. Hess and I have what should be the very last fucking meeting on this contract."

"Good," Kian said. The ongoing contract negotiations had obviously exhausted and annoyed Bastian, even though mostly he seemed to argue with his lawyer over conceding anything.

"Maybe if it actually goes well, we'll come to Terroir for dinner to celebrate."

Kian grinned. "Isn't it a little tactless to rub your perfection in the face of the man you've just defeated?"

"Is that what that is?" Bastian asked, but he was smiling too, the giddy, gleeful smile of a man who knew he had his opponent's number.

"Prevarication isn't your strong suit," Kian said seriously, reaching out and brushing some invisible lint off Bastian's shoulders. Today he was dressed not for the kitchen, but for business in a dark navy suit with crisp white shirt underneath, a few of the buttons popped open in deference to the more casual tone of Napa.

"No," Bastian admitted. "I see what I want and I take it."

For a second, Kian considered reminding him that out of the two of them, it had definitely been him who'd done the lion's share of the demanding. Demanding credit, demanding respect, and demanding

Bastian in his bed. But Bastian looked so adorably smug and certain of Hess' upcoming defeat that Kian refrained.

"Good luck," he said reluctantly brushing a single kiss across Bastian's mouth. "Own his ass, please."

"Done." Bastian really was unbearably egotistical sometimes, but at least he'd never directed it at Kian before. Kian didn't know exactly why, but he imagined that Bastian knew better than to try.

❧❧❧ ❦❦❦

Prep started out like most prep did, an interminable parade of mostly dull tasks, all to be completed with efficient speed and measured against exacting standards.

Derek had been doing better the last few weeks, and Kian took the risk to assign him some of the more complicated prep, working on the Japanese mandolin.

He looked very skeptical as Kian carefully explained how it worked, and what needed to be done with the crates of eggplants piled on the counter. "Isn't that what you cut yourself on?" he asked, eyeing the shining blade dubiously.

"I wasn't wearing the gloves. You're going to wear the gloves."

"Like a pussy," Mark inserted.

It was the most questionable thing that he'd said in days, long enough that Kian had almost begun to believe that the days of snarky, rude comments were over, and that he'd finally given up on questioning Kian's authority.

That had apparently been too good to hope for.

"Not like a pussy," Kian said between gritted teeth. "Like a smart, intelligent person who would like to keep all their fingers."

"I heard Aquino *carried* you to the ER," Mark said slyly.

Derek had the nerve to look guilty. So Mark hadn't been behaving after all—he'd just been going behind Kian's back to extract every bit of gossip that he could out of the rest of the staff.

He understood why the kitchen staff gossiped; their jobs were hard, if not actually impossible at points, and gossip helped alleviate some of that unrelenting pressure. And, it had been the moment of a lifetime to watch their notoriously hardheaded head chef lose his mind over an injury.

"I don't remember that, actually," Kian said.

"Yeah," Mark agreed, "because you fainted, like a *pussy*."

It was hard, but not impossible, to keep his voice level and calm. "I'm confused here, Mark. Who's the pussy here? First it's Derek, for using the gloves. But then it's me, for *not* using the gloves and cutting myself so badly I passed out."

Mark's glare was belligerent. It was clearly going to be one of *those* days, like somehow Mark had been in the bathroom this morning with him and Bastian and had heard Bastian wouldn't be around to witness his shitty behavior.

It was unbelievably annoying, but Kian refused to let him see how it was getting to him.

If he did, Mark would never let it go, and Kian would be forced to either fire him, or report him to Bastian—both of which meant that Bastian would find out that Kian hadn't been able to handle the problem himself.

Kian wasn't ready to accept that yet, but it felt like today, Mark wanted to keep pushing him.

"Put the gloves on," Kian directed to Derek. "Try the first eggplant, I want to make sure the settings are perfect."

Derek did as directed, while Kian continued to feel the heat of Mark's glare.

"There, that's good. Just keep your movement steady and you should be fine," Kian said.

"Is that what Bastian tells you?" Mark asked snidely.

The problem with Mark was that he wasn't dumb at all. He was annoyingly intelligent; usually smart enough to make sure that anything he said that was really offensive had another potential meaning.

Kian ignored him and continued to focus on Derek.

The other problem was that Mark seemed to have a knack for knowing just the moment when he'd pushed Kian too far and he always retreated. He had to know that if he pushed too hard and too far, Kian would just snap and fire him on the spot, no matter the consequences.

But he always made sure Kian wouldn't.

He did this time too, retreating after that last, infuriating comment back to his own station, and his own tasks.

After making sure Derek was all set, Kian stalked off, taking a five-minute breather in Bastian's office and then venturing out to start the soup.

But maybe he was actually the dumb one, because he'd expected that Mark would mostly leave it alone, at the most do something questionable during service, like forget every fucking ticket Kian called out to him.

And that definitely would have been shitty enough, but Kian would have dealt with it. Maybe he might have broken another plate, even though he still felt a sickening knot of guilt from the last one.

If Mark continued to fuck up the sauté station, all he'd do was make himself look incompetent and lazy. Somehow, he must have figured that out, because he didn't throttle it back and he didn't do anything during service.

Kian had made an extra batch of the curry carrot soup for family meal, which paired well with the big salad Derek threw together, and the flank steaks Michel grilled, slicing them thin, still nearly bloody in the middle.

It was a Saturday night, and the reservation list was completely booked, which meant it would be a difficult, stressful service. Too many tables, and not quite enough staff—not quite enough *competent* staff, Kian corrected—to deal with it.

He'd probably end up at sauté and leave Michelle to give a straightforward if rudimentary glance over the dishes before they went up to the dining room. She'd worked at Terroir for awhile, and he'd seen Bastian rely on her before, so Kian felt okay doing it.

Not great, just okay, but he couldn't dig Mark out of his mess of tickets and monitor the dishes at the same time. And if Bastian didn't like that, Kian thought with a sigh, trying to stretch out the kink in his neck as he sat down to dinner, then that was too goddamn bad, and he should have made sure Kian had the staff he needed to succeed.

He definitely wasn't counting Mark as a plus in that particular column.

Speak of the devil. Mark sat down next to him, a deceptively innocent look on his face. Of course Kian knew better, but he also couldn't physically force Mark to shut up. Well, he *could,* but that would be a Human Resources nightmare.

"Neck stiff?" he asked innocently.

Kian looked over at him, inherently suspicious. "Must have slept on it wrong."

Almost everyone was at the table, absorbed in the soup and the salad and Michel's excellent meat, paired with the good bread. "Or," Mark suggested slyly, "maybe you were too busy sucking Aquino's cock to worry about how bad your neck would feel in the morning."

You could hear a pin drop at the table. Almost everyone at it had been present, two months previous, when Kian had cut himself on the Japanese mandolin. They'd all witnessed Bastian losing his mind, the hottest gossip in ages. Even Kian had heard about it, because while he'd certainly not witnessed it, being passed the fuck out, the story had spread like wildfire. They'd seen Bastian pick Kian up bridal style and reject outright anyone else who attempted to help. They'd known Bastian had waited with Kian at the emergency room, and had driven him home afterwards, to the point of being late for a service. Something that had never actually happened before that particular day.

As Kian met each set of eyes at the table, he realized that they all knew. They knew and they'd all been talking about it, not only among themselves, but to Mark. Mark who would take this potentially salacious bit of gossip and turn it inside out, until it was the worst version of itself.

He'd make Kian look like a cock-sucking sycophant, who'd do whatever it took to get ahead. And Bastian? Bastian would be his normal asshole self, willing to take advantage of a much younger employee whom he was currently mentoring—to the point of demanding sexual favors for career favors.

Kian felt sick to his stomach. It wasn't like some of these people didn't respect him, but they'd clearly begun to form some other kind of opinion of him, and it wasn't good.

He stood up slowly. "Excuse me?"

Mark leaned back, indulgent and smug. "You heard me. Are you really going to deny it?"

It sounded so sordid when Kian thought about it, which was exactly why he'd wanted to keep it a secret. Nobody knew that they'd resisted doing a single thing about their feelings for over two years. Nobody knew that Bastian was a better person than they'd ever imagined. Nobody knew Kian would have rather quit than take this job because he was sleeping with the boss.

But none of that mattered, because it sure as hell didn't look like any of that.

"You are." Mark laughed incredulously. Kian clenched his fists and tried to remind himself what a nightmare it would be if he punched his own *sous*. "You're really going to stand there and try to pretend that the vaunted and much-worshipped pecking order at Terroir can't be undone as easily as Aquino undoes his pants at night?"

It was beyond stupid to engage. Even though it was a Saturday night, and they were going to be packed to the rafters with guests tonight, what he should do was fire Mark's traitorous ass and call Bastian in to help, screw closing his deal with Nathan Hess.

Unexpectedly, Kian felt so betrayed, and not only by the staff he'd been working with so many months—years, even, for some of them. No, the main betrayal was Bastian's. He'd saddled Kian with this *dick* and then manipulated the situation so Kian didn't feel like going to him for assistance was even an option. It was fucking unfair and even though Kian had claimed it would never happen, he felt a surge of something that felt a lot like hatred.

Which was why he did the opposite of what he knew he should do.

"It's not like that," he said, and instantly knew it was wrong. He'd not only confirmed Mark's version of the story, despite saying otherwise, and he'd gone on the defensive.

Mark, clearly sensing blood, pounced. "So you're saying it *is* happening. You're sleeping with Aquino."

There was nowhere to go, except right through the shit, and try not to slide off the edge in the process.

"I can't believe it," Michel said, and he didn't sound happy. *Michel*, who was someone Kian would have loved to have as his *sous*. But it would never happen now because there was a look of sheer disbelief on his face now—as if Kian had just betrayed everything he'd ever believed in.

"It's not like that," Kian repeated stubbornly, despite knowing that there was no way he could win from this position. He'd already admitted defeat.

"Oh, what's it like?" Mark asked creamily. "Do you really love each other?"

Kian looked around the table and knew nobody would believe him if he claimed that was true. They'd already made up their minds, and they weren't siding with him.

Somehow, he'd become the villain of the entire shitshow, which made no fucking sense to him at all. But if he was going to get labeled that way, he might as well go whole hog.

Kian had never punched anyone before, but with the adrenaline surging through his veins, it turned out it wasn't all that hard. His hand didn't even really hurt, he thought as he gazed at his scraped knuckles, at the speckles of blood, because of course once he'd hit Mark, he hadn't wanted to stop. The blood, and him collapsing onto the floor were finally enough for him to pull back, panting.

He stared down at the floor, at Mark's bloody, obnoxious face, and wished he could keep going until he was just a red smear on the floor. A burst tomato, strewn across the concrete.

Michel grabbed his arm and held him back, even though he'd already stopped. Mark was both taller and looked stronger, but that hadn't mattered. Probably because the last thing he'd ever expected Kian to do was punch him in the nose.

"Holy shit," Michel whispered, and for a blissful second, Kian thought he only sounded so shocked because he too had been surprised that Kian could punch the daylights out of Mark.

But that wasn't why. Kian looked up and Bastian was standing at the pass-through, stunned expression on his face. Then his eyes hardened, and in his place was a man Kian didn't recognize.

That wasn't exactly true, though. He was familiar, like a blast from the past. This was the Bastian Kian had met that very first day, who hadn't given a shit. Who hadn't been in love with Kian. Who wanted to remind him who was boss, who was really in charge.

Fucking hell.

Bastian had been through a lot of bad, weird, and confusing situations in his twenty-plus years in the culinary industry. He had never once, not in all that time, ever come face-to-face with one and found himself speechless.

He was speechless now, rooted to the spot he'd stopped short at a minute before, when he'd listened to Kian give Mark all the ammunition he'd ever need, and then lose every single fucking ounce of control.

It wasn't like he didn't *also* want to punch Mark in the face, but he couldn't exactly do it after he was already on the floor, bleeding.

"My office *now*," he finally said, and didn't miss the swift, guilty look Kian shot in his direction. Or the wounded expression Mark pasted on after being helped to his feet, with a rag to staunch the blood currently gushing out of his nose.

Bastian stomped over to his office, yanking the door open and pulling down the blinds so forcefully the bottom edges all crashed to the floor.

Was this what Kian had been holding back from him? That Mark had been trying to convince the rest of the staff to join his mutiny? That he was heckling him during his shift?

Bastian had told him to suck it up, to deal with Mark not liking him, but this was something entirely different, and he hoped, feeling a surge of guilt himself, that Kian would have known to come to him about it.

But he hadn't, and now the Terroir kitchen had been witness to more than just broken plates.

Kian and then Mark slunk into his office, as Bastian stood at the doorway.

He looked out at the rest of the crew, who were understandably gaping at this turn of events. "Finish your meal and get prepped for service," Bastian snapped. "And stop fucking staring."

He closed the door behind him and didn't even bother sitting down in his chair. He stood, facing his *chef de cuisine* and his *sous chef*—the two members of the kitchen staff who should have been working out problems with the *rest* of the employees, not letting their petty fight poison his restaurant.

"What the fuck," he finally spit out. "What the ever-loving fuck is wrong with you two?"

Kian opened his mouth, like he wanted to explain, but then he shut it again, inexplicably. Considering his position at Terroir, it *was* his responsibility to explain what had happened—never mind that it had been his fist that had met Mark's face.

But instead of opening up, instead of offering any apologies or reasoning why he'd suddenly lost his fucking mind, he said nothing.

Bastian watched as Mark eyed Kian, trying to figure out if he was going to say anything, and when he didn't, he jumped in.

"Chef, it was just some harmless gossip that some people took a lot more seriously," Mark said, innocence dripping from his voice. Bastian guessed that he was referring to Kian, and maybe if he didn't know Kian as well as he did, believing him would have been easier.

The thing he didn't understand was Kian's continued silence.

"Kian?" Bastian finally asked and felt another surge of frustrated anger that he'd had to *ask*. Didn't the man have any sense of self-preservation? One of the two of them would have to go, and despite the blood currently smearing his knuckles, Bastian was almost certain that it shouldn't be Kian. But if he didn't fucking speak up and defend himself with his side of the story, how could Bastian keep him?

It felt like a betrayal, like suddenly Kian didn't care enough to bother fighting.

Don't you dare put me in this fucking spot, he thought. *I can't beg you. I won't.*

Kian shrugged, and Bastian might have believed he didn't care at all, except the devastation in his eyes.

Like he'd already been fired. Like Bastian had already given up on him. When Bastian had actually been fighting for him every step of the way, and the only one who'd given up was Kian.

"Mark," he said, "go pack your things. You're fired."

Frowning, Mark didn't move. Not very smart of him, because even though Kian was a good seventy pounds lighter and a few inches shorter, Kian had already taken him out tonight. And Kian had stopped after a handful of hits; Bastian wasn't sure he could, not with the toxic brew of fury and aggravation boiling inside him. During the best of times, he had a temper; this definitely wasn't the best anything.

"Excuse me, sir," Mark said, "I just don't think that's fair. I know you're . . . involved, and I shouldn't be dismissed just because you don't want to fire who you're sleeping with."

It was becoming clearer just how this asshole had managed to get deep enough under Kian's skin to drive him to bloody his nose. He was a *dick*, with somehow even less self-preservation than Kian. Bastian straightened his back and gave Mark the coldest glare in his entire arsenal.

"Get the fuck out of my sight," was all he said, but Bastian had a feeling it would be more than enough to demolish any bravery this asshole had left.

Mark blanched, but *still* didn't seem to get how badly he'd fucked up, because he asked, "What about a reference?"

It was impossible to miss the shock crossing over Kian's face. Bastian didn't even know if what he really felt was shock; shock felt too small, too insignificant.

"Let me make sure I understand you," Bastian said, voice silky smooth with rage. "I hire you to come and be Kian's *sous*, with the belief you will support him with the staff and in the operation of this top-tier restaurant. But instead of doing any of that, you've been lazy, slow, and too busy gossiping to do your job properly. Then, to top off your sniveling, pathetic little machinations, you think it's a good idea to cause mutiny among the rest of the staff, with some nasty, completely untrue gossip that Kian was promoted because he's good at sucking my dick. Did I get all that correct?"

Bastian couldn't meet Kian's eyes as Mark stared at him. It had been easy enough to put together, and for some goddamned unknown reason, Kian hadn't come to him. One word of this and Bastian would have been happy to fire Mark himself, and even call Michael Mina to tell him what a snake his former employee was. Not even a snake, Bastian corrected, a *worm*. Maybe even a disease on a worm.

"That's not . . ." Mark hesitated. "That's not entirely how it was."

"If I call Derek or Michel in here, what will they tell me?" *Since you*, Bastian thought pointedly at Kian, *won't fucking defend your own ass.*

"It just didn't seem . . . fair." Mark hesitated. "Sir."

Bastian rolled his eyes. "So it *is* true. Well get this, *life isn't fucking fair.* I can't believe that even after all of that shit, you have the nerve to ask me for a *reference*. Like I would ever lower myself to even speak your name ever again. And don't expect one from Michael Mina either, because he's going to be hearing about this little stunt. Hope you have enough money saved for a ticket far, far away, because you're never fucking working in California again, if I have anything to say about it."

Mark chose that particular moment to flee the office, and Bastian was left staring at his *chef de cuisine*, his lover, who'd betrayed him as much as he could be betrayed.

He walked around the desk, until he was right in front of Kian, who looked suddenly, visibly nervous. He should have been nervous a hell of a lot sooner, as far as Bastian was concerned. Maybe Kian thought he'd neutered him over the last few weeks, but Bastian was still in charge.

"Anything to say for yourself?"

Kian actually glared. "What, you wanted me to roll on him? Why should I even bother? You never wanted to hear the shit he did, you told me to put up with it. So I did."

"I sure didn't tell you to punch him in the face." A terrible realization was dawning on Bastian. He'd done this. He'd put Kian in charge of something he couldn't hope to control—he didn't have the experience or the will or the skills yet—and then he'd compounded the problem by hiring Mark.

Why had he been so blind? Was it really like Mark said? Had he promoted Kian because he was good at sucking cock? Or had it been because he loved him and wanted desperately to believe in a slightly different, slightly better version of Kian? A Kian that didn't exist quite yet?

Regardless, this experiment was over, and Bastian didn't know how to end it without ending everything else. His stomach twisted. Maybe losing Kian was inevitable. He'd always been too young, too vibrant, too goddamned sweet, and it was probably only time before he realized that he was too good for Bastian, who deep down, was just a mean old grump. But he'd believed he'd get more time first, more days, more weeks, that he could file away and pull out when he got too lonely to function.

"No, but you set me up to fail," Kian said, and he sounded really pissed. Bastian wasn't even sure he was wrong; but regardless of whose fault the catastrophe was, *it existed*, and Bastian had to fix it.

"I'm going to go upstairs, tell Nathan Hess that the deal is off, because I have shit to sort out of my own. You'll be my *sous*, if you feel like you can possibly control yourself going forward."

"And if I don't want to take the demotion?" Kian demanded. Bastian wanted to believe he didn't understand why he *wouldn't*, but he did. Kian wanted so desperately to feel like they were on equal footing, but the truth was, they were never going to be able to exist that way. The situation had been prepped ahead of time to never be equal.

"You either accept the demotion, or you're fired." Bastian told himself that he wouldn't take that awful step, but deep down, he knew better. Kian had his same pride, his same iron will, the same determination, the same inability to accept defeat.

Maman, you were wrong, Bastian thought bitterly as he saw the acceptance in Kian's eyes.

"You can't fire me," Kian announced, breaking the heart that Bastian had never even believed existed until they'd met, "because I quit."

"Fine." The word made Bastian ill, but what else could he say? He couldn't refuse to accept Kian leaving. He'd already ruined every-thing enough.

"I'll be by later to pick up my stuff from your house." The jut of Kian's chin was so prideful, Bastian knew he recognized it from his own reflection. *Don't do this*, he wanted to beg, to plead, *don't be the worst version of yourself. Don't be like me.* But he was Bastian Aquino, head chef of Terroir, and he didn't beg anyone for anything, ever. Even the man he loved.

"Is that really necessary?" he finally asked, even though he already knew the answer.

Kian laughed without humor. "Did you really believe that we could keep this separate? Lovers at home, professionals at Terroir? It was doomed to fail from the beginning, and I know you're not stupid. You warned me. You knew it would happen."

What could he say? He'd wanted so badly to believe otherwise? Wanted it so much that he'd believed he could *hope* it into reality?

"That's what I thought," Kian said bitterly, turning and leaving.

Bastian was left alone, again, inevitably, and this time he won-dered, *what the fuck am I going to do now?*

Before, he'd always known. But Kian had demolished every structure he'd ever erected. He was a mess of crumbled rubble, all his walls demolished, his infrastructure blown to bits.

And still, if anyone asked him, which he hoped to God they wouldn't, he still believed it had been worth it.

He pushed away from the desk, and feeling every one of his years, marched out into the kitchen to save Terroir from certain disaster. It was what he'd always been the best at, and now it was all he had left.

Chapter Fifteen

Kian didn't start crying until he walked into the kitchen and saw the coffee mug Bastian had drunk out of just yesterday sitting in the sink.

It hit him then, like an inescapable blow to the head. He'd never pour Bastian another cup of coffee and tease him about liking it dark as mud. He'd never wake up tucked up next to him. He'd never kiss him again. He'd never smile at him over some boring prep at the restaurant. He'd never again set foot into the Terroir kitchen.

Because it wasn't just one blow; it was a thousand, big and small and every size in between, and every single one fucking hurt. Kian stood there and felt each one as they hit him, hard.

Nobody was home, and there was nobody to see him cry. Xander would be at the Barrel House, Nate was probably at the winery, where he worked in the tasting room. He'd have hours and hours before anyone came home to bother him, and that seemed like both the best and the worst thing to happen to him.

He could go to Bastian's house and get all the stuff he'd left there. He still had the code, and that way he'd avoid having to go over everything again with Bastian. But going to Bastian's would be even worse than spotting his mug in the sink.

He'd been spinning fantasies in his mind, imagining someday moving into Bastian's house and making it a real home, instead of the soulless box that Bastian had called it. He'd imagined a life they could share, where they gave and took in equal measures.

At the time, he'd wanted so desperately to believe that it was possible, but it wasn't. He'd been blinding himself to the realities of their situation. They'd never been even remotely equal. The only equality that had existed between them were advantages that Bastian had willingly ceded to him.

There shouldn't have been anything else but pain, but now there was the inevitable streak of humiliation winding its way through him. He'd been full of wishes and hope this whole time, but Bastian had only been pretending.

Kian stumbled into his bedroom, and lurched back, like he'd been burned by the lingering smell of Bastian in the air. It had been almost forty-eight hours since he'd been in here, but it didn't matter. The whole room would need to be aired out, every inch of fabric washed, the walls scrubbed, the carpet cleaned. Even then, he'd never be able to eradicate the memories—and Bastian had only spent a handful of nights here.

Hours before anyone would be home, so many useless hours spreading out in front of him. He needed to do something, keep busy. Keep himself from thinking; if he could keep his mind blank, he thought as he dried his eyes with the edge of his t-shirt, he might not break down.

He pulled off the sheets, stuffing them in the washing machine down the hall. Next, he went to his closet to find the other set he vaguely remembered having. Sorting through the random crap that accumulated, he accidentally nudged a cardboard box on one shelf, sending it careening to the floor, all its contents spilling out.

Kian groaned and righted the box. He didn't have the energy to deal with this today.

Except one of the items that had fallen out was his old Institute apron. As he crumpled up the fabric, planning to shove it right back where it came from, he heard the crinkle of paper.

Shit.

It had been two years since he'd even considered any of the overseas job applications he'd sent, or the letters he'd received as a response. He'd never even opened them, too blown away and excited by the possibility of working for Bastian Aquino at Terroir. He hadn't cared one way or the other if he'd been hired.

He'd shoved the responses away in a pocket of his apron and totally forgotten about them.

One by one, he pulled them out. Three in total. Still sealed. For the first time, Kian really faced what his sudden change of heart had cost him. He could be working and training in Europe right now, at restaurants far more prestigious than Terroir. Restaurants with decades of brilliance stretching behind them. He'd given all that up because Bastian had walked into his class, and he'd gotten an instant hard-on.

Why hadn't anyone stopped him? Why hadn't anyone pulled him aside and insisted that working for someone solely because you had a personal and professional crush was a terrible idea? He hadn't told his mom why he'd changed his mind on Europe because he'd been sure she'd be upset. Later, he knew Xander and Wyatt had conspired to try to find him a job in LA, a misguided attempt to get him away from Bastian. By then it had been too late, he'd fallen in love and he'd refused to even discuss leaving.

But at the beginning? There'd been room then, even in the first, full-body flush of his infatuation. He might have listened to reason. He might have changed his mind.

He might not have wasted the last two years.

Right now, they felt like a waste. Yeah, he'd become *chef de cuisine*, but he no longer believed that Bastian had promoted him because he deserved it. Mark, as galling as it was, had been fucking right. He'd gotten the *chef de cuisine* job because he was sucking Bastian's cock.

What did it matter, Kian thought bitterly, if you lied to yourself because you knew better or because you hoped for better? It turned out the same in the end.

He should have taken one look at Luc and not been horribly, terribly envious; he should have taken one look at Luc and understood he was a cautionary tale. Bastian was like a hurricane. He swept into a life and then out of it and left no structures standing in his wake.

Kian fingered the wrinkled paper of the envelopes. There was a part of him that was dying to open them, dying to know what he'd chosen Bastian over. But there was another part of him that dreaded facing the truth, and that actively didn't want to know what he'd given up without a thought.

A voice in his head called him a coward, and Kian flinched because it sounded too much like Bastian. But then, he'd been an excellent mentor. He'd taught him never to be afraid of the truth.

That was ironic, Kian thought, and ripped one envelope open, and then another, and then the last.

They were all job offers. They'd all wanted to hire him.

A sob escaped his throat, and then another. He sank to his knees, crying over everything he'd lost today, and two years ago—before he'd even known better.

Kian sat there for a very long time. He stopped crying, eventually, but he still didn't move. The house grew dark and he stayed right where he was.

Eventually, he heard a car pull into the driveway, and assumed it would be Xander. It was late, but not quite late enough for Nate to come home.

Footsteps echoed down the hall, and before Kian could brace for it, the hall light turned on, leaving him flinching into the sudden brightness.

"What's going on?" Xander asked, kneeling down and taking in the situation. The sheet-less bed. The letters spread out on the floor in front of Kian.

"The inevitable," Kian said dully. He couldn't look at Xander. "I quit, and I guess we broke up."

"You guess?"

"At the beginning, we told ourselves that it would stay separate. Work at Terroir, personal at home. But it didn't, it couldn't. It was all tangled together, from the very beginning." Kian had never felt so bleak, so hopeless before.

"You didn't know any better, but the Bastard did," Xander growled, and Kian knew just how angry he was. He wanted to tell him that it wasn't just Bastian's fault; it was his own too. After all, he'd just punched Mark in the face and then refused to give any explanation at all. He'd lost control of the kitchen, and Bastian had been right to demote him.

But instead of explaining, Kian just shrugged. It hurt too much to try to explain, even if he knew what side Xander would inevitably be on.

"And all this?" Xander asked, pointing to the letters.

Kian glanced up, his eyes full of pain. "Did I ever tell you that at one point, I was going to Europe?"

❧❧❧❧❧❧ ❧❧❧❧❧❧

Kian had been expecting the call all day, so it was easy enough to hit ignore half a dozen times.

When the unknown number started calling, Kian let it go to voicemail three times before he finally answered.

"Xander called you," Kian said in an edgy, annoyed voice.

"How did you even know it was me?" Wyatt asked, mystified.

"Xander has a method," Kian retorted. "He offered me another bottle of Nate's wine last night. I'm not sure he has any other comforting methods in his repertoire. He's run out, so he called you."

Wyatt sighed on the other end of the line. "This *is* Xander we're talking about. Not exactly the most comforting person in the world."

"Right." Kian knew he didn't sound convinced, and he found he didn't give a fuck. There was a huge number of things piling up that, in the last two days, he'd discovered that he didn't give a fuck about.

Everyone had always thought he was sweet and naïve and a little blind. The truth was, he'd just stupidly, optimistically, believed in the best in people, and in the world. And now he knew he'd been so fucking wrong, this whole damn time.

"Xander called me because he's worried about you," Wyatt soothed.

"I've got money saved, I'm good for my share of rent." Kian dipped his sponge back in the bucket of soapy water at his feet. He'd already finished airing out and cleaning every inch of his bedroom, and he'd moved on to the living room because doing nothing wasn't acceptable, and he didn't have anything else to do.

If he stopped, he'd think, and thinking was so wretched Kian was determined never to do it again.

"I don't think that was what he was worried about," Wyatt said wryly.

"I'm fine," Kian said, not giving a single shit that he didn't sound fine. "In a week or so I'll look for a new job."

He'd do it, because he was bored and there was only so much cleaning to do, even though the thought of another kitchen—a kitchen without Bastian at the head of it—made him sick to his stomach. He could do it because he was a goddamn professional. That was what Bastian had trained him to be, even though he'd failed at the end.

"I know Xander is desperate to hire you," Wyatt said.

"Did you call for any actual purpose or just to make yourself feel better?" Kian demanded, inexplicably furious all of a sudden. "Because you're not making *me* feel any better."

There was a long silence on the other end of the phone. Kian pinched off the disappointment that Wyatt didn't really care either and tossed it away. He didn't need that on top of everything else.

When Wyatt finally spoke again, it was slowly, like he was carefully picking every single word. "Xander told me about your European jobs. That you think you've wasted the last two years."

"I did," Kian retorted bitterly.

"Actually," Wyatt said and then hesitated. "I really don't think you did."

"You don't really believe that." The only reason Wyatt would say that would be to try to talk Kian out of feeling that way. And Kian wasn't dumb, not anymore. His eyes had been forcibly opened wide.

"I do. Do you love him?"

"I don't see why that matters." Kian swallowed back the unexpected tears lingering in the back of his throat. Suddenly it didn't matter if Wyatt *did* care about him, he just couldn't talk about this anymore.

"You might as well just tell me, because we all know you do." Wyatt sighed. "Does he love you?"

Kian nearly hung up the phone. It was only the impossible kindness in Wyatt's voice that kept him from doing it. "He said he did, but I'm not sure I believe him anymore."

"He must love you, because he gave you a job you weren't really qualified for, but that you wanted a lot. He didn't give it to you because you guys were fucking; he gave it to you because that's what you do with someone you love—you give them what they want, even if it isn't always good for them."

Kian hated the sob that escaped him. Even more than he hated that Wyatt was right. He'd been ill-prepared, even with all of Bastian's training, and he'd known that when it had been offered to him. He should have turned it down, but there'd been that irresistible glow of living up to the man on Bastian's pedestal.

That had turned out so well, too.

"I've fucked it all up," he cried. "I knew it was too soon, I knew it was a mistake. I should have told him."

"You can't go back and change the past," Wyatt said softly, "you can only change the future. So what are you going to do with it?"

"I guess . . ." Kian took a deep breath. "I guess I could contact these restaurants in Europe again. See if they'd consider hiring me still."

"Do you want to go to Europe?"

Truthfully Kian didn't know what he wanted. No—that wasn't true. He wanted things to not change, but Wyatt was right; he could only change the future, not the past.

"I don't know," Kian said. "Bastian said they'd have me doing dishes for a year."

"At least," Wyatt said with a chuckle, then his voice grew serious. "You didn't waste your time at Terroir. Bastian was a good mentor to you. He taught you an enormous amount, and you were already talented. It wasn't a waste, because you got to do more in two years than anyone in Europe would do in five."

"Swear to god?" Kian demanded.

"Swear to god." Wyatt laughed again. "Seriously, go work for Xander while you figure it out. You could do it in your sleep and it'll keep you occupied and sane. Somewhat, anyway. It *is* still Xander's restaurant."

Kian had considered that too. Working for Xander at the Barrel House might hurt the least, out of all the options available to him. Was that a pussy move? He wasn't sure anymore. Self-preservation, while not something that Bastian had ever encouraged or cultivated in himself, wasn't so bad.

"I'll think about it," Kian promised. "I'm not ready to be *chef de cuisine* and I'm done doing dishes. I'm not sure where I belong anymore."

"Somewhere in between. But I know you'll figure it out, you're the smartest guy I know," Wyatt said.

Kian scoffed. "That's bullshit. I went to my boss' house and *took my clothes off.*"

There was silence on the other end of the line. So Xander hadn't told Wyatt *everything*.

"I reserve the right to take back that statement," Wyatt said. "Nobody ever said you didn't have balls, though. Wow."

"Love makes you do really stupid things," Kian pointed out and Wyatt agreed.

"You know you can text me anytime," Wyatt stated. "I have to go make sure Tony doesn't blow up our food truck. He's deep frying a turkey or . . . maybe a whole ham. Or something."

"Go save your truck," Kian said. "And yes, I do."

Wyatt was right, Kian realized after he'd set the phone down and had continued scrubbing the living room wall. He hadn't wasted the time. It helped alleviate some of the humiliating sting, but the yawning chasm of pain was still right there, hovering on the edge of Kian's consciousness. Not thinking he'd wasted his time wasn't the same as not missing Bastian so much he could barely breathe sometimes.

Maybe Wyatt was right about something else too. Working for Xander wouldn't be so bad; it would at least be better than continuing to scrub this wall.

❧ ❦

Bastian didn't know how it happened, but his whole life had suddenly become a fucking disaster. Wyatt and Xander were long gone. Kian was gone. That worm Mark was gone. He was left with a bare bones staff, not nearly enough to run a restaurant the size of Terroir. Also spring and the tourists were coming and they'd be able to open up the patio in a few weeks. That meant even more tables to service, and not nearly enough people to service them.

He'd considered begging Kian to come back, not just because things were bad on the staffing front, but because every time he thought so much as his name, Bastian felt like throwing up. And since he thought about him all the damn time, that was a problem.

Terroir needed Bastian to be leading it, not hiding in the bathroom, curled inwards around his traitorous stomach. He never actually threw up, he just *wanted* to, constantly.

After the second day without Kian, Bastian finally assumed that this horrible feeling must be what a broken heart felt like and stopped going to the bathroom to hunch over the toilet in vain.

He was a master at ignoring things that might have bothered others: sickness, exhaustion, injuries, personal problems. He couldn't even remember the last time he'd actually *had* a personal problem, but he'd always assumed he could push those petty hurts away, like he did everything else.

But Kian wasn't a petty hurt, he was a gaping hole in Bastian's chest, a maelstrom of regret and guilt.

On the third day, his mother called, and he'd ignored it. She called again, and then again, and then again. Biting off a whole string of bad words, he left the prep station, hoping that Derek wouldn't fuck anything up in the five minutes he was gone.

He exited out the back door, and leaned on the brick wall, taking a deep breath of fresh air. He'd been working almost nonstop since Kian had walked out, and somehow, even though two years ago, Bastian had done everything without Kian, it turned out that he'd come to rely on him so much that now the burden felt too heavy to bear.

Not a realization that Bastian was particularly happy to come to.

"What is it, *maman*?" he asked when she picked up the phone on the second ring. "I'm very busy, the restaurant is swamped, and we've had some . . ." Bastian paused, he didn't want to tell her about Kian in the context of complaining they didn't have enough staff, but what else was there? He wasn't going to sit at her knee and cry into her lap. He'd never been that child, and he certainly wasn't that child now. "We've had some staffing problems."

It was foolish to hope she'd let it go at that vague statement, but he'd cross that bridge when they came to it. Yet another painful inevitability he'd need to face; admitting to his mother that he'd fucked up everything with the love of his life.

"Bastian," she staid sternly, "I am hearing the strangest rumors."

Sighing, Bastian scrubbed a hand over his face. He couldn't remember the last time he'd really slept. Probably before Kian had quit. "I wish you wouldn't listen to those."

"I went to Barrel House last night," she continued, like he hadn't said a word. "And for once the rumors were correct. Kian, he is not working for you anymore? He was working at Xander Bridges' restaurant? What has happened?"

It was inevitable that Kian would go to work for Xander. Bastian had theoretically prepared himself for that eventuality, but it stung so much more than he'd ever imagined it would. Salt on an open wound, sprinkled liberally.

"I really don't have time for this right now, *maman*," he said, trying with one last ditch effort to dodge the question.

"Bastian Pierre Aquino," Celeste said sternly. "Do I need to come down there and harass you until you tell me?"

Bastian laughed because otherwise he was going to cry, and he couldn't remember the last time he'd ever cried in front of someone. Frankly, before this week, he couldn't remember the last time he'd cried at all, but he'd passed that milestone the first night without Kian beside him.

It was shameful, but at least it was honest, Bastian thought bleakly. He deserved the misery; he'd fucked this whole thing up, and he didn't really blame Kian for quitting.

For leaving him too, maybe. But Kian was almost certainly right, their personal relationship would never have survived their professional one imploding.

That didn't mean Bastian had forgiven him for it, or himself.

"He quit," he finally admitted quietly, "probably because I drove him to it. I set him up in a position where he was doomed to fail." Deep ragged breath, to try to suppress the tears that threatened. He had yet to cry at Terroir and he was determined that it *would not* happen. "I don't even blame him for being pissed off at me. I was very stupid."

"Oh, Bastian," Celeste said softly. "I am so sorry. Will he not forgive you?"

Bastian thought of all the times he'd seen himself reflected in Kian. "I doubt it." He hadn't tried, because he didn't know what to say, and he definitely didn't know how to fix the situation. Kian would chafe as *sous*, that was something Bastian believed fully, and he wasn't ready to be *chef de cuisine*. What else was there?

"You haven't even tried," Celeste said with damning judgement in her voice. "Bastian."

"There is no way to fix this," Bastian swore. "If there was, I would have thought of it. I would have done it already. I'm dying here."

"I'm sure you are, my darling. Go back to work, and I will think on it."

"*Maman*," Bastian argued, because the last thing this fucked-up situation needed was interference. But she had already hung up, and checking his watch, there really wasn't time to call her back. Frankly, there hadn't really been time to talk to her in the first place. He took one last breath of fresh air, and then went back inside.

He had a lot of work to do.

***

Working for Xander was like slipping back into a familiar position that he recognized—but the edges didn't quite fit properly and they chafed. The kitchen was too small. The fact that the diners could see everything they were doing in the kitchen was weird, and Kian didn't like it. He didn't know how Xander stood it. He did understand why Xander had designed it that way; the chefs were held accountable for their behavior with so many eyes watching, and he could never lose his temper the way that Bastian did frequently.

The same devastating wave of pain swept over him the same as it did every time he thought of Bastian, but a week had gone by now. It didn't hurt any less, but he was starting to get used to it.

"Chicken special," Xander called out. "Three top."

Xander ran a good kitchen. The food was delicious and high quality but a little more relaxed than Terroir had been. It was a good fit for Kian, but he already knew this was temporary. He didn't really want to stay forever.

Xander kept telling him that eventually he'd feel differently, that when he finally got Bastian out of his system, he'd see how good it was to work for someone else.

He'd sounded so sure of this theory that Kian hadn't wanted to contradict him. But he was never going to get Bastian out of his system. Even when he hated him—and there had been one or two or ten moments of that—he still loved him. He didn't believe that was going to change anytime soon, no matter what Xander claimed.

One of the waiters approached the pass-through as Kian put on three sauté pans, starting the chicken.

"There is a lady that wanted to send compliments to the chef," he said, smile glimmering in the corners of his mouth.

Kian frowned. "She wants to send compliments to Xander, you mean."

"No," he said, shaking his head. "She was very specific about sending compliments to *you*. Kian Reynolds. She said you have a mutual acquaintance you both care about."

Kian's hand froze on one of the sauté pans. "How old was she?"

"Oh, maybe sixty? Beautiful. Distinguished."

It had to be Bastian's mother. The age was right. The description was right.

"Did she speak with an accent?"

"Yeah," the waiter said. "How did you know? She's French."

Something everyone learned about Bastian Aquino at some point—his mother was French, his father Spanish. A conflagration of hot temperaments swirling inside him, fighting containment.

"Xander," Kian said, "come take over these pans."

Xander didn't look happy but he came over anyway. "You already took a break," he objected, but there was something to be said for working for your best friend.

"Yeah, and I'm sorry, but I need another. I just need . . . five minutes, if that's okay?"

Muttering under his breath, Xander didn't respond, but bumped Kian out of the way with a hip check.

"I'll be quick," Kian promised, and wiped his hands on a towel, unwinding his apron and hanging it on a hook before walking into the dining room.

Bastian's mother was everything he'd been told, and sitting alone at a corner table, a half-drunk glass of one of Xander's creative mocktails at her elbow.

"Hello," Kian said, and she looked up. He could see hints of Bastian in her face, her dark hair, streaked with gray.

"You are Kian," she said, clearly delighted, starting to stand up.

"No, no, please," he said, sliding into the chair opposite her. "I only have a minute. I just . . . I wanted to meet you."

"And I you. I am Celeste Aquino, but please call me Celeste," she said warmly, reaching out for his hands. "You are just as Bastian described to me."

Kian thought he'd been prepared, but he really wasn't. Bastian had described him to his mother? Sometimes it was easier for him to believe that Bastian had never really been serious, that Kian had imagined the way Bastian looked at him. But if he'd told his mother about him, then Kian hadn't misremembered anything. It had all been real, and that hurt worse than believing that Bastian had lied to him.

"Oh, darling, you are just as sad as he is." She frowned. "He is devastated without you."

Kian cleared his throat. "Sometimes things just don't work out. He told me that it wouldn't, the first month I worked for him. It shouldn't have been a surprise that it all fell apart."

"I would like you to come to my house, for tea. When are you free?" she asked, and for a second, Kian nearly turned her down. What point was there in making this harder than it already was? Sitting in Bastian's mother's house, wishing that he'd introduced them before everything had gone to hell? Forming a friendship with Celeste, even though there seemed to be little point to it?

It was a bad idea, but Kian was learning that even acknowledging that fact didn't always stop him. It sure hadn't stopped him with Bastian.

"Tomorrow," he said. "I have the afternoon off. Is that too soon?"

"No," she said, clearly delighted. "You will come tomorrow. One o'clock." She slid a piece of paper across the table. "My address."

Kian stared at the paper, realizing that she had come here tonight with the express purpose of talking to him, and not for a few minutes that he could steal from the kitchen. She wanted to get to know him and knew he wouldn't be able to do it during service.

His heart beat a little faster, even though he told himself firmly that he should not get his hopes up.

But it was too late, and hope was too addictive in the face of despair.

Chapter Sixteen

"Darling, come in," Celeste Aquino said, opening the door to Kian.

Bastian's mother's house wasn't the soulless modern box that his own was. It was painted French blue, with charming white shutters, and a proliferation of gardens surrounding it, from the start of the drive all the way up to the house.

"Thank you for inviting me," Kian said, hating how stiff and nervous he sounded. Since accepting the invitation the night before, the only thing that had stopped him from canceling was the fact that he didn't know her phone number. And he couldn't exactly call Bastian and ask *him*.

"Don't worry, he is not here. He is working, of course," she said, leading him through the interior of the house, which was laid out just as open as Bastian's own, but decorated in her own style. Celeste took him out onto the back terrace, and they sat at a table and chairs for two, set with delicate china and a center serving tray filled with petit fours and tea sandwiches.

"See, isn't this lovely?" Celeste asked and Kian nodded mutely. This shouldn't feel like a test, but it was. He'd never imagined meeting Bastian's mother without Bastian actually being present.

"It's a beautiful view," Kian added. "And your gardens are stunning."

Celeste poured tea into his cup. "This ground is so fertile, I enjoy it so much," she said. "When Bastian said he wanted me to come with him to California, of course I agreed, but I had no idea I would like it so much here."

She handed him the cup, and then offered him a choice of sandwiches. Like Bastian, she was clearly a perfectionist, because everything was elegant and beautifully prepared.

"I taught him to cook, you know," she said conspiratorially. "Though he will deny it now."

Kian took a bite of smoked salmon, chewed, and then swallowed. "Why would he?" He didn't add that she was hardly the type of mother that he could ever be ashamed of.

"You know Bastian," she said with a little airy wave of her hand. "No doubt he wants everyone to believe he came out of the womb knowing how to cook. He lets none of that show through his armor."

He'd let a little of it show, with Kian. But not much, and not, Kian had realized during the last week, enough for Kian to feel comfortable showing any of his own weakness. That was why he'd resisted telling him about Mark causing so much difficulty. Bastian's expectations of perfectionism were difficult to face, but even tougher because his own personal standards were so high. You could hardly blame someone for expecting too much when they expected even more out of themselves.

"No, he doesn't," Kian admitted softly.

"I know it's painful to talk about him," she said, kindness echoing through every syllable of her words. "If you really don't want to, I won't blame you, but I think it would help if I told you a little of his past. I'm assuming he has never told you, *non*?"

"I know what's on his Wikipedia page," Kian admitted wryly.

"It would be nice for these conversations to come up naturally, for him to tell you himself, in his own time, but I think, I *think* he will eventually come to you, and you knowing these things will help."

Kian knew he was staring incredulously at her. "Why would he come to me?"

She laughed. "Bastian, you know he does not let things go. He does not give up. He does not quit. He is searching for a solution to your professional problem, a place you will fit, a place you fit with him, and I know he will find one eventually. Because he is Bastian."

Kian knew him well too, obviously not as well as his mother knew him, but he wasn't so certain.

"I see you doubt," she said, leaning forward a little. "But that is alright. Still, I would like to tell you, if that is alright?"

"Yes," Kian agreed. "it's alright."

Celeste took her time, pouring more tea, popping a sugar cube into her own cup with a delicate pair of silver tongs, offering him another sandwich. Finally, she spoke. "Bastian's father, I assume he has not told you of him."

"No." Before, he hadn't really found that odd because they were still getting to know each other more personally than as just mentor and trainee, and Kian had believed they had all the time in the world to have those conversations. But then nothing had turned out the way he'd expected it to.

"He was . . . to put it mildly, a brute. Mean and cruel and rigid. Bastian has a terrible fear of being like him, while at the very same time, being very nearly like him."

"He isn't mean or cruel or rigid," Kian protested. "He's got a temper, yes, and he comes down on you if you mess up, but he's not, he's not really like that."

"*Vraiment*," Celeste agreed. "He is not. He has his father's drive for perfection, his commitment to excellence, his need to be the very best at what he begins. He is neither cruel nor mean—but he fights it, every single day." She took a sip of tea. "It is why he feels the need to control everything so completely. Even you."

Kian nodded slowly. Hearing about Bastian's father did help explain some of why he behaved the way he did.

"You love to work with him, yes?"

"I did," Kian said. He thought about what Xander had said, how he would eventually want to move on, to work for someone new, but he knew he never would. He was always going to want to be somehow adjacent to Bastian. They understood each other, on a very elemental level, in a way that few others did. Their creativity echoed in one another, one side complementing the other.

Celeste eyed him steadily across her teacup. "Why did you not take the *sous* position then?"

Why hadn't he? It wouldn't have been a great fit—he would have felt shamed and embarrassed and like a failure if he had. But it also would have meant they could have tried to work things out.

"It was embarrassing to fail. And to fail that way," Kian finally admitted.

"Ah," she said. "So, ego. The first day you met, Bastian came to me and said you were alike, and I thought, there is no way this is possible, you are too young, you are much sweeter than Bastian, but I see now I was wrong. You want your personal and professional relationships to feel equal."

"It's . . . I know it's impossible," Kian said.

"This is why he struggles. He wishes to find you a place where you feel respected and not still his trainee, but also a place you deserve." She winced. "It will not be easy."

Kian finished his tea. It was one thing to know that everything with Bastian was over, it was another to hear his mother say it, in that sad, regretful voice. He stood. "Thank you for the tea," he said, "but I really need to be going."

"Of course, your new job," Celeste said, her voice brightening. "And you will promise me to come by sometime, again?"

"Yes, I'll try," Kian promised as they walked through the house together.

As he went to open the door, she surprised him by placing her hand against it, keeping it only partially open. "You also must promise me that if he comes to you, and he tries to make it work, you'll remember what I told you."

Why this continued insistence Bastian would eventually contact him? It had been over a week since Kian had quit and there had been only silence. He didn't expect that would change, not at this point. Celeste had even admitted that the solution was difficult, if not impossible.

"I will, though I don't think he intends to contact me," Kian said wryly.

"He loves you," Celeste said. "He won't let you go, I know he won't."

As he walked back to his car, Kian wanted to believe her, because she so clearly believed her own words, but instead, there was only doubt.

Bastian had never really wanted to love him; he'd only done it because Kian had finally forced him to acknowledge it by coming to his home and taking all his clothes off. He'd set them on this path, and maybe Bastian resented that; maybe he wished that they'd continued on as they were, loving each other from afar, and never doing anything about it.

At least then, he'd still have Kian at Terroir.

It was a week later that the recruiter called.

Kian nearly told her to forget it, because he already had a job at Barrel House, but she kept insisting that the offer was lucrative and promising and that he would want to at least listen to it.

"I'm nobody," he'd said wryly into the phone, right before his shift started, "why would you even know to contact me?"

"Everyone knows about you," she said with certainty, "and you're who the client wants."

Kian was not convinced but he finally agreed to hear the proposal. She gave him an address of a little café outside of town, and said they would be using a back room, for privacy.

Frankly, he thought the whole thing smelled fishy, but when he told Xander, he'd just shrugged.

"So, someone wants to interview you," he said. "Word gets around. You dealt with the Bastard longer than most people. He personally trained you. You're young and fresh and hungry. It's not like I don't want to keep you here, but I get the feeling you don't intend to stay."

Xander wasn't wrong.

"I guess," Kian said dubiously.

"What's the worst that can happen?" Xander demanded. "It's a shitty job and you say no?"

Kian wasn't sure what he was afraid of, but instead of looking forward to the meeting with the recruiter, he dreaded it. He nearly called her twice to call it off, but then Wyatt had sent a text, wishing him good luck on the interview, and after that, it had seemed silly to cancel it.

Xander was right. All he had to do was say no if it was a job he wasn't interested in.

The café was one he'd been to before, though he'd never been ushered by the hostess with such deference to the back room, where a young woman with auburn hair and black-framed glasses was sitting at the end of the long table.

"Hello, I'm Lindsay Frost," she said, "and you must be Kian Reynolds."

"Yes," he said, reaching out to shake her hand. "It's nice to meet you."

"The honor is all mine. Wow, Terroir. What a way to start your career." She motioned towards the only other place at the table that had been set. He sat down, but still couldn't shake the feeling there was something going on that he didn't understand.

"I've been very lucky," Kian said.

"Bastian Aquino as your mentor? You sure have. And to be *chef de cuisine*, his appointed choice, at your age? Wow, I have a whole list of people who want to talk to you," she said with a laugh.

Kian knew going into this that he'd need to be honest. He'd need to tell the truth about what happened and how he'd quit Terroir. He took a deep breath and tried to find a way to confess that didn't make him look all bad.

"I only worked as *chef de cuisine* for a few weeks," he admitted. "But I was fully in charge of the kitchen for quite awhile before that."

She seemed completely unconcerned by his confession, and that made no sense. He wasn't crazy, because he knew that most of the time, interviewers wanted to know why you'd left a job abruptly, after only a few weeks. Especially one as prestigious as the one he'd quit.

"And now you're working at Barrel House?" she asked, consulting notes on a pad of paper in front of her.

"Xander Bridges is a friend," Kian said. "I'm not sure where I want to go next, and that seemed like as good of a place as any to spin my wheels while I figured it out."

"You've definitely been working with some exalted company," Lindsay said.

Kian wanted to say that none of them really seemed all that exalted, especially Xander, who still insisted on wearing that awful chili pepper headwrap, but that wasn't going to convince anyone to hire him.

"Can you tell me a little more about the job?" Kian asked.

"Oh yes, of course. Sorry. Just so excited to meet you." Lindsay glanced at her notes again. "It's a small restaurant, much smaller than Terroir, a little more casual than fine dining, but still high-end cuisine. Dinner only. Approximately fifty seats. A five-person staff. You'd be in charge of developing the menu, though it was suggested that some sort of rotating small plates menu would be preferred, and in charge of the kitchen and the staff."

On the surface, exactly the sort of position Kian was looking for. He hadn't been ready to be *chef de cuisine* at someplace like Terroir, with three hundred seats, and catering events, and twenty people to manage in the kitchen, but he could do something small. It would be a great learning experience. And small plates, he loved those, and could very easily develop a menu around that concept.

Still, something held him back.

"I'm assuming there's an owner or investor?" Kian asked. "When can I meet them?"

"Well, um," Lindsay hesitated, which was *so* weird. "Yes. There is. They're very busy, out of town a lot. Unfortunately they couldn't be at this meeting, but they gave me the power to offer you the contract, if you'd like to take a look at it. It's very generous."

More alarms pinged in Kian's head. They wanted to hire a head chef they'd never even met before? That seemed like a bizarre choice.

Still, Kian looked over the contract when Lindsay pushed it across the table. It was very generous. The salary was good. His decisions on menu and personnel were final, that was actually written into the contract. There was a business manager to oversee those choices, but if he wanted to do something, he could do it, immediately.

"Do they own other restaurants?" Kian wondered. The business manager position was odd, though maybe not so odd considering that the owner hadn't even bothered to meet with him today. But then if they hadn't, why was the business manager not here in their place?

"Oh yes," Lindsay said, and it seemed like she was going to continue but she shut her mouth abruptly.

Xander had told him that the worst that could happen today would be for Kian to turn down the job. Simple enough, to just say no, and there was a part of Kian that was tempted, even though there were a lot of factors that made it seem like a perfect job for him.

Tailor made in fact. Like the job had been designed with exactly his skill set and his experience in mind. It would be a little bit of a stretch, but nothing he couldn't handle.

"Could I meet the owner if I wanted to?" Kian asked.

Lindsay's eyes grew wider, like saucers, and that was when he knew. There was something going on, and he wanted to know what it was before he signed anything.

"He's not available," she finally stuttered out.

"He, huh?" Kian asked.

Suddenly, he knew who was behind this mysterious new restaurant, this mysterious new job. Of course getting Lindsay to admit that wasn't going to be easy, because of course, she was terrified of letting the secret out—and of him.

There was really only one person it could be.

"Who owns this restaurant?" Kian demanded.

Lindsay looked lost and decidedly out of her element, which jived with the rest of this charade, which hadn't been anything like any interview Kian had ever heard of before. Which meant she probably wasn't a recruiter, but only pretending to be one.

"I do."

Kian glanced up and Bastian was standing in the doorway. He had the nerve to look sheepish, but Kian's temper flared anyway. He knew he'd promised Celeste that he'd listen, that he'd consider what Bastian said when he came to him, but all he could think was, *why the fuck was all this necessary?*

"You own it," Kian said flatly. "No wonder. The job seems perfect for me, probably because it was *designed* for me."

Bastian shot Lindsay a single look and she fled, grabbing her purse and exiting the private room, shutting the door behind her.

Kian rolled his eyes. "You have it all figured out, don't you?" he accused. "You even hired some random person to try to recruit me, because you didn't want to recruit me yourself."

Bastian sat down and Kian flinched. It hurt, having him so close, and knowing he was so far away. Even further than he'd been this morning.

"Please," Bastian begged, and there were so few times Kian had ever heard that note in his voice that it was impossible not to at least listen. "Please, give this a chance. I've been tearing my hair out for the last two weeks, trying to find a way to do this with you, trying to find a way to work this out, and this is the only way I could find."

"You don't even *own* a restaurant of this description," Kian said, tossing the contract in front of him.

"Yes, I do." Bastian's voice was steadier now. Surer. "They broke ground today."

"What?"

"It's an expansion of Terroir, sort of. A more casual, friendlier version, right next door. The kitchens are being expanded." Bastian's gaze on him was warm, so warm. Warmer than he'd ever seen before. "We'll share initially, but we've shared before."

"But I'm still in charge." Kian still felt incredulous. "I'm in charge of my part of that kitchen."

Bastian nodded earnestly. "You'd be completely in charge of *your* kitchen. You'd call all the shots."

"But you'd still own it." Kian didn't know how that was going to make this slightly different version of what they'd already tried any better.

"Technically yes." Bastian sighed. "Your immediate boss would be my business manager. But yes, I'd still own it."

"And if I turned this down?" Kian demanded. "What would happen then?"

"I love you. Whether you work with me or not. I want you to be in my life. If you keep working at Barrel House, we'll figure out a way to make it work—if that's what you want." Bastian paused, like he was trying to come to terms with the possibility that Kian wouldn't, and it was *hard*.

Kian felt a pulse of satisfaction that this whole fucking situation didn't just feel impossible for him, that at least Bastian was right there in the trenches with him.

Did he want to keep working at Barrel House? Work with Xander and date Bastian? It would fix the professional and personal messiness that had caused their breakup the first time around, but Kian wasn't sure it would fix the gaping hole in his chest. He wanted to learn more from Bastian; he'd left and it had felt wrong, all the way, and he still didn't feel right.

Maybe Xander was right, and with time, the hole would heal and ache less. But Kian really didn't think so. He'd always believed that when the time came for him to move on from Terroir, he'd know—and while he'd still quit, none of it had felt right.

"I don't know what I want," Kian admitted softly. "I liked the sound of the job, and then I found out you were behind it the whole time . . . fixing everything without even giving me a chance to tell you what I wanted."

Bastian's eyes grew wide, and then wider. "I . . . I guess I did, didn't I?" He sounded so ashamed, and Kian couldn't help but feel a little guilty. Bastian had been trying, and that was what Kian had wanted, wasn't it? When his mother had promised Kian that he'd be in touch eventually, he hadn't believed it, even though he'd desperately wanted Bastian to make the effort.

To come to him. To *want* him. To tell him that he couldn't live without him.

"You did," Kian said, and tried to soften his voice. It wasn't entirely Bastian's fault, not after what Celeste had told him, that he wanted to control everything. It was his natural inclination, and right now, he was fighting it, all for Kian. What else could he really ask for?

"I'm sorry. It was my fault you failed, and all I wanted was to go back and fix it. But I couldn't. All I could do was try to make it better going forward, and that was what I focused on. Making it better. Making it work; making *us* work."

There were worse things, Kian realized, than a partner who tore themselves apart trying to fix a problem that had made you both miserable.

"This is always how it's going to be, isn't it?" he asked, even though he already knew the answer. "Neither of us have really changed. I'm still going to challenge you and you're still going to hate it."

"I don't hate it," Bastian claimed, even though Kian knew it was a lie.

"It makes you uncomfortable," Kian corrected. "I know it does."

Bastian actually squirmed in the chair, like he was uncomfortable now. "Not always."

"I'm not talking about when we're at your house or my house or in bed. I'm talking about when we're working. Because that's what we're talking about right now. How to fix our professional relationship."

Bastian's face fell, devastation filling his eyes, and Kian realized what he'd just said.

"No, no," he said quickly, reaching for Bastian, and cradling his big hands in his smaller ones. "No. I don't know what's going on between us, not professionally, but I know I love you, and I know that you love me. We *fit* together, which is why our personal relationship is so much easier to figure out."

"I'm not sure what you're saying."

"I'm saying you can't leave me, because I won't let you," Kian promised, squeezing his hands. "How does that sound?"

Bastian choked out a laugh that actually sounded a lot more like a sob. He hadn't said, because that wasn't Bastian's way, but Kian knew instinctively how much he'd been suffering. Being apart was like living without a limb, and on top of that, he'd been working nearly nonstop—while also trying to figure out a way to give Kian exactly what he wanted and needed.

"It's good. Good. I . . ." Bastian took a deep breath. "I missed you so fucking much."

Kian pulled him in for an embrace and felt Bastian's full-body shudder. "It's okay," he soothed. "We've got each other again."

When Bastian finally pulled away, his eyes were damp, and Kian's own weren't exactly dry either.

"I tried to control you," Bastian admitted after a long silence. "I tried to control the restaurant through you." His voice grew rougher. "I'm not a perfect man, Kian, as much as I want to believe otherwise. I make mistakes. I made a big one, but it wasn't *this*. I wouldn't change that for the world. I should have known we couldn't keep everything separate. It's too messy, and it's messy because it's real."

Kian raised an eyebrow. "And you think this will fix it?" He still wasn't convinced. He desperately wanted to go back to work for Bastian, he desperately wanted to take this job, but there was still a part of him that believed what Bastian had claimed two years ago.

They couldn't work together and have *this* too. It wouldn't ever work.

"I'm not expecting it to work out all the time," Bastian said, "but I know I have to try. I can't let you walk out again, not like before. That . . . it killed me. I thought the worst was when we kept our hands off each other, but that wasn't the worst. Not having you here, in my life, that was the worst."

"Neither of us has changed," Kian said slowly, "I don't know how this won't end in disaster, all over again. And if it does, I'm not sure I can handle it."

Bastian's eyes were intense on his. "I'm not a different man. I can't be a different man. I am the man I am, the good and the bad. But I'm more aware now. That's all I can be. And you've grown up. You're assertive and confident and challenge me in ways that I never expected."

"And you're okay with that?" There was no way to keep the disbelief from his voice. Bastian had claimed to try before and had failed utterly.

"I don't hate it as much as I thought I would," Bastian admitted. "I know we can't . . . we can't ever really be equals. Not really. I know that's what you wanted. I know that now. But I think this gives us the best chance to be more equal. Your best chance to grow, a little bit outside of my shadow."

Kian didn't say anything for a long moment. There was a part of this that felt too good to be true, too perfect almost, but this didn't feel like it had with the *chef de cuisine* job which he'd known wasn't right. This felt far more like the right sort of beginning.

There were so many paths open to him right now. He could keep working for Barrel House. He could find a job at another restaurant. He could take this job now, that Bastian was offering him.

The truth was, he knew what he wanted, but he was fucking terrified of losing Bastian again. Of losing everything he'd ever cared about.

"I'm afraid," Kian admitted, his voice cracking. He'd never let Bastian see any weakness, always afraid that it would mean Bastian's admiration and his respect and his love would die in the face of it. And maybe it would have, before, but Bastian *was* growing.

All Kian could do was trust that he was ready to see it. And if there wasn't any trust between them, how could they ever hope to have a personal *or* a professional relationship?

"I know," Bastian said very softly. "I am too. Absolutely fucking terrified."

And suddenly, shockingly, the way forward felt very clear. Kian knew what he should do, what was absolutely the right move for him, and it also happened to be exactly what he wanted.

He reached over and grabbed the pen that Lindsay had left on the table, and without a word, signed the contract, pushing it over towards Bastian after he was done.

Bastian grinned, so bright it nearly hurt. "You won't regret it, I swear," he promised, and Kian leaned forward, his mouth only an inch or so away from Bastian's.

"I probably will, at some point," Kian said thoughtfully, "but you're worth the risk."

Bastian's eyes were dark, deep wells, staring right into Kian's. "I am?" For the first time, the inherent cockiness in his tone was more subdued. And that, Kian realized, was his fear talking.

Fear of things falling apart, fear of the messiness overwhelming them, fear of failure, fear of not being enough, of Kian not loving him enough to stick out all the times when he wanted to quit because it was too hard.

Bastian probably felt that the fear he felt was an embarrassing weakness, something to push Kian away, but in the end all it did was convince Kian completely that they'd both do whatever it took to make this work.

"You're worth everything," Kian admitted and leaned forward that last inch to kiss him. It had been too long since the last time they'd kissed, and even though he knew now that they had all the time in the world, he didn't want to wait another second.

EPILOGUE

EIGHTEEN MONTHS LATER

"I think this is a very bad idea." Bastian wasn't perfect, would never be perfect, and still liked to construct all sorts of walls to keep his deeper feelings from the world. The only difference now was that at least when he constructed the walls, he built them with Kian inside.

Kian rolled his eyes. "It's going to be great. How could it not? It's a wedding."

"Your friends all hate me," Bastian said, and, unusually, sounded like he actually regretted this.

It was hard, but not impossible, to keep his chuckle hidden inside. It was just so unusual to see Bastian on such shaky ground, uncertain of how he'd be received. What Kian had discovered more and more over the months, as their personal relationship deepened and their professional relationship flourished, was that he'd always had these feelings, he just was total shit at expressing them. But now he'd started to, with Kian as the only witness.

"You didn't seem to mind them hating you when they all worked for you," Kian pointed out wryly.

Bastian thought about this for a long moment, then gave a sharp nod, his eyes following Kian from the closet to the suitcase on the bed, as he packed for their trip down to southern California.

Bastian had gotten home a little earlier, so he was already packed, and he kept eyeing his duffel, sitting on the floor by the bedroom door, with extreme trepidation.

"Did you do laundry this week?" Kian asked from the depths of the closet. The shelf holding his jeans was pretty bare. He'd meant to do some earlier, but Cluster, the small plates bistro adjacent to Terroir, was in the middle of a menu overhaul, and he'd been too busy.

"Did I do laundry?" Bastian appeared in the doorway, arms crossed over his bare chest. "Do I ever do laundry?"

"Not if you can help it," Kian sighed.

"I have time to throw in a quick load now," Bastian offered.

Four years ago when Kian had walked into Terroir for the first time, he never would have dreamt that one day Bastian would be offering to do his laundry.

The problem was that even though he was a relentless perfectionist in the kitchen, it turned out that Bastian was fucking awful at chores like laundry. Last year, he'd even managed to turn an entire load of whites bright pink even though there had been nothing red to be found.

Socks regularly disappeared, stains didn't come out, and even though Bastian, who hated failure with the fire of a thousand suns, meticulously folded every item, somehow everything always came out wrinkled.

Kian shot him a loving look. It was sort of adorable how bad Bastian was at laundry. "I think I'm going to have to pass on that offer."

A frustrated noise escaped Bastian. "I was going to be careful."

When you were dating and living together with someone like Bastian Aquino, diplomacy was of the utmost importance. "I'm sure you were," Kian said, with the straightest face he could manage.

"I know it's mind-boggling that someone with Michelin stars is unable to do a load of laundry," Bastian said with a disgusted sigh. "God knows I know how pathetic I am."

"Hey," Kian said, reaching up and brushing a lingering kiss on his cheek, rough with stubble after a very long day, "if the worst thing you ever do is fuck up my clothes, I'm good with that. I'm just going to run a load myself. There's time before we leave tomorrow for it to dry."

Kian pulled a selection of jeans and shirts out of the hamper and then Bastian trailed after him as he went down the hall to start the washing machine.

"It wasn't that I didn't care that they hated me, before," Bastian said.

Oh, so they were back to the prior subject of conversation—that all of Kian's best friends didn't like him, their dislike long predating Kian and Bastian's relationship.

Kian shot him a look over his shoulder. He hadn't given a single fuck that they'd hated him. He'd been not-so-affectionately called the Bastard and he'd carried the insult of that nickname regally, like a fur cloak.

"Oh, really?" Kian asked, turning back to him after hitting the start button on the washer.

"I didn't *like* it," Bastian claimed.

Kian rolled his eyes as they returned to the bedroom so he could finish packing. "They don't hate you. It'll be fine."

Celeste had texted him this morning, telling him that she'd told Bastian the same thing. Apparently this was something he was really worried about.

"Listen," Kian continued, pushing Bastian down on the edge of the bed they shared, and climbing onto his lap. He'd grown another inch and had begun to fill out his lanky body a little, but Bastian would always be bigger than him—something Kian hoped would never stop being hot. "This is a really happy occasion that is actually *not about you*. Just relax and try to have a little fun. That's what you typically do at weddings."

Bastian glared. "I know what to do at a wedding."

"Oh?" Kian raised his eyebrow. "And how many of them have you taken off to go to in the last . . . let's say . . . ten years?"

"I've been a little busy." Despite his words, Bastian's grumpy expression was beginning to crack, and Kian could see the beginnings of a smile. And he could *feel* the beginnings of something else stirring under his crotch. This position turned Bastian on just as much as it did Kian.

"A little advice then," Kian murmured, leaning in a little until they were almost kissing. Nearly, but not close enough. "Smile. Laugh. Eat. Drink. Enjoy yourself."

Bastian's arms wound around his middle and pushed Kian down, brushing their growing erections together. "Are you going to be there?"

"Yeah, I am."

"Then it shouldn't be very hard for me to do any of those things," Bastian admitted.

Even though they'd been together a year and a half, Bastian being sappy and sweet still turned Kian's world upside down. It shouldn't have been unexpected by this point, but it always was, in the best possible way.

Kian leaned down and kissed him long and slow and filthy. "I love you," he whispered against his lips.

Bastian didn't answer but from the way he crawled up his body, Kian knew exactly what his answer was.

Bastian hated weddings.

If there'd been a way to avoid this one without hurting Kian's feelings or looking like a complete asshole, he would've done it. But considering that one of the grooms was a former employee of Terroir, and one of Kian's best friends, it was impossible. Add to those facts the other fact that both grooms were up-and-coming in the culinary scene, and this was *the* wedding.

That still didn't mean that Bastian had to like it.

"It's awful, isn't it?"

Bastian glanced up from where he'd been minutely examining his program, stuffed and uncomfortable in his suit, and saw a blonde woman, a rueful expression on her face wearing a turquoise dress with flowers strewn across it.

"You must be Kian's boyfriend," she said, settling in next to him. Bastian, who'd been actively trying to keep his expression neutral, frowned.

"I'm Tabitha King," she said, holding out her hand.

Bastian let his frown deepen, even though there was a strong possibility that Kian would see it and be disappointed in him. This was a *wedding*, and it was supposed to be filled with love and beauty and happiness, right?

Bastian was more intimately acquainted with those concepts than he'd ever been, but the visible outpouring still made him nervous.

"Do I know you?" he asked, shaking her hand briskly. She had a surprisingly firm handshake and a way of looking at you that stripped most pretense away.

"I'm Ryan's best friend," she said.

It took him a long moment to place who Ryan was, and then he remembered Kian mentioning that Wyatt, his old employee, had ended up dating Ryan Flores, the baseball player.

"But this isn't Wyatt's wedding," Bastian objected.

She tilted her head and the look in her blue eyes was as sharp as one of his Japanese steel knives. "Correct. I also work at Five Points, which is why I'm here."

"So you work with Miles and Evan, then," Bastian said, a little pleased that he'd finally managed to figure out the somewhat complex personal relationships. He'd never claim to be a very good boyfriend in that regard. His focus was too single-minded. It had expanded to include Kian, but not Kian's circle of friends, most of whom, unfortunately, were ex-employees and hated him.

Tabitha shrugged. "Not really, but they're two really nice guys."

It dawned on Bastian that not only was she clearly friendly with Wyatt, she would also be friendly with Miles. Therefore she knew exactly who he was, yet she'd still identified him as "Kian's boyfriend," and not as Bastian Aquino, head chef of Terroir.

"Miles used to work for me," Bastian admitted, even though technically Miles had worked for René, the head of pastry at Terroir.

"I know." Tabitha eyed him steadily.

Bastian sighed. "Then you know three quarters of the wedding party hates my guts."

"Thus making you the most interesting person at this wedding," Tabitha pointed out, "and why I'm over here talking to you, instead of sucking up to my boss."

"I'm flattered," Bastian said dryly.

"At least I'm not asking you when you're going to do this," she said, giving a general wave around the wedding preparations.

He adored Kian, and he was almost completely certain that Kian adored him, but this sort of event, with the proliferation of flowers and silky tents and strung lights and a full wedding party—not his type of thing at all.

"So you thought you'd come over here *not* to ask when we're getting married and also because I'm the most interesting yet most hated person at the wedding?"

She laughed. "Something like that. And because you were sitting alone, and I know what that's like."

When Kian had told him that Miles had asked him to be one of his attendants, it hadn't struck him right away that meant that he would be on his own, surrounded by people who either knew him personally and didn't like him or who had definitely heard the worst of the rumors about him.

He'd fully expected to have to sit through the ceremony by himself, even though Kian had insisted that he could sit with Damon and Ryan. He and Damon had come to an uneasy truce, but they weren't ever going to be friends, and after getting a glimpse of Ryan, in sunglasses and a very sharp suit, with a trail of fans following him around, Bastian had decided he wasn't going to go to the trouble to introduce himself.

"Well, thank you," Bastian said stiffly.

She laughed again. "I couldn't drag my husband to this—he hates weddings too—and he's working besides, so you're stuck with me. Though," she added speculatively, "you need to let me introduce you to Ryan after the ceremony."

It would be so easy to brush her off. It wasn't like Bastian hadn't been doing it his whole damn life, never letting a single person close.

He'd thought he could just let Kian in, and leave the rest of the world out, but the longer they dated, the more impossible that seemed.

This wedding was the prime example of that, and he was beginning to realize that loving Kian came with all this other stuff too—and other *people,* one of whom was sitting next to him right now.

"Sure, I'd like that," Bastian said, voice gruff and suddenly swamped with emotion because Kian had brought *life* with him when he'd let him in.

He'd brought people and joy and vitality and a messiness that Bastian didn't always like, but in the end, enjoyed nevertheless.

"I knew you'd come around," Tabitha said impudently. "You're really not as scary as your reputation promised."

Bastian opened his mouth, very willing to promise that he was as scary as it took, but then the music started—a goddamn string trio complete with harpist.

He leaned closer to her, and said under his breath, "I didn't realize that Miles was the string trio type."

Tabitha smothered a laugh. "You clearly haven't spent much time with Evan."

So apparently *Evan* was the string trio type in their relationship. Frankly, Bastian thought as the ceremony began, he wasn't sure he could picture Miles settling down with a string trio type. Even when Miles had been filming his pastry videos, he'd always been so casual and laid-back.

But then Evan and Miles approached the officiant, dressed similarly in gray suits, and their hands gripped tightly together. Evan's white shirt was buttoned up and topped off with a pale yellow bow tie. Miles had not only eschewed the bow tie, he'd left the top two buttons of his shirt unbuttoned.

And somehow, despite that clear outer difference illustrating their inner differences, they couldn't take their eyes off each other, the love radiating out of them so palpable, that Bastian had to wonder if he and Kian were so obvious.

They'd spent forever hiding their feelings, so maybe they weren't. Or maybe, like Michel had told him wryly and more than once, they'd always been shitty at hiding. Everyone had always known, but it had only been that worm Mark who had figured out a way to twist it, to make their feelings for each other so negative.

Right before he spoke, Bastian realized that he recognized the officiant. That was Reed Ryan, and somehow Evan and Miles had managed to drag him out of the kitchen, which was impressive.

"Ladies and gentlemen, family and friends, welcome," the officiant said, smiling wide. "I'm Reed Ryan, and I've had the pleasure and the pride of knowing Evan and Miles for several years now, and I was so touched when they asked me to officiate their wedding. Of course, I was also terrified because I'm the worst public speaker ever, so please bear with me."

The assembled friends and family laughed, but Bastian knew from the strain on Reed's face that he wasn't trying to lower expectations; this truly wasn't easy for him.

"Today," Reed continued, "we've all gathered here to witness the loving union between Evan and Miles. Every single one of you is here because you've all had a special part of their lives, and they've asked you not only to bear witness to their union, but to help create beautiful memories of this special day."

Bastian shifted uncomfortably in his chair. He didn't think he'd been asked to come to help create beautiful memories. He'd been asked because despite everyone's beliefs and against all the odds, he and Kian had created a lasting relationship together.

He knew how long Xander and Wyatt and to a lesser extent, Miles, had fought against Kian having feelings for him. Just because they'd finally accepted that Kian wasn't leaving Bastian anytime soon didn't mean they suddenly approved of whom he'd picked to be his partner.

And there was nothing like a wedding to drill that point home.

He wouldn't be particularly surprised if that was another reason why the woman next to him had chosen this particular seat.

Kian, standing in the front next to Xander and Wyatt, smiled at him, and even though he wasn't enjoying himself, Bastian couldn't help but smile back.

"First," Reed continued, "is there anybody who has an objection to this couple joining their lives together?"

It was difficult to imagine standing up where Evan and Miles were in a few years, but Bastian still made a mental note to make sure that particular sentence was erased from the ceremony, as he could imagine more than one person deciding that they definitely had an objection. Or ten.

Bastian couldn't imagine anyone objecting to Miles and Evan. So he was shocked, along with the rest of the audience, when Wyatt stepped forward, his blond hair shaggy and longer than it had ever been when he'd worked at Terroir.

"I do," Wyatt said, clearly and loudly, with a voice that carried. Several rows away, Bastian heard his boyfriend, Ryan, laugh out loud.

What was going on?

Reed must have anticipated this because he just smiled, and said, "What is your objection?"

"I object," Wyatt said, clearly trying for a serious tone, but failing because he kept smiling so brightly, "because you should be ridiculously in love to get married."

Miles laughed then, Evan's warm gaze never leaving his future husband's. As if there was *any* doubt they were ridiculously in love.

"If I am, how do you suggest I prove it?" Miles asked, his voice amused and curious.

"Maybe spirit him away to a tropical island and spoil him horribly?" Wyatt suggested. "Oh wait, you already did that. I guess," he said with a shrug, "it's inevitable, you *should* marry him."

"Thanks," Miles said dryly.

"Any other objections?" Reed asked, but Bastian had figured out there were going to be at least two others, the exact number of remaining attendants who had yet to speak.

"I have one," Xander said next.

"Of course you do," Evan said, loud enough for the audience to hear and chuckle along with the wedding party.

"I'm somewhat infamous for my objections," Xander continued, "so don't think I present this lightly. But I think two people who are getting married should spend more time together than you do. Be partners, in the truest sense of the word."

This time it was Evan who responded. "You mean, more than live together and work together? What sort of partnership would you suggest, Bridges?"

Xander's gaze was steady, and clearly not on the couple standing in front of Reed, but his fiancé, one row up from Bastian. "True partnership means you support each other through thick and thin, even when it's hard, and especially when it feels impossible. You need to have each other's backs, every single time, no matter the obstacle."

Miles' voice wasn't quite steady as he answered Xander. "I think we can do that, don't you?" he asked his husband-to-be in a hushed voice.

"I think with you next to me, we can do anything," Evan said.

"Then I withdraw my objection," Xander said, and the look he directed towards Damon was practically a caress.

"Let me guess," Reed said, "there's one more objection."

"Yeah, I've definitely got one," Kian said, and even though Bastian had been anticipating this, his heart started beating harder. A hand reached for his and gave it a little squeeze. It must have been Tabitha. Maybe she'd even been put next to him so he wouldn't do anything crazy like leap up in the middle of Evan and Miles' wedding and do something insane that would make everyone hate him even more, like proposing to Kian.

He wasn't sure anymore it was the proposing part everyone would hate him for. But interrupting Evan and Miles' wedding and making it all about him? That was a fairly good reason.

"What's your objection?" Reed asked.

Kian gazed right at him, and maybe Michel was right, Bastian thought in a haze, maybe they had always been terrible at hiding their feelings. "From my own relationship, I know just how important loyalty is. Without it, you might as well give up now, because you're never going to be able to stay together. True loyalty is protecting the person you love with every fiber of your being, but also knowing when to let them go and set them free. Supporting them, even if their choices aren't your own."

Miles' look at Evan was both dry and a little watery. "I can't imagine knowing anything about that."

"We've made it work, we'll make it work every day," Evan promised. "Because I love you."

"I guess," Kian said, his own glance an invisible caress against Bastian's cheek, "I don't have an objection after all."

The assembled guests all chuckled, and Reed said, "Then it's time for your vows."

Bastian reached over and gripped Tabitha's hand. "Thank you," he murmured to her.

Her smile back was brilliant. "Anytime."

And from the way Kian was looking at him, Bastian suddenly knew that it would only be a matter of time before they did this too. Maybe not with the string trio and the bow ties, but definitely surrounded by the people they cared about, who cared about them.

"After the ceremony, I also want to introduce you to my husband," she said quietly.

"You said he hadn't come?" Bastian questioned.

Tabitha rolled her eyes. "Like I would ever let him out of a wedding."

Watching Evan and Miles exchange rings, Bastian realized that Kian had known how uncomfortable he'd feel during the ceremony, having to sit alone, and that he wouldn't ever seek out Damon or Ryan. So he'd asked Tabitha, whom he probably knew through Ryan and Miles and Evan, to sit with him. To make sure that he felt relaxed and comfortable.

Love swirled all around him and all through him, lighting him up inside, and Bastian knew he could never go back to the lonely workaholic he'd been before Kian. Kian had changed his life, had opened him up *to* life—and love, and a thousand other things that he'd been missing before.

"And I want you to meet Kian," Bastian said, because he could no longer help playing along. "He's the love of my life."

Want to read more chef-themed books? Make sure you check out **Drive Me Crazy,** the first book of the Food Truck Warriors spinoff series!

INTERESTED IN READING MORE OF
BETH'S BOOKS?

CHECK OUT A FULL LIST OF TILES
BY SCANNING THE QR CODE
OR VISITING HER WEBSITE

WWW.BETHBOLDEN.COM/BOOKLIST

WANT TO FOLLOW BETH?

MAKE SURE YOU NEVER
MISS A RELEASE?

SCAN THE QR CODE BELOW
OR VISIT HER WEBSITE
FOR A SOCIAL MEDIA LIST,
NEWSLETTER SIGNUP,
AND SO MUCH MORE!

WWW.BETHBOLDEN.COM/ABOUT